SUZANNE BROCKMANN

TALL, DARK AND DEADLY

HQN™

CONTENTS

GET LUCKY

PROLOGUE

IT WAS LIKE BEING HIT by a professional linebacker.

The man barreled down the stairs and bulldozed right into Sydney, nearly knocking her onto her rear end.

To add insult to injury, he mistook her for a man.

"Sorry, bud," he tossed back over his shoulder as he kept going down the stairs.

She heard the front door of the apartment building open and then slam shut.

It was the perfect end to the evening. Girls' night out—plural—had turned into girl's night out—singular. Bette had left a message on Syd's answering machine announcing that she couldn't make it to the movies tonight. Something had come up. Something that was no doubt, six-foot-three, broad-shouldered, wearing a cowboy hat and named Scott or Brad or Wayne.

And Syd had received a call from Hilary on her cell phone as she was pulling into the multiplex parking lot. *Her* excuse for cancelling was a kid with a fever of one hundred and two.

Turning around and going home would have been too depressing. So Syd had gone to the movie alone. And ended up even *more* depressed.

The show had been interminably long and pointless, with buff young actors flexing their way across the screen. She'd alternately been bored by the story and embarrassed,

those tidy, quietly rich women who wore a giant diamond ring and drove a car that cost more than Syd could make in three very good years as a freelance journalist.

The he-man who'd barrelled down the stairs wasn't what Syd would have expected a boyfriend of Gina's to look like. He was older than Gina by about ten years, too, but this could well be more proof that opposites did, indeed, attract.

This old building made so many weird noises during the night. Still, she could've sworn she'd heard a distinctly human sound coming from Gina's apartment. Syd stepped closer to the open door and peeked in, but the apartment was completely dark. "Gina?"

She listened harder. There it was again. A definite sob. No doubt the son of a bitch who'd nearly knocked her over had just broken up with Gina. Leave it to a man to be in such a hurry to be gone that he'd leave the door wide open.

"Gina, your door's unlatched. Is everything okay in here?" Syd knocked more loudly as she pushed the door open even farther.

The dim light from the hallway shone into the living room and...

The place was trashed. Furniture knocked over, lamps broken, a bookshelf overturned. Dear God, the man hurrying down the stairs hadn't been Gina's boyfriend. He'd been a burglar.

Or worse...

Hair rising on the back of her neck, Syd dug through her purse for her cell phone. Please God, don't let Gina have been home. Please God, let that funny little sound be the ancient swamp cooler or the pipes or the wind wheezing through the vent in the crawl space between the ceiling and the eaves....

CHAPTER ONE

ALL EARLY-MORNING CONVERSATION in Captain Joe Catalanotto's outer office stopped dead as everyone turned to look at Lucky.

It was a festival of raised eyebrows and opened mouths. The astonishment level wouldn't have been any higher if Lieutenant Luke "Lucky" O'Donlon of SEAL Team Ten's Alpha Squad had announced he was quitting the units to become a monk.

All the guys were staring at him—Jones and Blue and Skelly. A flash of surprise had even crossed Crash Hawken's imperturbable face. Frisco was there, too, having come out of a meeting with Joe and Harvard, the team's senior chief. Lucky had caught them all off guard. It would've been funny—except he wasn't feeling much like laughing.

"Look, it's no big deal," Lucky said with a shrug, wishing that simply saying the words would make it so, wishing he could feel as nonchalant as he sounded.

No one said a word. Even recently promoted Chief Wes Skelly was uncharacteristically silent. But Lucky didn't need to be telepathic to know what his teammates were thinking.

He'd lobbied loud and long for a chance to be included in Alpha Squad's current mission—a covert assignment for which Joe Cat himself didn't even know the details. He'd only been told to ready a five-man team to insert

as marriage. He'd gone fully intending to be persuasive. She was impossibly young. How could she be ready to commit to one man—one who wore sweaters to work, at that—when she hadn't had a chance yet to truly live?

But Ellen was Ellen, and Ellen had made up her mind. She was so certain, so unafraid. And as Lucky had watched her smile at the man she was determined to spend the rest of her life with, he'd marveled at the fact that they'd had the same mother. Of course, maybe it was the fact they had different fathers that made them such opposites when it came to commitment. Because, although Ellen was ready to get married at twenty-two, Lucky could imagine feeling too young to be tied down at age eighty-two.

Still, he'd been the one to give in.

It was Greg who had convinced him. It was the way he looked at Ellen, the way the man's love for Lucky's little sister shone in his eyes that had the SEAL giving them both his blessing—and his promise that he'd be at the wedding to give the bride away.

Never mind the fact that he'd have to turn down what was shaping up to be the most exciting assignment of the year.

"I'm the only family she's got," Lucky said quietly. "I've got to be there for her wedding, if I can. At least I've got to *try*."

The Captain nodded. "Okay," he said. That was explanation enough for him. "Jones, ready your gear."

Wes Skelly made a squawk of disappointment that was cut off by one sharp look from the senior chief. He turned away abruptly.

Captain Catalanotto glanced at Frisco, who worked as a classroom instructor when he wasn't busy helping run the SEAL BUD/S training facility. "What do you think about using O'Donlon for your little project?"

Lucky took one last look around Alpha Squad's office. Harvard was already handling the paperwork that would put him temporarily under Frisco's command. Joe Cat was deep in discussion with Wes Skelly, who still looked unhappy that he'd been passed over yet again. Blue McCoy, Alpha Squad's executive officer, was on the phone, his voice lowered—probably talking to Lucy. He had on that telltale frown of concern he wore so often these days when he spoke to his wife. She was a San Felipe police detective, involved with some big secret case that had the usually unflappable Blue on edge.

Crash sat communing with his computer. Jones had left in a rush, but now he returned, his gear already organized. No doubt the dweeb had already packed last night, just in case, like a good little Boy Scout. Ever since the man had gotten married, he hurried home whenever he had the chance, instead of partying hard with Lucky and Bob and Wes. Jones's nickname was Cowboy, but his wild and woolly days of drinking and chasing women were long gone. Lucky had always considered the smooth-talking, good-looking Jones to be something of a rival both in love and war, but he was completely agreeable these days, walking around with a permanent smile on his face, as if he knew something Lucky didn't.

Even when Lucky had won the spot on the current team—the spot he'd just given up—Jones had smiled and shaken his hand.

The truth was, Lucky resented Cowboy Jones. By all rights, he should be miserable—a man like that—roped into marriage, tied down with a drooling kid in diapers.

Yeah, he resented Cowboy, no doubt about it.

Resented, and envied him his complete happiness.

Frisco was waiting impatiently by the door, but Lucky took his time. "Stay cool, guys."

asked about the rumored connection of the serial rapist to the Coronado naval base, and in particular to the teams of SEALs stationed there, the police spokesman replied, 'Our investigation will be thorough, and the military base is a good place to start.'

"Known for their unconventional fighting techniques as well as their lack of discipline, the SEALs have had their presence felt in the towns of Coronado and San Felipe many times in the past, with late-night and early-morning explosions often startling the guests at the famed Hotel del Coronado. Lieutenant Commander Alan Francisco of the SEALs could not be reached for comment."

Lucky swore again. "Way to make us look like the spawn of Satan. And let me guess just how hard—" he looked at the top of the article for the reporter's name "—this S. Jameson guy tried to reach you for comment."

"Oh, the reporter tried," Frisco countered as he began moving toward the jeep that would take him across the base to his office. Lucky could tell from the way he leaned on his cane that his knee was hurting today. "But I stayed hidden. I didn't want to say anything to alienate the police until I had the chance to talk to Admiral Forrest. And he agreed with my plan."

"Which is…?"

"There's a task force being formed to catch this son of a bitch," Frisco told him. "Both the Coronado and San Felipe police are part of it—as well as the state police, and a special unit from FInCOM. The admiral pulled some strings, and got us included. That's why I went to see Cat and Harvard. I need an officer I can count on to be part of this task force. Someone I can trust."

Someone exactly like Lucky. He nodded. "When do I start?"

"There's a meeting in the San Felipe police station

clean of makeup, her shirt buttoned wrong—and spitting mad that she hadn't been called sooner.

Syd had been fiercely guarding Gina, who was frighteningly glassy-eyed and silent after the trauma of her attack.

The male detectives had tried to be gentle, but even gentle couldn't cut it at a time like this. *Can you tell us what happened, miss?*

Sheesh. As if Gina would be able to look up at these men and tell them how she'd turned to find a man in her living room, how he'd grabbed her before she could run, slapped his hand across her mouth before she could scream, and then...

And then that Neanderthal who had nearly run Syd down on the stairs had raped this girl. Brutally. Violently. Syd would've bet good money that she had been a virgin, poor shy little thing. What an awful way to be introduced to sex.

Syd had wrapped her arms tightly around the girl, and told the detectives in no uncertain terms that they had better get a woman down here, pronto. After what Gina had been through, she didn't need to suffer the embarrassment of having to talk about it with a man.

But Gina had told Detective Lucy McCoy all of it, in a voice that was completely devoid of emotion—as if she were reporting facts that had happened to someone else, not herself.

She'd tried to hide. She'd cowered in the corner, and he hit her. And hit her. And then he was on top of her, tearing her clothing and forcing himself between her legs. With his hands around her throat, she'd struggled even just to breathe, and he'd...

Lucy had quietly explained about the rape kit, explained about the doctor's examination that Gina still had

"It's our guy again," Lucy McCoy had grimly told the other detectives. "Gina's been burned with a Budweiser, too."

Our guy *again*. When Syd asked if there had been other similar attacks, Lucy had bluntly told her that she wasn't at liberty to discuss that.

Syd had gone to the hospital with the girl, staying with her until her mother arrived.

But then, despite the fact that it was three o'clock in the morning, there were too many unanswered questions for Syd to go home and go to sleep. As a former investigative reporter, she knew a thing or two about finding answers to unanswered questions. A few well-placed phone calls connected her to Silva Fontaine, a woman on the late-night shift at the hospital's Rape Counseling Center. Silva had informed Syd that six women had come in in half as many weeks. Six women who hadn't been attacked by husbands or boyfriends or relatives or co-workers. Six women who had been attacked in their own homes by an unknown assailant. Same as Gina.

A little research on the Internet had turned up the fact that a *budweiser* wasn't just a bottle of beer. U.S. Navy personnel who went through the rigorous Basic Underwater Demolition Training over at the SEAL facility in nearby Coronado were given a pin in the shape of a flying eagle carrying a trident and a stylized gun, upon their entrance into the SEAL units.

This pin was nicknamed a budweiser.

Every U.S. Navy SEAL had one. It represented the SEAL acronym of sea, air and land, the three environments in which the commando-like men expertly operated. In other words, they jumped out of planes, soaring through the air with specially designed parachutes as easily as they

Zale had demanded Syd hold all the detailed information about the recent attacks. Syd had countered with a request to write the exclusive story after the rapist was caught, to sit in with the task force being formed to apprehend the rapist—provided she could write a series of police-approved articles for the local papers, now warning women of the threat.

Zale had had a cow.

Syd had stood firm despite being blustered at for several hours, and eventually Zale had conceded. But, wow, had he been ticked off.

Still, here she was. Sitting in with the task force.

She recognized the police chief and several detectives from Coronado, as well as several representatives from the California State Police. And although no one introduced her, she caught the names of a trio of FInCOM Agents, as well. Huang, Sudenberg and Novak—she jotted their names in her notebook.

It was funny to watch them interact. Coronado didn't think much of San Felipe, and vice versa. However, both groups preferred each other over the state troopers. The Finks simply remained aloof. Yet solidarity was formed—at least in part—when the U.S. Navy made the scene.

"Sorry, I'm late." The man in the doorway was blindingly handsome—the blinding due in part to the bright white of his naval uniform and the dazzling rows of colorful ribbons on his chest. But only in part. His face was that of a movie star, with an elegantly thin nose that hinted of aristocracy, and eyes that redefined the word *blue*. His hair was sunstreaked and stylishly long in front. Right now it was combed neatly back, but with one puff of wind, or even a brief blast of humidity, it would be dancing around his face, waving tendrils of spun gold. His skin was per-

at the table, directly across from Sydney, as he glanced around the room. "I'm sure you all understand Lieutenant Commander Francisco's need to look into this situation immediately."

Syd tried not to stare, but it was hard. At three feet away, she should have been able to see this man's imperfections—if not quite a wart, then maybe a chipped tooth. Some nose hair at least.

But at three feet away, he was even more gorgeous. *And* he smelled good, too.

Chief Zale gave him a baleful look. "And you are...?"

Navy Ken half stood up again. "I'm sorry. Of course, I should have introduced myself." His smile was sheepish. Gosh darn it, it said, I plumb forgot that not everybody here knows who I am, wonderful though I may be. "Lieutenant Luke O'Donlon, of the U.S. Navy SEALs."

Syd didn't have to be an expert at reading body language to know that everyone in the room—at least everyone male—hated the Navy. And if they hadn't before, they sure did now. The jealousy in the room was practically palpable. Lieutenant Luke O'Donlon gleamed. He shone. He was all white and gold and sunlight and sky-blue eyes.

He was a god. The mighty king of all Ken dolls.

And he knew it.

His glance touched Syd only briefly as he looked around the room, taking inventory of the police and FInCOM personnel. But as Zale's assistant passed out manila files, Navy Ken's gaze settled back on Syd. He smiled, and it was such a perfect, slightly puzzled smile, Syd nearly laughed aloud. Any second now and he was going to ask her who she was.

"Are you FInCOM?" he mouthed to her, taking the file

about everyone else here, but we haven't been introduced. Are you a police psychologist?"

Zale didn't let Syd reply. "Ms. Jameson is going to be working very closely with you, Lieutenant."

Ms. not Doctor. Syd saw that information register in the SEAL's eyes.

But then she realized what Zale had said and sat back in her chair. "I am?"

O'Donlon leaned forward. "Excuse me?"

Zale looked a little too pleased with himself. "Lieutenant Commander Francisco put in an official request to have a SEAL team be part of this task force. Detective McCoy convinced me that it might be a good idea. If our man is or was a SEAL, you may have better luck finding him."

"I assure you, luck won't be part of it, sir."

Syd couldn't believe O'Donlon's audacity. The amazing part was that he spoke with such conviction. He actually believed himself.

"That remains to be seen," Zale countered. "I've decided to give you permission to form this team, provided you keep Detective McCoy informed of your whereabouts and progress."

"I can manage that." O'Donlon flashed another of his smiles at Lucy McCoy. "In fact, it'll be a pleasure."

"Oh, ack." Syd didn't realize she'd spoken aloud until Navy Ken glanced at her in surprise.

"And provided," Zale continued, "you agree to include Ms. Jameson in your team."

The SEAL laughed. Yes, his teeth *were* perfect. "No," he said, "Chief. You don't understand. A SEAL team is a team of *SEALs*. Only SEALs. Ms. Jameson will—no offense, ma'am—only get in the way."

"That's something you're just going to have to deal

"My God," he whispered. "I didn't…I'm sorry—I had no idea…."

He was ashamed. And embarrassed. Honestly shaken. "I feel like I should apologize for all men, everywhere."

Amazing. Navy Ken wasn't all plastic. He was at least part human. Go figure.

Obviously, he thought she had been one of the rapist's victims.

"No," she said quickly. "I mean, thanks, but I'm an eyewitness because my neighbor was attacked. I was coming up the stairs as the man who raped her was coming down. And I'm afraid I didn't even get that good a look at him."

"God," O'Donlon said. "*Thank* God. When Chief Zale said…I thought…" He drew in a deep breath and let it out forcefully. "I'm sorry. I just can't imagine…" He recovered quickly, then leaned forward slightly, his face speculative. "So…you've actually *seen* this guy."

Syd nodded. "Like I said, I didn't—"

O'Donlon turned to Zale. "And you're giving her to *me?*"

Syd laughed in disbelief. "Excuse me, I would appreciate it if you could rephrase that…."

Zale stood up. Meeting over. "Yeah. She's all yours."

Her hair was thick and dark, curling around her face, unstyled and casual—cut short enough so that she probably could get away with little more than raking her fingers through it after climbing out of bed.

Her eyes were dark brown and impossibly large in a face that could only be called pixielike.

Provided, of course, that pixies had a solid dose of unresolved resentment. She didn't like him. She hadn't liked him from the moment he'd walked into the San Felipe police-station conference room.

"Cindy, wasn't it?" He knew damn well that her name was Sydney. But what kind of woman was named *Sydney?* If he was going to have to baby-sit the woman who could potentially ID the San Felipe Rapist, why couldn't she be named Crystal or Mellisande—and dress accordingly?

"No," she said tightly, in a voice that was deceptively low and husky, unfairly sexy considering she clearly didn't want anyone looking at her to think even remotely about sex, "it wasn't. And no, I've never been hypnotized."

"Great," he said, trying to sound as enthusiastic as possible as he parked in the lot near Frisco's office. *His* office now, too, at least temporarily. "Then we're going to have some fun. A real adventure. Uncharted territory. Boldly going, etcetera."

Now Sydney was looking at him with something akin to horror in her eyes. "You can't be serious."

Lucky took the keys out of the ignition and opened the truck's door. "Of course not. Not completely. Who'd ever want to be completely serious about anything?" He climbed out and looked back inside at her. "But the part I'm not completely serious about is whether it's going to be fun. In fact, I suspect it's going to be pretty low key. Probably dull. Unless while you're under, I can convince the hypnotist to make you quack like a duck."

pregnant woman with a stunner from his vast repertoire of smiles.

"Hey, gorgeous—what are you doing here?" He wrapped his arms around her and planted a kiss full on her lips.

His wife. Had to be.

It was funny, Syd wouldn't have believed this man capable of marriage. And it still didn't make sense. He didn't walk like a married man. He certainly didn't talk like a married man. Everything about him, from the way he sat as he drove his truck to the way he smiled at anything and everything even remotely female, screamed bachelor. *Terminal* bachelor.

Yet as Syd watched, he crouched down and pressed his face against the woman's burgeoning belly. "Hello in there!"

Whoever she was, she *was* gorgeous. Long, straight, dark hair cascaded down her back. Her delicately featured face held a hint of the Far East. She rolled her beautiful, exotic eyes as she laughed.

"This is why I don't come out here that often," she said to Syd over the top of O'Donlon's head as he pressed his ear to her stomach, listening now. "I'm Mia Francisco, by the way."

Francisco. The Lieutenant Commander's wife.

"He's singing that Shania Twain song," O'Donlon reported, looking past Syd and grinning. "The one Frisco says never leaves your CD player?"

Syd turned to see a teenaged girl standing behind her— all long legs and skinny arms, surrounded by an amazing cloud of curly red hair.

The girl smiled, but it was decidedly half-hearted. "Ha, ha, Lucky," she said. "Very funny."

"We heard about the diving accident," Mia explained

"Tell Alan it's my fault you're late."

"Yeah, great." Lucky laughed as he waved good-bye, leading Syd down one of the corridors. "I'll tell him I'm delayed because I stopped to flirt with his wife. *That'll* go over just swell."

Syd had to run to keep up. She had no doubt that whatever excuse O'Donlon gave for being late, he would be instantly forgiven. Grown men didn't keep nicknames like Lucky well past adolescence for no reason.

Lucky.

Sheesh.

Back in seventh grade, Syd had had a nickname.

Stinky.

She'd forgotten to wear deodorant one day. Just one *day,* and she was Stinky until the end of the school year.

Speaking of stinky, she'd have dressed differently if she'd known she was going to be running a marathon today. Lieutenant Lucky O'Donlon was well out in front of her and showed no sign of slowing down. How big was this place, anyway?

Not content to wait for an elevator, he led the way into a stairwell and headed up.

Syd was already out of breath, but she pushed herself to keep up, afraid if she let him out of her sight, she'd lose him. She tried to keep her eyes glued to his broad back, but it was hard, particularly since his perfect rear end was directly in her line of sight.

Of course he had a perfect rear end—trim and tiny, about one one-hundredth the size of hers, and a perfect match for his narrow hips. She shouldn't have expected anything less from a man named Lucky.

She followed his microbutt back out into the hallway and into an empty outer office and…

Syd caught her breath as he knocked on a closed door.

And just like that, he was gone. It wasn't until he was out the far door that Syd realized he'd moved stiffly, leaning heavily on a cane.

With a jolt, she realized she was standing there gazing after Alan Francisco. Lucky had already gone into the lieutenant commander's office, and she followed, shutting the door behind her.

Surprise, surprise—Lucky had his arms wrapped around Detective McCoy. As Syd watched, he gave her a hello kiss.

"I didn't get to say hello properly before," he murmured. "You are looking too good for words, babe." Keeping his arm looped around her shoulders, he turned to Syd. "Lucy's husband, Blue, is XO of SEAL Team Ten's Alpha Squad."

Lucy's husband. Syd blinked. Lucy had a husband, who was also a SEAL. And presumably the two men were acquaintances, if not friends. This guy was too much.

"XO means executive officer," Lucy explained, giving Lucky a quick hug before slipping free from his grasp, reaching up to adjust the long brown hair that had slipped free from her ponytail holder. She really did have remarkably pretty eyes. "Blue's second in command of Alpha Squad."

"Blue," Syd repeated. "His name's really *Blue?*"

"It's a nickname," Lucy told her with a smile. "SEALs tend to get nicknames when they first go through BUD/S training. Let's see, we've got Cat, Cowboy, Frisco—" she ticked the names off on her fingers "—Blue, Lucky, Harvard, Crow, Fingers, Snakefoot, Wizard, Elmer, the Priest, Doc, Spaceman, Crash..."

"So your husband works here on the Navy base," Syd clarified.

"Some of the time," Lucy said. She glanced at Lucky and

with *my* rules. You let me form a team of SEALs, you don't hammer me with a lot of useless rules and hamper me with unqualified people who will only slow us down—" he shot Syd an apologetic version of his smile "—no offense—and then we'll catch your guy."

Lucy didn't blink. "The members of your team have to meet Chief Zale's approval."

"Oh, no way!"

"He—and *I*—believe that since we don't know who we're dealing with, and since you have plenty of alternatives for personnel, you should construct your team from SEALs or SEAL candidates who *absolutely*—no question—do not fit the rapist's description."

Syd sat down across from Lucky. "So in other words, no one white, powerfully built, with a crew cut."

Lucky sputtered. "That eliminates the majority of the men stationed in Coronado."

Lucy nodded serenely. "That's right. And the majority of the men are all potential suspects."

"You honestly think a real SEAL could have raped those women?"

"I think until we know more, we need to be conservative as to whom we allow into our information loop," she told him. "You'd be a suspect yourself, Luke, but your hair's too long."

"Gee, thanks for the vote of confidence."

"The second rule is about weapons," Lucy continued. "We don't want you running around town armed to the teeth. And that means knives as well as sidearms."

"Sure," he said. "Great. And when we apprehend this guy, we'll throw spoons at him."

"You won't apprehend him," she countered. "The task force will. Your team's job is to help locate him. Track him down. Try to think like this son of a bitch and anticipate

nineteen years old, Luke. Sydney was there when I arrived, and oddly enough, I didn't think to inquire as to whether she was with UPI or Associated Press."

"So what did you do?" Lucky turned back to Syd. "Blackmail your way onto the task force?"

"Damn straight." Syd lifted her chin. "Seven rapes and not a single word of warning in any of the papers. It was a story that needed to be written—desperately. I figured I'd write it—*and* I'll write the exclusive behind-the-scenes story about tracking and catching the rapist, too."

He shook his head, obviously in disgust, and Syd's temper flared. "You know, if I were a man," she snapped, "you'd be impressed by my assertive behavior."

"So did you actually see this guy, or did you just make that part up?" he asked.

Syd refused to let him see how completely annoyed he made her feel. She forced her voice to sound even, controlled. "He nearly knocked me over coming down the stairs. But like I told the police, the light's bad in the hallways. I didn't get a real clear look at him."

"Is there a chance it was good enough for you to look at a lineup of my men and eliminate them as potential suspects?" he demanded.

Lucy sighed. "Lucky, I don't—"

"I want Bobby Taylor and Wes Skelly on my team."

"Bobby's fine. He's Native American," she told Syd. "Long dark hair, about eight feet tall and seven feet wide—definitely not our man. But Wes..."

"Wes shouldn't be a suspect," Lucky argued.

"Police investigations don't work that way," Lucy argued in response. "Yes, he *shouldn't* be a suspect. But Chief Zale wants every individual on your team to be completely, obviously not the man we're looking for."

"This is a man who's put his life on the line for me—for

"I've worked for years as an investigative reporter," Syd told them both. "Hasn't it occurred to either one of you that I might actually be able to help?"

"In *every* state it's old enough," Syd said. What do you know? She was actually listening. At least partly.

"Yeah," Lucky said. "I know. That was a joke."

"Oh," she said and looked back out the window.

O-kay.

Lucky kept on talking, filling the cab of the truck with friendly noise. "I went into San Diego to see her, intending to tell her no way. I was planning at least to talk her into waiting a year, and you know what she tells me? I bet you can't guess in a million years."

"Oh, I bet I can't either," Syd said. Her words had a faintly hostile ring, but at least she was talking to him.

"She said, we can't wait a year." Lucky laughed. "And I'm thinking murder, right? I'm thinking where's my gun, I'm going to at the very least scare the hell out of this guy for getting my kid sister pregnant, and then Ellen tells me that if they wait a year, this guy Greg's sperm will expire."

He had Syd's full attention now.

"Apparently, Greg had leukemia as a teenager, years and years ago. And before he started the treatment that would save him but pretty much sterilize him, he made a few deposits in a sperm bank. The technology's much better now and frozen sperm has a longer, um, shelf life, so to speak, but Ellen's chances of having a baby with the sperm that Greg banked back when he was fifteen is already dropping."

Lucky glanced at Syd, and she looked away. Come on, he silently implored her. Play nice. Be friends. I'm a nice guy.

"Ellen really loves this guy," he continued, "and you should see the way he looks at her. He's too old for her by about seventeen years, but it's so damn obvious that

away. It's a survival instinct. If we can't learn to ID you, we can't know to take cover or brace for impact when you make the scene."

Sydney might've actually laughed at that. But he wasn't sure. Her smile had widened though, and he'd been dead right about it. It was a good one. It lit her up completely, and made her extremely attractive—at least in a small, dark, non-blond-beauty-queen sort of way.

And as Lucky smiled back into Sydney's eyes, the answer to all his problems became crystal clear.

Boyfriend.

It was highly likely that he could get further faster if he managed to become Sydney Jameson's boyfriend. Sex could be quite a powerful weapon. And he knew she was attracted to him, despite her attempts to hide it. He'd caught her checking him out more than once when she thought he wasn't paying attention.

This was definitely an option that was entirely appealing on more than one level. He didn't have to think twice.

"Do you have plans for tonight?" he asked, slipping smoothly out of best-friend mode and into low-scale, friendly seduction. The difference was subtle, but there *was* a difference. "Because I don't have any plans for tonight and I'm starving. What do you say we go grab some dinner? I know this great seafood place right on the water in San Felipe. You can tell me about growing up in New York over grilled swordfish."

"Oh," she said, "I don't think—"

"Do you have other plans?"

"No," she said, "but—"

"This is perfect," he bulldozed cheerfully right over her. "If we're going to work together, we need to get to know each other better. *Much* better. I just need to stop at

seduction. That wasn't going to happen. Not in a million years. Who did she think she was, anyway? Barbie to his Ken? Not even close. She wouldn't even qualify for Skipper's weird cousin.

Lucky held the door for her, smiling. It was a self-confident smile, a warm smile…an *interested* smile?

No, she had to be imagining that.

But she didn't have time for a double take, because, again, his living room completely surprised her. The furniture was neat but definitely aging. Nothing matched, some of the upholstery was positively flowery. There was nothing even remotely art deco in the entire room. It was homey and warm and just plain comfortable.

And instead of Ansel Adams prints on the wall, there were family photographs. Lucky as a flaxen-haired child, holding a chubby toddler as dark as he was fair. Lucky with a laughing blonde who had to be his mother. Lucky as an already too-handsome thirteen-year-old, caught in the warm, wrestling embrace of a swarthy, dark-haired man.

"Hey, you know, I've got an open bottle of white wine," Lucky called from the kitchen, "if you'd like a glass of that instead of lemonade…?"

What? Syd wasn't aware she had spoken aloud until he repeated himself, dangling both the bottle in question and an extremely friendly smile from the kitchen doorway.

The interest in his smile was *not* her imagination. Nor was the warmth in his eyes.

God, Navy Ken was an outrageously handsome man. And when he looked at her like that, it was very, very hard to look away.

He must've seen the effect he had on her in her eyes. Or maybe it was the fact that she was drooling that gave her away. Because the heat in *his* eyes went up a notch.

He continued to gaze at her as he took a sip of his wine.

His eyes were a shade of blue she'd never seen before. It was impossible to gaze back at him and not get just a little bit lost. But that was okay, she decided, as long as she realized that this was a game, as long as she was playing, too, and not merely being played.

He set his wineglass down on the counter. "I've got to change out of my Good Humor man costume. Excuse me for a minute, will you? Dress whites and grilling dinner aren't a good mix. Go on out to the deck—I'll be there in a flash."

He was so confident. He walked out of the kitchen without looking back, assuming she'd obediently do as he commanded.

Syd took a sip of the wine as she leaned back against the counter. It was shockingly delicious. Didn't it figure?

She could hear Lucky sing a few bars of something that sounded suspiciously like an old Beach Boys tune. Didn't that figure also? We'll have fun, fun, fun indeed.

He stopped singing as he pushed the button on his answering machine. There were two calls from a breathy-voiced woman named Heather, a third from an equally vapid-sounding Vareena, a brief "call me at home," from an unidentified man, and then a cheerful female voice.

"Hi, Luke, it's Lucy McCoy. I just spoke to Alan Francisco, and he told me about Admiral Stonegate's little bomb. I honestly don't think this is going to be a problem for you—I've met the candidates he's targeted and they're good men. Anyway, the reason I'm calling is I've found out a few more details about this case that I think you should know, and it's occurred to me that it might be a good idea for the grown-ups—assuming Bobby's part of your team—to meet tonight. I'm on duty until late, so why

Syd took little sips of her wine as Lucky gave a running discourse on his decision four years ago to build this deck, the hummingbird feeders he'd put in the garden, and the fact that they'd had far too little rain this year.

As he lit the grill, he oh-so-casually pointed out that the fence around the backyard made his swimming pool completely private from the eyes of his neighbors, and how—wink, wink—that helped him maintain his all-over tan.

Syd was willing to bet it wouldn't take much to get him to drop his pants and show off the tan in question. Lord, this guy was too much.

And she had absolutely no intention of skinny dipping with him. Not now, not ever, thanks.

"Have you tried it recently?" he asked.

Syd blinked at him, trying to remember his last conversational bounce. Massage. He'd just mentioned some really terrific massage therapy he'd had a few months ago, after a particularly strenuous SEAL mission. She wasn't sure exactly what he'd just asked, but it didn't matter. He didn't wait for her to answer.

"Here, let me show you." He set his glass on the railing of the deck and turned her so that she was facing away from him.

It didn't occur to him that she might not want him to touch her. His grip was firm, his hands warm through the thin cotton of her shirt and jacket as he massaged her shoulders. He touched her firmly at first, then harder, applying pressure with his thumbs.

"Man, you're tense." His hands moved up her neck, to the back of her head, his fingers against her skin, in her hair.

Oh. My. God.

touched hers. She meant to step back and freeze him with a single, disbelieving, uncomprehending look.

Instead, she melted completely in his arms. The bones in her body completely turned to mush.

He tasted like the wine, sweet and strong. He smelled like sunblock and fresh ocean air. He felt so solid beneath her hands—all those muscles underneath the silk of his shirt, shoulders wider than she'd ever imagined. He was all power, all male.

And she lost her mind. There was no other explanation. Insanity temporarily took a tight hold. Because she kissed him back. Fiercely, yes. Possessively, absolutely. Ravenously, no doubt about it. She didn't just kiss him, she inhaled the man.

She slanted her head to give him better access to her mouth as he pulled her more tightly against him.

It was crazy. It was impossibly exciting—he was undeniably even more delicious than that excellent wine. His hands skimmed her back, cupping the curve of her rear end, pressing her against his arousal and—

And sanity returned with a crash. Syd pulled back, breathing hard, furious with him, even more furious with herself.

This man was willing to take her to bed, to be physically intimate with her—all simply to control her. Sex meant so little to him that he could cheerfully use himself as a means to an end.

And as for herself—her body had betrayed her, damn it. She'd been hiding it, denying it, but the awful truth was, this man was hot. She'd never been up close to a man as completely sexy and breathtakingly handsome as Lucky O'Donlon. He was physical perfection, pure dazzling masculine beauty. His looks were movie-star

with big hips." Syd didn't let him answer. She went back into the house, raising her voice so he could hear her. "I'll catch a cab back to the police-station parking lot."

She heard him turn off the grill, but then he followed her. "Don't be ridiculous. I'll give you a ride to your car."

Syd pushed her way out the front door. "Do you think you can manage to do that without embarrassing us both again?"

He locked it behind him. "I'm sorry if I embarrassed you or offended you or—"

"You did both, Lieutenant. How about we just not say anything else right now, all right?"

He stiffly opened the passenger-side door to his truck and stood aside so that she could get in. He was dying to speak, and Syd gave him about four seconds before he gave in to the urge to keep the conversation going.

"I happen to find you very attractive," Luke said as he climbed behind the wheel.

Two and a half seconds. She knew he'd give in. She should have pointedly ignored him, but she, too, couldn't keep herself from countering.

"Yeah," she said. "Right. Next you'll tell me it's my delicate and ladylike disposition that turns you on."

"You have no idea what's going on in my head." He started his truck with a roar. "Maybe it is."

Syd uttered a very non-ladylike word.

The lieutenant glanced at her several times, and cranked the air-conditioning up a notch as Syd sat and stewed. God, the next few weeks were going to be dreadful. Even if he didn't hit on her again, she was going to have to live with the memory of that kiss.

That amazing kiss.

Her knees still felt a little weak.

was just a lovers' tryst myself, but she mentioned what's-his-name, Bobby, would be there."

"Lovers' tryst...?" He actually looked affronted. "If you're implying that there's something improper between Lucy and me—"

Syd rolled her eyes. "Oh, come on. It's a little obvious there's something going on. I wonder if she knows what you were trying to do with me. I suppose she couldn't complain because she's married to—"

"How dare you?"

"Your...what did you call it? XO? She's married to your XO."

"Lucy and I are *friends*." His face was a thundercloud—his self-righteous outrage wasn't an act. "She loves her husband. And Blue...he's...he's the best."

His anger had faded, replaced by something quiet, something distant. "I'd follow Blue McCoy into hell if he asked me to," Luke said softly. "I'd never dishonor him by fooling around with his wife. Never."

"I'm sorry," Syd told him. "I guess... You just... You told me you never take anything too seriously, so I thought—"

"Yeah, well, you were wrong." He stared out the front windshield, holding tightly to the steering wheel with both hands. "Imagine that."

Syd nodded. And then she dug through her purse, coming up with a small spiral notebook and a pen. She flipped to a blank page and wrote down the date.

Luke glanced at her, frowning slightly. "What...?"

"I'm so rarely wrong," she told him. "When I am, it's worth taking note of."

She carefully kept her face expressionless as he studied her for several long moments.

CHAPTER FOUR

LUCKY HADN'T REALLY EXPECTED to win, so he wasn't surprised when he followed Heather into La Cantina and saw Sydney already sitting at one of the little tables with Lucy McCoy.

He'd more than half expected the reporter to second-guess his decision to change the meeting's location and track them down, and she hadn't disappointed him. That was part of the reason he'd called Heather for dinner and then dragged her here, to this just-short-of-seedy San Felipe bar.

Syd had accused him of being desperate as she'd completely and brutally rejected his advances. The fact that she was right—that he had had a motive when he lowered his mouth to kiss her—only somehow served to make it all that much worse.

Even though he knew it was foolish, he wanted to make sure she knew just how completely non-desperate he was, and how little her rejection had mattered to him, by casually showing up with a drop-dead gorgeous, blond beauty queen on his arm.

He also wanted to make sure there was no doubt left lingering in her nosy reporter's brain that there was something going on between him and Blue McCoy's wife.

Just the thought of such a betrayal made him feel ill.

Of course, maybe it was Heather's constant, mindless

And yet, after kissing him as if the world were coming to an end, Syd had pushed him away.

"Heather and I had dinner at Smokey Joe's," Lucky told them. "Heather Seeley, this is Lucy McCoy and Sydney Jameson."

But Heather was already looking away, her MTV-length attention span caught by the mirrors on the wall and her distant but gorgeous reflection...

Syd finally spoke. "Gee, I had no idea we could bring a date to a task-force meeting."

"Heather's got some phone calls to make," Lucky explained. "I figured this wasn't going to take too long, and after..." He shrugged.

After, he could return to his evening with Heather, bring her home, go for a swim in the moonlight, lose himself in her perfect body. "You don't mind giving us some privacy, right, babe?" He pulled Heather close and brushed her silicone-enhanced lips with his. Her perfect, *plastic* body...

Sydney sharply looked away from them, suddenly completely absorbed by the circles of moisture her glass had made on the table.

And Lucky felt stupid. As Heather headed for the bar, already dialing her cell phone, he sat down next to Lucy and across from Syd and felt like a complete jackass.

He'd brought Heather here tonight to show Syd...what? That he was a jackass? Mission accomplished.

Okay, yes, he *had* taken Syd into his arms on his deck earlier this evening in an effort to win her alliance. But somehow, some way, in the middle of that giddy, free-fall-inducing kiss, his strictly business motives had changed. He thought it had probably happened when her mouth had opened so warmly and willingly beneath his.

invisible, outshone by Heather's golden glory. Standing side by side, there should have been no contest.

Except, one of the two women made Lucky feel completely alive. And it wasn't Heather.

"Hey, Lucy. Lieutenant." U.S. Navy SEAL Chief Bobby Taylor smiled at Sydney as he slipped into the fourth seat at the table. "You must be Sydney. Were my directions okay?" he asked her.

Syd nodded. She looked up at Lucky almost challengingly. "I wasn't sure exactly where the bar was," she told him, "so I called Chief Taylor and asked for directions."

So that's how she found him. Well, wasn't she proud of herself? Lucky made a mental note to beat Bobby to death later.

"Call me Bob. Please." The enormous SEAL smiled at Syd again, and she smiled happily back at him, ignoring Lucky completely.

"No nickname?" she teased. "Like Hawk or Cyclops or Panther?"

And Lucky felt it. Jealousy. Stabbing and hot, like a lightning bolt to his already churning stomach. My God. Was it possible Sydney Jameson found Bob Taylor attractive? More attractive than she found Lucky?

Bobby laughed. "Just Bobby. Some guys during BUD/S tried to call me Tonto, which I objected to somewhat... forcefully." He flexed his fists meaningfully.

Bobby *was* a good-looking man despite the fact that his nose had been broken four or five too many times. He was darkly handsome, with high cheekbones, craggy features, and deep-brown eyes that broadcast his mother's Native American heritage. He had a quiet calmness to him, a Zen-like quality that *was* very attractive.

And then there was his size. Massive was the word for the man. Some women really went for that. Of course, if

meet with Admiral Stonegate," Lucy explained. "Ron Stonegate's not exactly a big fan of the SEAL teams."

"What'd Stonehead do this time?" Bobby asked.

"Easy on the insults," Lucky murmured. He glanced at Syd, wishing she weren't a reporter, knowing that anything they said could conceivably end up in a news story. "We've been ordered by the…admiral to use this assignment as a special training operation," he said, choosing his words carefully, leaving out all the expletives and less-than-flattering adjectives he would have used had she not been there, "for a trio of SEAL candidates who are just about to finish up their second phase of BUD/S."

"King, Lee and Rosetti," Bobby said, nodding his approval.

Lucky nodded. Bobby had been working as an instructor with this particular group of candidates right from the start of phase one. He wasn't surprised the chief should know the men in question.

"Tell me about them," Lucky commanded. He'd made a quick stop at the base and had pulled the three candidates' files after he'd talked to Frisco and before he'd picked up Heather. But you could only tell so much about a man from words on a piece of paper. He wanted to hear Bobby's opinion.

"They were all part of the same boat team during phase one," Bobby told him. "Mike Lee's the oldest and a lieutenant, Junior Grade, and he was buddied up with Ensign Thomas King—a local kid, much younger. African American. Both have IQs that are off the chart, and both have enough smarts to recognize each other's strengths and weaknesses. It was a good match. Petty Officer Rio Rosetti, on the other hand, is barely twenty-one, barely graduated from high school, struggles to spell his own name, but he can build anything out of nothing. He's magic. He

her head in frustration. "I don't know why some women don't report sexual assault when it happens."

"Is it our guy?" Syd asked. "Same MO?"

"Three of the women were branded with the budweiser. Those three attacks took place within the past four weeks. The fourth was earlier. I'm certain the same perp was responsible for all four attacks," Lucy told them. "And frankly, it's a little alarming that the severity of the beatings he gives his victims seems to be increasing."

"Any pattern among the victims as to location, physical appearance, anything?" Lucky asked.

"If there is, we can't find anything other than that the victims are all females between the ages of eighteen and forty-three, and the attacks all took place in either San Felipe or Coronado," the detective replied. "I'll get you the complete files first thing in the morning. You might as well try searching for a pattern, too. I don't think you're going to find one, but it sure beats sitting around waiting for this guy to strike again."

Bobby's pager went off. He glanced at it as he shut it off, then stood. "If that's all for now, Lieutenant…"

Lucky gestured with his head toward the pager. "Anything I should know about?"

"Just Wes," the bigger man said. "It's been a rough tour for him. Coronado's the last place he wanted to be, and he's been here for nearly three months now." He nodded at Sydney. "Nice meeting you. See you later, Luce." He turned back. "Do me a favor and lock your windows tonight, ladies."

"And every night until we catch this guy," Lucky added as the chief headed for the door. He stood up. "I'm going to take off, too."

"See you tomorrow." Syd barely even looked at him as she turned to Lucy. "Are you in a hurry to get home,

loaded with promise. A smile he knew that Syd had not missed.

Good. Let her know that he was going to get some tonight. Let her know he didn't need her to make fireworks.

"Absolutely." Lucky put his arm around her waist.

He glanced at Syd, but she was already back to her discussion with Lucy, and she didn't look up.

As Heather dragged him to the door, Lucky knew he was the envy of every man in the bar. He was going home with a beautiful woman who wanted to have wild sex with him.

He should have been running for his car. He should have been in a hurry to get her naked.

But as he reached the door, he couldn't stop himself from hesitating, from looking back at Syd.

She glanced up at that exact moment, and their eyes met and held. The connection was instantaneous. It was cracklingly powerful, burningly intense.

He didn't look away, and neither did she.

It was far more intimate than he'd ever been with Heather, and they'd spent days together naked.

Heather tugged at his arm, pressed her body against him, pulled his head down for a kiss.

Lucky responded instinctively, and when he looked back at Syd, she had turned away.

"Come on, baby," Heather murmured. "I'm in a hurry."

Lucky let her pull him out the door.

THE PICKUP TRUCK WAS following her.

Syd had first noticed the headlights in her rearview mirror as she'd pulled out of La Cantina's parking lot.

The truck had stayed several car lengths behind her as

without emotion? A balloon that, when popped, revealed nothing but slightly foul-smelling air.

She was glad she'd seen Luke O'Donlon with his Barbie doll. It was healthy, it was realistic and just maybe it would keep her damned subconscious from dreaming erotic dreams about him tonight.

Syd took a right turn onto Pacific, pulling into the right lane and slowing down enough so that anyone in their right mind would pass her, but the truck stayed behind her.

Think. She had to think. Or rather, she had to stop thinking about Luke O'Donlon and his perfect butt and focus on the fact that a sociopathic serial rapist could well be following her through the nearly deserted streets of San Felipe.

She'd written an article dealing with this very subject just minutes ago.

If you think someone is following you, she'd said, do not go home. Drive directly to the police station. If you have a cell phone, use it to call for help.

Syd fumbled in her shoulder bag for her cell phone, hesitating only slightly before she pushed the speed-dial button she'd programmed with Lucky O'Donlon's home phone number. It would serve him right if she interrupted him.

His machine picked up after only two rings, and she skipped over his sexy-voiced message.

"O'Donlon, it's Syd. If you're there, pick up." Nothing. "Lieutenant, I know my voice is the last thing you probably want to hear right now, but I'm being followed." Oh, crud, her voice cracked slightly, and her fear and apprehension peeked through. She took a deep breath, hoping to sound calm and collected, but only managing to sound very small and pitiful. "Are you there?"

could go for miles on a sixteenth of a tank. She had no reason to be afraid. At any minute, the San Felipe police were going to come to the rescue.

Any minute. Any. Minute.

She heard it then—sirens in the distance, getting louder and deafeningly louder as the police cars moved closer.

Three of them came from behind. She watched in her rear-view mirror as they surrounded the truck, their lights flashing.

She slowed to a stop at the side of the road as the truck did the same, twisting to look back through her rear window as the police officers approached, their weapons drawn, bright searchlights aimed at the truck.

She could see the shadow of the man in the cab. He had both hands on his head in a position of surrender. The police pulled open the truck's door, pulled him out alongside the truck where he braced himself, assuming the position for a full-body search.

Syd turned off the ignition and got out, wanting to get closer now that she knew the man following her wasn't armed, wanting to hear what he was saying, wanting to get a good look at him—see if he was the same man who'd nearly knocked her down the stairs after attacking her neighbor.

The man was talking. She could see from the police officers standing around him that he was keeping up a steady stream of conversation. Explanation, no doubt, for why he was out driving around so late at night. Following someone? Officer, that was just an unfortunate coincidence. I was going to the supermarket to pick up some ice cream.

Yeah, right.

As Syd moved closer, one of the police officers approached her.

"No," she said, nodding yes. "I think you should make him stay like that for about two hours as punishment."

"Punishment?" Luke let out a stream of sailor's language as he straightened up. "For doing something *nice?* For worrying so much about you and Lucy going home from that bar alone that I dropped Heather off at her apartment and came straight back to make sure you'd be okay?"

He hadn't gone home with Miss Ventura County. He'd given up a night of steamy, mindless, emotionless sex because he had been worried about her.

Syd didn't know whether to laugh or hit him.

"Heather wasn't happy," he told her. "That's your answer for 'what about Heather?'" He smiled ruefully. "I don't think she's ever been turned down before."

He *had* heard her question.

She'd spent most of the past hour trying her hardest not to imagine his long, muscular legs entangled with Heather's, his skin slick and his hair damp with perspiration as he...

She'd tried her hardest, but she'd always had a very good imagination.

It was stupid. She'd told herself that it didn't matter, that *he* didn't matter. She didn't even like him. But now here he was, standing in front of her, gazing at her with those impossibly blue eyes, with that twenty-four-carat sun-gilded hair curling in his face from the ocean's humidity.

"You scared me," she said again.

"You?" He laughed. "Something tells me you're unscareable." He looked around them at the three police cars, lights still spinning, the officers talking on their radios. He shook his head with what looked an awful lot like admiration. "You actually had the presence of mind

CHAPTER FIVE

"SIT ON THE COUCH—or in the chair," Dr. Lana Quinn directed Sydney. "Wherever you think you'll be more comfortable."

"I appreciate your finding the time to do this on such short notice," Lucky said.

"You got lucky," Lana told him with a smile. "Wes called right after my regular one o'clock cancelled. I was a little surprised actually—it's been a while since I've heard from him."

Lucky didn't know the pretty young psychologist very well. She was married to a SEAL named Wizard with whom he'd never worked. But Wizard had been in the same BUD/S class with Bobby and Wes, and the three men had remained close. And when Lucky had stopped Wes in the hall to inquire jokingly if he knew a hypnotist, Wes had surprised him by saying, yes, as a matter of fact, he did.

"How is Wes?" Lana asked.

Lucky was no shrink himself, but the question was just a little too casual.

She must have realized the way her words had sounded and hastened to explain. "He was in such a rush when he called, I didn't even have time to ask. We used to talk on the phone all the time back when my husband was in Team Six, you know, when he was gone more often than not—I think it was because Wes and I both missed Quinn. And

busy Alpha Squad office and Blue would look across the room and smile, and she'd smile back. Or Joe Cat. Calling Veronica every chance he got, from a pay phone in downtown Paris, from the Australian outback after a training op. He'd lower his voice, but Lucky had overheard far more than once. *Hey babe, ya miss me? God, I miss you....*

Lucky had come embarrassingly close to getting a lump in his throat more than once.

Despite his rather desperate-sounding mantra, Joe and Blue and Frisco and all of the other married SEALs made the perils of commitment look too damn good.

As Lucky watched, across the room Sydney perched on the very edge of the couch, arms folded tightly across her chest as she looked around Lana's homey office. She didn't want to be here, didn't want to be hypnotized. Her body language couldn't be any more clear.

He settled into the chair across from her. "Thanks for agreeing to this."

He could see her trepidation in the tightness of her mouth as she shook her head. "I don't think it's going to work."

"Yeah, well, maybe it will."

"Don't be too disappointed if it doesn't."

She was afraid of failing. Lucky could understand that. Failure was something he feared as well.

"Why don't you take off your jacket," Lana suggested to Sydney. "Get loose—unbutton your shirt a little, roll up your sleeves. I want you to try to get as comfortable as possible. Kick off your boots, try to relax."

"I don't think this is going to work," Sydney said again, this time to Lana, as she slipped her arms out of her jacket.

"Don't worry about that," Lana told her, sitting down in the chair closest to Sydney. "Before we go any further,

Syd thought about that, chewing for a moment on her lower lip. "More like alarmed," she said. "He was big. But I wasn't afraid of him because I thought he was dangerous. It was more like the flash of fear you get when a car swerves into your lane and there's nowhere to go to avoid hitting it."

"Picture the moment that you first heard him coming," Lana suggested, "and try to flip it into slow motion. You hear him, then you see him. What are you thinking? Right at that second when you first spot him coming down the stairs?"

Syd looked up from untying the laces of her boots. "Kevin Manse," she said.

She was still leaning over, and Lucky got a sudden brief look down the open front of her shirt. She was wearing a black bra, and he got a very clear look at black lace against smooth pale skin. As she moved to untie her other boot, Lucky tried to look away. Tried and failed. He found himself watching her, hoping for another enticing glimpse of her small but perfectly, delicately, deliciously shaped, lace-covered breasts.

Sydney Jameson was enormously attractive, he realized with a jolt as he examined her face. Sure he'd always preferred women with a long mane of hair, but hers was darkly sleek and especially lustrous, and the short cut suited the shape of her face. Her eyes were the color of black coffee, with lashes that didn't need any makeup to look thick and dark.

She wasn't traditionally pretty, but whenever she stopped scowling and smiled, she was breathtaking.

And as far as her clothes…

Lucky had never particularly liked the Annie Hall look before, but with a flash of awareness, he suddenly completely understood its appeal. Buried beneath Syd's baggy,

Laughing, Lana crossed the room and turned off the light. "Actually, I use a mirror ball, a flashlight and voiced suggestions. Lieutenant, I have to recommend that you step out into the waiting room for a few minutes. I've found that SEALs are highly susceptible to this form of light-induced hypnotism. My theory is that it has to do with the way you've trained yourself to take combat naps." She sat down again across from Syd. "They fall, quickly, into deep REM sleep for short periods of time," she explained before looking back at Lucky. "There may be a form of self-hypnosis involved when you do that." She smiled wryly. "I'm not sure though. Quinn won't let me experiment on him. You can try staying in here, but…"

"I'll leave the room—temporarily," Lucky said.

"Good idea. I'm sure Dr. Quinn doesn't want both of us waddling around quacking like ducks," Syd said.

Hot damn, she'd made a joke. Lucky laughed, and Syd actually smiled back at him. But her smile was far too small and it faded far too quickly.

"Seriously," she added. "If I do something to really embarrass myself, don't rub it in, all right?"

"I won't," he told her. "As long as you promise to return the same favor some day."

"I guess that's fair."

"Step outside, Lieutenant."

"You'll wait to ask her any questions until I come back in?"

Lana Quinn nodded. "I will."

"Quack, quack," Syd said.

Lucky closed the door behind him.

As he paced, he punched a number into his cell phone. Frisco picked up the phone on his office desk after only half a ring.

"Francisco."

"Whoops," Lucky said to Frisco. "I've got to go. It's hypno-time. Later, man."

He hung up on his commanding officer and snapped his phone shut, slipping it into his pocket.

"Move slowly," Lana told him. "She's pretty securely under, but no quick motions or sudden noises, please."

The blinds were down in the office and, with the overhead lights off, Lucky had to blink for a moment to let his eyes adjust to the dimness.

He moved carefully into the room, standing off to the side, as Lana sat down near Syd.

She was stretched out on the couch, her eyes closed, as if she were asleep. She looked deceptively peaceful and possibly even angelic. Lucky, however, knew better.

"Sydney, I want to go back, just a short amount of time, to the night you were coming home from the movies. Do you remember that night?"

As Lucky sat down, Syd was silent.

"Do you remember that night?" Lana persisted. "You were nearly knocked over by the man coming down the stairs."

"Kevin Manse," Syd said. Her eyes were still tightly shut, but her voice was strong and clear.

"That's right," Lana said. "He reminded you of Kevin Manse. Can you see him, Syd?"

Sydney nodded. "He nearly knocks me over on the stairs. He's angry. And drunk. I know he's drunk. I'm drunk, too. It's my first frat-house party."

"What the—"

Lana silenced Lucky with one swift motion. "How old are you, Sydney?"

"I'm eighteen," she told them, her husky voice breathless and young-sounding. "He apologizes—oh, God, he's *so* cute, and we start talking. He's an honors student as

was breathing hard, with a slight sheen of perspiration on her face. "Okay," he said, unable to stand this another second. "Okay, Syd. You do the deed with Mr. Wonderful. It's over. Let's move on."

"He's so sweet," Syd sighed. "He says he's afraid people will talk if I stay there all night, so he asks a friend to drive me back to my dorm. He says he'll call me, and he kisses me good night and I'm…I'm so amazed at how good that felt, at how much I love him— I can't wait to do it again."

Okay. So now he knew that not only was Sydney hot, she was hot-blooded as well.

"Sydney," Lana's voice left no room for argument. "Now it's just a little less than a week ago. You're on the stairs, in your apartment building. You're coming home from the movies—"

"God." Sydney laughed aloud. "Did that movie *suck*. I can't believe I spent all that money on it. The highlight was that pop singer who used to be a model who now thinks he's an actor. And I'm not talking about his acting. I'm talking about the scene that featured his bare butt. It alone was truly worthy of the big screen. And," she laughed again, a rich, sexy sound, "if you want to know the truth, these days the movies is the closest I seem to be able to get to a naked man."

Lucky knew one easy way to change that, fast. But he kept his mouth shut and let Lana do her shrink thing.

"You're climbing the stairs to your apartment," she told Syd. "It's late, and you're heading home and you hear a noise."

"Footsteps," Syd responded. "Someone's coming down the stairs. Kevin Manse—no, he just looks for half a second like Kevin Manse, but he's not."

Lana shot him an appalled "what are you doing?" look. He didn't give a damn. He wanted to know.

"It's safe," Syd told him.

"Safe."

"Lieutenant," Lana said sternly.

"Back to the guy on the stairs," Lucky said. "What's *he* wearing?"

"Jeans," Syd said without hesitating. "And a plain dark sweatshirt."

"Tattoos?" Lucky asked.

"His sleeves are down."

"On his feet?"

She was silent for several long seconds. "I don't know."

"You turn away," Lana said. "But do you look back at him as he goes down the stairs?"

"No. I hear him, though. He slams the front door on his way out. I'm glad—it sometimes doesn't latch and then anyone can get in."

"Do you hear anything else?" Lucky asked. "Stop and listen carefully."

Syd was silent. "A car starts. And then pulls away. A fan belt must be loose or old or something because it squeals a little. I'm glad when it's gone. It's an annoying sound—it's not an expensive part, and it doesn't take much to learn how to—"

"When you're home, do you park in a garage," Lucky interrupted, "or on the street?"

"Street," she told him.

"When you pulled up," he asked, "after the movie, were there any cars near your apartment building that you didn't recognize?"

Syd chewed on her lip, frowning slightly. "I don't remember."

okay. Look at her! *Look* at her!" She started to cry; deep, racking sobs that shook her entire body, a fountain of emotion brimming over and spilling down her cheeks. "What kind of monster could have done this to this girl? Look in her eyes—all of her hopes, her dreams, her *life,* they're *gone!* And you know with that mother of hers, she's going to live the rest of her life hiding from the world, too afraid ever to come back out again. And why? Because she left the window in the kitchen unlocked. She wasn't careful, because nobody had *bothered* to warn any of us that this son of a bitch was out there! They knew, the police *knew,* but nobody said a single word!"

Lucky couldn't stop himself. He sat next to Sydney, and pulled her into his arms. "Oh, Syd, I'm sorry," he said.

But she pushed him away, curling into herself, turning into a small ball in the corner of the couch, completely inconsolable.

Lucky looked at Lana helplessly.

"Syd," she said loudly. "I'm going to clap my hands twice, and you're going to fall asleep. You'll wake up in one minute, feeling completely refreshed. You won't remember any of this."

Lana clapped her hands, and just like that, Syd's body relaxed. The room was suddenly very silent.

Lucky sat back, resting his head against the back of the couch. He drew in a deep breath and let it out with a whoosh. "I had no idea," he said. Syd was always so strong, so in control.... He remembered that message he'd found on his answering machine last night when he'd gotten home. The way she hadn't quite managed to hide the fear in her voice when she'd called him for help, thinking she was being followed by a stranger. *You scared me to death,* she'd told him, but he hadn't really believed it until he'd heard that phone message.

CHAPTER SIX

"WHERE ARE WE GOING?" Syd asked, following Luke down toward the beach.

"I want to show you something," he said.

He'd been quiet ever since they'd left Lana Quinn's office—not just quiet, but subdued. Introspective. Brooding.

It made her nervous. What exactly had she said and done while under the hypnotist's spell to make the ever-smiling Navy Ken *brood?*

Syd had come out of the session feeling a little disoriented. At first she'd thought the hypnosis hadn't worked, but then she'd realized that about half an hour had passed from the time she'd first sat down. A half hour of which she remembered nothing.

To Syd's disappointment, Lana told her she *hadn't* got a clear look at the rapist's unmasked face as he'd come down the stairs. They weren't any closer to identifying the man.

Luke O'Donlon hadn't said a word to her. Not in Lana's office, not in his truck as they'd headed back here to the base. He'd parked by the beach and gotten out, saying only, "Come on."

They stood now at the edge of the sand, watching the activity. And there was a great deal of activity on this beach, although there was nary a beach ball, a bikini-clad girl, a picnic basket or a colorful umbrella in sight.

stayed in, but this flu came with a dangerously high fever. Medical wouldn't let them stay. Those guys were rolled back to the next class—most of them are going through the first weeks of phase one again right now. To top that off, this particular class also just lost six men in the fallout from that diving accident. So their number's low."

Syd watched the men who were running through the water—the candidates Luke had said were in the second phase of BUD/S training. "Somehow I was under the impression that the physical training ended after Hell Week."

Luke laughed. "Are you kidding? PT never ends. Being a SEAL is kind of like being a continuous work in progress. You always keep running—every day. You've got to be able to do consistent seven-and-a-half-minute miles tomorrow and next month—and next year. If you let it slip, your whole team suffers. See, a SEAL team can only move as fast as its slowest man when it's moving as a unit."

He gestured toward the men still carrying the black rubber boats above their heads. "That's what these guys are starting to learn. Teamwork. Identify an individual's strengths and weaknesses and use that information to keep your team operating at its highest potential."

A red-haired girl on a bicycle rode into the parking lot. She skidded to a stop in the soft sand a few yards away from Luke and Syd, and sat down, watching the men on the beach.

"Yo, Tash!" Luke called to her.

She barely even glanced up, barely waved, so intent was she on watching the men on the beach. It was the girl Syd had met yesterday, the one who'd been at the base with Lieutenant Commander Francisco's wife. She was looking for someone, searching the beach, shading her eyes with her hand.

"Are you crazy?" His less-than-friendly greeting was accompanied by a scowl. "What did I tell you about riding your bike out here alone? And that was *before* this psycho-on-the-loose crap."

"No one wanted to ride all the way out here with me." Tasha lifted her chin. They were both speaking loudly enough for Syd to easily overhear. "Besides, I'm fast. If I see any weirdos, I can get away, no problem."

Sweat was literally pouring off the young man's face as he bent over to catch his breath, hands on his knees. "You're fast," he repeated skeptically. "Faster than a car?"

She was exasperated. "No."

"No." He glared at her. "Then it's *not* no problem, is it?"

"I don't see what the big deal—"

The black man exploded. "The *big deal* is that there's some son-of-a-bitch psycho running around town raping and beating the hell out of women. The *big* deal is that, as a female, you're a potential target. As a pretty, young female who's riding her bike alone, you're an attractive, easy target. You might as well wear a sign around your neck that says *victim*."

"I read this guy breaks into women's homes," Tasha countered. "I don't see what that has to do with me riding my bike."

Syd couldn't keep her mouth shut any longer. "Actually," she said, "serial rapists tend to do something called *troll* for victims. That means they drive around and look for a likely target—someone who's alone and potentially defenseless—and they follow her home. It's possible once they pick a victim, they follow her for several days or even weeks, searching for the time and place she's the most vulnerable. Just because all of the other attacks we know

girl's attachment to this man was much stronger. But he was being careful not to touch her, careful to use words like *friends,* careful to keep his distance.

"How about I call you?" he suggested, kindly. "Three times a week, a few minutes before 2100—nine o'clock? Check in and let you know how I'm doing. Would that work?"

Tasha chewed on her lower lip. "Make it five times a week, and you've got a deal."

"I'll try for four," he countered. "But—"

She shook her head. "*Five.*"

He looked at her crossed arms, at the angle of her tough-kid chin and assumed the same pose. "*Four.* But I don't get every evening off, you know, so some weeks it might be only three. But if I get weekend liberty, I'll drop by, okay? In return, you've got to promise me you don't go anywhere alone until this bad guy is caught."

She gave in, nodding her acceptance, gazing up at him as if she were memorizing his face.

"Say it," he insisted.

"I promise."

"I promise, too," he said then glanced at his watch. "Damn, I gotta go."

He turned, focusing on Luke and Syd as if for the first time. "Hey, Uncle Lucky. Drive Tasha home."

It was, without a doubt, a direct order. Luke saluted. "Yes, sir, *Ensign* King, sir."

Thomas's harshly featured face relaxed into a smile that made him look his age. "Sorry, Lieutenant," he said. "I meant, *please* drive Tasha home, *sir.* It's not safe right now for a young woman to ride all that distance alone."

Luke nodded. "Consider it done."

"Thank you, sir." The young man pointed his finger

your strengths and being completely honest about your weaknesses."

"But—" This time Syd cut her own self off. Did he say *make this work?*

"Here's what I think we should do," Luke said. He was completely serious. "I think we should put you to work doing what you do best. Investigative reporting. Research. I want you to be in charge of finding a pattern, finding *some*thing among the facts we know that will bring us closer to the rapist."

"But the police are already doing that."

"We need to do it, too." The breeze off the ocean stirred his already tousled hair. "There's got to be something they've missed, and I'm counting on you to find it. I know you will, because I know how badly you want to catch this guy." He gazed back at the ocean. "You, uh, kind of gave that away in Lana Quinn's office."

"Oh," Syd said. "God." What else had she said or done? She couldn't bring herself to ask.

"We're both on the same page, Syd," Luke said quietly, intensely. "I really want to catch this guy, too. And I'm willing to have you on my team, but only if you're willing to be a team player. That means you contribute by using your strengths—your brain and your ability to research. And you contribute equally by sitting back and letting the rest of us handle the physical stuff. You stay out of danger. We get a lead, you stay back at the base or in the equipment van. No arguments. You haven't trained for combat, you haven't done enough PT to keep up, and I won't have you endanger the rest of the team or yourself."

"I'm not *that* out of shape," she protested.

"You want to prove it?" he countered. "If you can run four miles in thirty minutes while wearing boots, and complete the BUD/S obstacle course in ten minutes—"

officers and enlisted men currently stationed in Coronado to any hint of a sex crime.

Admiral Stonegate's handpicked trio of SEAL candidates spent their off hours helping. They were a solid group—good, reliable men, despite their connection to Admiral Stonehead.

And after only two days, Syd was best friends with all three of them. And Bobby, too.

She laughed, she smiled, she joked, she fumed at the computers. It was only with Lucky that she was strictly business. All "yes, sir," and "no, sir," and that too-polite, slightly forced smile, even when they were alone and still working at oh-one-hundred....

Lucky had managed to negotiate a truce with her. They had a definite understanding, but he couldn't help but wish he could've gone with the girlfriend alliance scenario. Yes, it would've been messy further down the road, but it would have been much more fun.

Especially since he still hadn't been able to stop thinking about that kiss.

"Here's another 'what if' situation for you," Lucky heard Syd say. "You're a woman—"

"What?" Rio hooted. "I thought you wanted to know about being a SEAL?"

"This is related to this assignment," she explained. "Just hear me out. You're a woman, and you turn around to find a man wearing panty hose on his head in your apartment in the middle of the night."

"You tell him, 'no darling, that shade of taupe simply doesn't work with your clothing.'" Rio laughed at his joke.

"You want me to kill him or muzzle him?" Thomas King asked.

"Rosetti, I'm serious here," Syd said. "This has hap-

A majority of the women fought back, but some of them didn't. One of them pretended to faint—went limp. Several others say they froze—they were so frightened they couldn't move. A few others, like Gina, just cowered."

"And?" Lucky said, dragging a chair up to the table.

"And I wish I could say that there's a direct relationship between the amount of violence the rapist inflicted on the victim and the amount that she fought back. In the first half-dozen or so attacks, it seemed as if the more the woman fought, the more viciously he beat her. And there were actually two cases where our perp walked away from women who didn't fight back. As if he didn't want to waste his time."

"So then it makes sense to advise women to submit," Lucky figured.

"Maybe at first, but I'm not so sure about that anymore. His pattern's changed over the past few weeks." Syd scowled down at the papers in front of her. "We have eleven victims, spanning a seven-week period. During those seven weeks, the level of violence our guy is using to dominate his victims has begun to intensify."

Lucky nodded. He'd overheard Syd and Lucy discussing this several nights ago.

"Out of the six most recent victims, we've had four who fought back right from the start, one who pretended to faint, and Gina, the most recent, who cowered and didn't resist. Out of those six, Gina got the worst beating. Yet—go figure—the other woman who didn't resist was barely touched."

"So if you fight this guy, you can guarantee you'll be hurt," Lucky concluded. "But if you submit, you've got a fifty-fifty chance of his walking away from you."

"And a chance of being beaten within an inch of your life," Syd said grimly. "Keep in mind, too, that we're

sure you don't want to follow them, Lieutenant? Read about this in my memo instead?"

Lucky stood up to pour himself a cup of coffee from the setup by the door. He had to search for a mug that was clean, and he was glad for the excuse to keep his back to her. "Nothing about this assignment has been pleasant. So if you think this is something I need to hear…"

"I do."

Lucky poured himself a cup of coffee, then, taking a deep breath, he turned to face her. He carried it back to the table and sat down across from her. "Okay," he said. "Shoot."

"According to the medical reports, our man didn't… shall we say, achieve sexual completion, unless the woman fought back," Syd told him.

Oh, God.

"We need to keep in mind," she continued, "the fact that rape isn't about sex. It's about violence and power. Domination. Truth is, many serial rapists never ejaculate at all. And in fact, out of these eleven cases of rape, we've got only four instances of sexual, um, completion. Like I said, all of them occurred when the victim fought back, or—and this is important—when the victim was *forced* to fight back."

"But wait. You said a majority of the victims fought back." Lucky leaned forward. "Couldn't he have been wearing a condom the other times?"

"Not according to the victims' statements." Syd stood up and started to pace. "There's more, Luke, listen to this. Gina said in her interview that she didn't resist. She cowered, and he hit her, and she cowered some more. And then, she says he spent about ten minutes trashing her apartment. I went in there. The place looked like there'd been one hell of a fight. But she *didn't fight back.*

CHAPTER SEVEN

LUKE O'DONLON WAS WAITING when Syd pulled up.

"Is she alive?" she asked as she got out of her car.

The quiet residential area was lit up, the street filled with police cars and ambulances, even a fire truck. Every light was blazing in the upscale house.

Luke nodded. "Yes."

"Thank God. Have you been inside?"

He shook his head. "Not yet. I took a...walk around the neighborhood. If he's still here, he's well hidden. I've got the rest of the team going over the area more carefully."

It was remarkable, really. When Syd had received Luke's phone call telling her Lucy had just called, that there'd been another attack, she'd been fast asleep. She'd quickly pulled on clothes, splashed water on her face and hurried out to her car. She felt rumpled and mismatched, slightly off-balance and sick to her stomach from exhaustion and fear that this time the attacker had gone too far.

Luke, on the other hand, looked as if he'd been grimly alert for hours. He was wearing what he'd referred to before as his summer uniform—short-sleeved, light fabric— definitely part of the Navy Ken clothing action pack. His shoes were polished and his hair was neatly combed. He'd even managed to shave, probably while he was driving over. Or maybe he shaved every night before he went to bed on the off chance he'd need to show up somewhere and be presentable at a moment's notice.

unless she did something fast, the big tough warrior was going to keel over in a dead faint.

"I am, too," Syd said. "Mind if we take a minute and sit down?" She took his arm and gently pulled him down next to her on the stairs that led to the front door, all but pushing his head down between his knees.

They sat there in silence for many long minutes after the ambulance pulled away. Syd carefully kept her eyes on the activity in the street—the neighbors who'd come out in their yards, the policemen keeping the more curious at a safe distance—looking anywhere but at Luke. She was aware of his breathing, aware that he'd dropped his head slightly in an attempt to fight his dizziness. She took many steadying breaths herself—but her own dizziness was more from her amazement that he could be affected this completely, this powerfully.

After what seemed like forever, she sensed more than saw Luke straighten up, heard him draw in one last deep breath and blow it out in a burst.

"Thanks," he said.

Syd finally risked a glance at him. Most of the color had returned to his face. He reached for her hand, loosely lacing her fingers with his as he gave her a rueful smile. "That would've been really embarrassing if I'd fainted."

"Oh," she said innocently, "were you feeling faint, too? I know I'm not taking enough time to eat right these days, and that plus the lack of sleep…."

He gently squeezed her hand. "And thanks, also, for not rubbing in the fact that right now *I'm* the one slowing *you* down."

"Well, now that you mention it…."

Luke laughed. God, he was good-looking when he laughed. Syd felt her hands start to sweat. If she hadn't been light-headed before, she sure as hell was now.

indelicate word. "Where's the connection with Mary Beth?"

"It's a stretch," Lucy admitted.

"Tell me."

"Former boyfriend. And I mean former. As in nearly ancient history. Although Mary Beth just got married, she's been living with her lawyer for close to four years. Way before that, she was hot and heavy with a captain who still works as a doctor at the military hospital. Captain Steven Horowitz."

Syd sighed. Four years ago. That *was* a stretch.

"Still think there's a connection?" Lucy asked.

"Yes."

Lucky poked his head in the door. "Ready to go?"

Like Syd, he'd been working nonstop since last night's late-night phone call about the most recent attack. But unlike Syd, he still looked crisp and fresh, as if he'd spent the afternoon napping rather than sifting through the remaining personnel files of the men on the naval base.

"I gotta run," Syd told Lucy. "I'm going back to the hypnotist, see if I noticed any strange cars parked in front of my house on the night Gina was attacked. Wish me luck."

"Good luck," Lucy said. "If you could remember the license-plate number, I'd be most appreciative."

"Yeah, what are the odds of that? I don't even know my own plate number. Later, Lucy." Syd hung up the phone, saved her computer file and stood, trying to stretch the kinks out of her back.

"Anything new turn up?" Lucky asked as they started down the hall.

"Four years ago, Mary Beth Hollis—victim twelve— used to date a Captain Horowitz."

You didn't see the plates—not that anyone expected you to—but I have to confess I'd hoped."

"Yeah, me, too." Syd tiredly pulled herself up into a sitting position. "I'm not a car person. I'm sorry—" She looked around. "Where's Luke?"

"Waiting room," Lana said as she pulled open the curtains, brightening up the room. "He fell asleep while he was out there—while I was putting you under. He looked so completely wiped out, I couldn't bring myself to wake him."

"It's been a tough couple of days," Syd told the doctor.

"I heard another woman was attacked last night."

"It's been frustrating," Syd admitted. "Particularly for Luke. We haven't had a whole lot of clues to go on. There's not much to do besides wait for this guy to screw up. I think if Luke had the manpower, he'd put every woman in both of these cities in protective custody. I keep expecting him to start driving around with a bullhorn warning women to leave town."

"Quinn's in DC this week," Lana said. "He's worried, too. He actually asked Wes Skelly to check up on me. I left for work earlier than usual this morning, and Wes was sitting in his truck in front of my house. It's crazy."

"Luke keeps trying to get me to stay overnight at the base," Syd told her, "and for the first time in his life, it's for platonic reasons."

Lana laughed as she opened the door to the waiting room. "I'm sorry to have to kick you out so soon, but I've got another patient."

"No problem. Dark, old-model sedan," Syd repeated. "Thanks again."

"Sorry I couldn't be of more help."

Syd went into the waiting room, where a painfully thin

But then he blinked and turned back into Luke O'Donlon, aka Lucky, aka her own living Navy Ken.

"Jeez." He lifted his arm from her throat so that she could breathe again. "What the hell were you trying to do?"

"Not this," Syd said, clearing her throat, her head starting to throb from where it had made hard contact with the floor. "In fact, I was trying to do the exact opposite of this. But I couldn't wake you up."

"Oh, man, I must've..." He shook his head, still groggy. "Usually I can take a combat nap and wake up at the least little noise."

"Not this time."

"Sometimes, if I'm really tired, and if I know I'm in a safe place, my body takes over and I go into a deep sleep and—" his eyes narrowed slightly. "You're supposed to be hypnotized," he remembered. "How come you're not hypnotized?"

As Syd stared up into the perfect blueness of his eyes, she wasn't sure she *wasn't* hypnotized. Why else would she just lie here on the floor with the full weight of his body pressing down on top of her without protesting even a little?

Maybe she'd gotten a concussion.

Maybe that was what had rendered her so completely stupid.

But maybe not. Her head hurt, but not that much. Maybe her stupidity was from more natural causes.

"Dark, old-model sedan," she told him. "Lana didn't want to wake you, and it's just as well. I'm an idiot when it comes to cars. That and calling it ugly was the best I could do."

Was he never going to get off her ever again? She could

considering you woke me up by sticking a gun barrel into my ribs."

"A *gun* barrel!" She laughed her disbelief. "Get real!"

"What the hell was that, anyway?"

Syd picked up the magazine and tightly rolled it, showing him.

"It felt like a gun barrel." He pulled himself to his feet and held out his hand to help Syd up. "Next time you want to wake me, and calling my name won't do it," he said, "think Sleeping Beauty. A kiss'll do the trick every time."

Yeah, right. Like she'd ever try to kiss Luke O'Donlon awake. He'd probably grab her and throw her down and...

And kiss her until the room spun, until she surrendered her clothes, her pride, her identity, her very soul. And probably her heart, as well.

"Maybe we shouldn't leave," she said tartly, as she followed Luke out the door. "It seems to me that the safest place for a Navy SEAL who fantasizes that he's Sleeping Beauty is right here, in a psychologist's waiting room."

"Ha," Luke said, "ha."

"What's on the schedule for this afternoon?" Syd asked as Luke pulled his truck into the parking lot by the administration building.

"I'm going to start hanging out in bars," Luke told her. "The seedier the better."

She turned to look at him. "Well, *that's* productive. Drinking yourself into oblivion while the rest of us sweat away in the office?"

He turned off the engine but didn't move to get out of the truck. "You know as well as I do that I have no intention of partying."

There was nothing in the bathroom that could be used as a weapon except for the heavy ceramic lid to the back of the toilet. She'd brandished it high over her head as she'd finally emerged from the bathroom to find she was, indeed, alone in her apartment. But she'd turned on every lamp in the place, checked all the window locks twice, and slept—badly—with the lights blazing.

"Nah," she said now. "I'm just not the type that scares easily."

He smiled as if he knew she was lying. "What, did you get spooked and sleep with all the lights on last night?" he asked.

"Me?" She tried to sound affronted. "No way."

"That's funny," he said. "Because when I drove past your place at about 1:00 a.m. it sure looked as if you had about four million watts of electricity working."

She was taken aback. "You drove past my apartment…?"

He realized he'd given himself away. "Well, yeah…I was in the neighborhood…."

"How many nights have you been spending your time cruising the streets of San Felipe instead of sleeping?" she asked.

He looked away, and she realized she'd collided with the truth. "No wonder you nearly fainted last night," she said. No wonder he'd looked as if he had been pulled from bed.

"I wasn't going to faint," he protested.

"You were *so* going to faint."

"No way. I was just a little dizzy."

She glared at him. "How on earth do you expect to catch this guy if you don't take care of yourself—if you don't get a good night's sleep?"

"How on earth can I get a good night's sleep," he said through gritted teeth, "*until* I catch this guy?"

"Right," she said. "And what exactly is it that I'm bothering to hide from you?"

"I think you're hiding," he paused dramatically, "the fact that you cry at movies."

She gave him her best "you must be crazy" look. "I do not."

"Or maybe I should just say *you cry*. You pretend to be so tough. So...unmovable. Methodically going about trying to find a connection between the rape victims, as if it's all just a giant puzzle to be solved, another step in the road to success which starts with you writing an exclusive story about the capture of the San Felipe Rapist. As if the human part of the story—these poor, traumatized women—doesn't make you want to cry."

She couldn't meet his gaze. "Even if I were the type of person who cried, there's no time," she said as briskly as she possibly could. She didn't want him to know she'd cried buckets for Gina and all of the other victims in the safety and privacy of her shower.

"I think you're secretly a softy," he continued. "I think you can't resist giving to every charity that sends you a piece of junk mail. But I also think someone once told you that you'll be bulldozed over for being too nice, so you try to be tough, when in truth you're a pushover."

Syd rolled her eyes. "If you really need to think that about me, go right a—"

"So what are *you* doing this afternoon?"

Syd opened the door to the cab, ready to end this conversation. How had it gotten so out of hand? "Nothing. Working. Learning all there is to know about serial rapists. Trying to figure out what it is I'm missing that ties the victims together."

"Frisco told me you asked his permission to bring Gina Sokoloski onto the base."

was as close to a fetal position as she could get. She was a picture of tension and fear.

But Syd was undaunted. She sprawled on her stomach, elbows propping up her chin, keeping up a nearly continuous stream of chatter.

Down on the beach, the phase-one SEAL candidates were doing a teamwork exercise with telephone poles. And, just for kicks, during a so-called break, Wes and Aztec and the other instructors had them do a set of sugar-cookie drills—running into the surf to get soaked, and then rolling over and over so that the white powdery sand stuck to every available inch of them, faces included. Faces in particular. Then it was back to the telephone poles.

Syd gestured toward the hard-working, sand-covered men with her cola can, and Lucky knew she was telling Gina about BUD/S. About Hell Week. About the will-power the men needed to get through the relentless discomfort and physical pain day after day after day after day, with only four blessed hours of sleep the whole week long.

Perseverance. If you had enough of that mysterious quality that made you persevere, you'd survive. You'd make it through.

You'd be wet, you'd be cold, you'd be shaking with fatigue, muscles cramping and aching, blisters not just on your feet, but in places you didn't ever imagine you could get blisters, and you'd break it all down into the tiniest segments possible. Life became not a day or an hour or even a minute.

It became a footstep. Right foot. Then left. Then right again.

It became a heartbeat, a lungful of air, a nanosecond of existence to be endured and triumphed over.

Lucky knew what Syd was telling Gina, because she'd

toward him, but then ran back to Gina, leaning over to say something to the young woman.

And then she was flying toward him, holding on to that silly floppy hat with one hand, her sunglasses falling into the sand. Her feet were bare and she hopped awkwardly and painfully over the gravel at the edge of the parking area to get closer to him.

"Luke, I think I've found it!"

He immediately knew which *it* she was talking about. The elusive connection among the rape victims.

"I've got to take Gina back home," she said, talking a mile a minute. "I need you to get some information for me. The two other women who had no obvious ties to the base? I need you to find out if they have or *had* a close relationship with someone who was stationed here four years ago."

She was so revved up, he hated to be a wet blanket, but he didn't get it. She looked at the expression on his face and laughed. "You think I'm nuts."

"I think it's a possibility."

"I'm not. Remember Mary Beth Hollis?"

"Yeah." He was never going to forget Mary Beth Hollis. The sight of her being carried to the ambulance was one he'd carry with him to his dying day.

"Remember she dated Captain Horowitz four years ago, before she was married?"

He remembered hearing about the woman's romantic connection to the navy doctor, but he hadn't committed the details to memory.

"Gina just told me that her mother's second husband was a master chief in the regular Navy," Syd continued. "Stationed where? Stationed *here*. He was transferred to the east coast when he and Gina's mom were divorced— when? Four years ago. Four. Years. Ago."

was good at providing comfort—particularly the kind that slid neatly into seduction.

God, what was he thinking? This was *Syd*.

Syd—who'd kissed him as if the world were coming to an end. Syd—whose body had felt so tempting beneath his just this morning. Syd—whose lit-up windows he'd stared at for nearly an hour last night, dying to ring her bell for more reasons than simply to make sure she was safe.

Okay. True confession time. Yes, it was Syd, and yes, he wanted to seduce her. But he liked her. A lot. Too much to trade in their solid friendship for his typical two-week, molten-lava, short-term fling.

He wasn't going to do it.

He was going to stay away from her, keep it platonic.

Yeah. Right.

long, heart-stopping moments, Syd was certain that he was going to kiss her.

Like the last time he'd kissed her, she saw it coming, but this go-round seemed so much more unrehearsed. The shift of emotions and the heightened awareness in his eyes couldn't possibly be an act, could it? Or the way his gaze dropped for just an instant to her lips, the way his own lips parted just a tiny bit, the tip of his tongue wetting them slightly in an unconscious move.

But then, instead of planting a big knee-weakening one on her, he released her. He let her go and even stepped back.

Whoa, what just happened here?

Luke grabbed her hand and pulled her over to the main computer. "Check *this* out. Show her the thing," he commanded the SEAL candidates.

Thomas was at the keyboard with Rio hovering over his shoulder, and they both moved slightly to the side so that Syd could see the screen. As if her eyes could focus on the screen.

She still felt completely disoriented. Luke hadn't kissed her. Of course, this was an office in a building on a U.S. naval base, she told herself, and he was the team's commanding officer. This was the U.S. Navy and there were probably rules about kissing.

Restrained, he'd said, indeed. Syd had to smile. Funny, she wouldn't have thought he'd have had it in him.

Thomas was talking to her, explaining what they'd done on the computer. "We pulled up the personnel files of all twelve of the servicemen and women—living and dead, active duty and retired—who're connected to the victims."

"All twelve," Rio chimed in, "were stationed here in Coronado during the same eight-week period in 1996."

"A percentage of a billion is still a huge number," Syd countered.

"There's not a billion names on that list," Luke told her.

She hefted the list. "It feels as if there is."

"Most of Alpha Squad's in there," Bobby told her. "The squad came to Coronado for a training op, I remember, and ended up pulling extra duty as BUD/S instructors. There was this one class, where the dropout rate was close to zero. I think three guys rang out, total. It was the most amazing thing, but as they went into Hell Week, we were completely understaffed."

"I remember that," Luke said. "Most of us had done a rotation assisting the instructors, so we ended up shanghaied into helping take these guys through their paces."

"Most of Alpha Squad," Syd echoed, realizing just what that meant. Anyone female and connected to anyone on this list was a potential target for attack. She looked at Luke. "Have you called—"

"Already done," he said, anticipating her question. "I've talked to all the guys' wives except Ronnie Catalanotto, and I left a pretty detailed message on her machine and told her to call me on my cell phone ASAP."

"You know, Lieutenant Lucky, sir," Rio said, "one way to catch this guy might be to set Syd here up as bait, make it look like she's your girlfriend and—"

"Uh-uh," Luke said. "No way."

Well, wasn't he vehemently opposed to *that?*

"I'm not talking about sending her out into the bad part of San Felipe in the middle of the night," Rio persisted. "In fact, she'll be safer than she is right now, considering we'll be watching her whenever she's alone."

"She lives on the third floor of a house in a neighborhood that's more concrete and asphalt than landscaping,"

job is research, remember? We had an agreement. You're supposed to be the one in the surveillance van, not the one used as bait. *Bait.* Dear Lord, save me from a conspiracy of fools!"

"Hey, what happened to brilliant?" Syd asked sharply.

He glared at her. "You tell me! You're the one who's lost your mind!"

"Maybe we could get Detective McCoy to pretend she's your girlfriend," Thomas volunteered.

"Oh, that would work," Syd rolled her eyes. "Clearly this guy pays attention to details. You don't think he'd notice that Luke sends out this 'come and get me and mine' message, and then starts getting chummy with the wife of one of his best friends? Oh, and she's a police detective, too. Anyone notice that not-too-fresh smell? Could that possibly be the stench of a *setup?*"

"Do you have *any* idea at all how much damage this dirtwad could do to you in the amount of time it would take the fastest SEAL team in the world to get from a van on the street to your third-floor apartment?" Luke asked hotly. "Do you know that this son of a bitch broke Mary Beth Hollis's cheekbone with his first punch? Do you really want to find out what that feels like? My God, Sydney! Think about *that,* will you *please?*"

"So maybe the setup should be at your house," she countered. "We can make like I move in with you, and set up a pattern where you come home extremely late—where there's a repeated block of time when I'm there alone. The team can hide in your backyard. Shoot, they can hide in your basement."

"No, they can't. I don't have a basement."

She nearly growled at him in exasperation. "Luke, think about this! If we can guarantee that the team will be close,

Syd rolled her eyes. "Anyone who knows him will take one look at me and realize something's up."

"Anyone who knows him," Bobby said, "will take one look at you, and think he's finally found someone worthy of his time."

LUCKY COULDN'T REMEMBER THE last time he'd felt this nervous because of a woman.

He had to park his truck three houses down from the Catalanottos'. Veronica's "little" cookout had turned into a full-blown party, judging from all the cars and trucks parked on the street. Bobby's truck and Wes's bike were there. PJ Becker's lime-green Volkswagen bug. Frisco's Jeep. Lucy McCoy's unassuming little subcompact.

"We'll just stop in so I can talk Veronica into leaving town for a week or so," he told Syd as they walked down the driveway toward the little house. "We can use this party as a dress rehearsal for when we go into town later. If we can fool this group of people into thinking we're together, we can fool anyone."

Syd looked over at him, one perfect eyebrow slightly raised. "Do you really think we can fool them? We don't look like we're together."

She was right. In fact, they looked about as un-together as a man and woman could. "What do you think I...? Should I put my arm around your shoulders?"

Yeesh, he hadn't sounded this stupidly uncertain since that eighth-grade dance he'd been invited to as a sixth-grader.

"I don't know," she admitted. "Would you put your arm around my shoulders if we really were together?"

"I'd..." He put his arm around her waist, tucking her body perfectly alongside his. He didn't mean for it to

"Look, Syd." He stopped about ten feet from the Catalanottos' front steps, pulling her to face him. "It's okay. You don't need to make up reasons why I shouldn't kiss you."

"I'm not making up reasons," she insisted.

"So then, if I don't mind about the alleged garlic-breath, *you* don't mind if I kiss you?"

The early evening shadows played artfully across Syd's face as she laughed. "I can't believe we're having this conversation."

And standing there, looking down at her, with his arm still around her waist, Lucky wanted to kiss her about as badly as he'd ever wanted to kiss anyone.

And damn it, as long as they were playing this pretend girlfriend game, he might as well take advantage of the fact that it would only *help* their cover if he *did* kiss her.

But how the hell did one go about kissing a friend? He knew all there was to know about how to kiss a stranger, but this was different. This was far more dangerous.

And suddenly he knew exactly what to do, what to say.

"You've got me dying to find out if you really do taste like garlic," he said.

"Oh, believe me, I do."

"Do you mind…?" He tipped her chin up to his. "For the sake of scientific experimentation…?"

She laughed. That was when he knew he had her. That was when he knew he *could* kiss her without having her get all ticked off at him. She might pull away really fast, but she wasn't going to hit him.

So he lowered his head those extra inches and covered her mouth with his.

And, oh, my. Just like when he'd kissed her on that deck just off his kitchen, she turned to fire in his arms.

behind Veronica. And Mia Francisco peeked through the front window, Frisco right behind her. Frisco gave him a smile and a thumbs-up.

Syd jettisoned herself from his arms, but he caught her hand and reeled her back in.

"It's okay," he murmured to her. "I knew someone would be bound to notice us. We're together, remember? You're my new girlfriend—I'm allowed to kiss you."

"Sorry," Veronica called through the screen in her crisp British accent. "Frankie came out onto the back deck, insisting that a man and a lady were making a baby in the front yard, and we just had to see for ourselves."

"Oh, my God," Syd said, her face turning bright pink.

"I obviously need to discuss the details of conception with him again," she said, laughter in her voice. "I'd thought we'd been over that 'kissing doesn't make a baby' stuff, but apparently it didn't stick. I suppose it's all right—he's only four."

"Do you want to come in?" PJ called out, "or should we just all go away? Give you some privacy—close the door and turn off the light?"

Lucky laughed as he pulled Syd to the door.

The introductions took no time, and then Veronica was pulling Syd through the house to the back deck. "You've got to see the view we've got of the ocean," she said, as if she'd known Syd for years, "and I've got to check the chicken that's on the grill."

"Bobby already checked the chicken," about four voices called out.

"Everyone here is convinced I can't cook," Veronica told Syd as she opened the slider. She made a face. "Unfortunately they're right."

He vanished into the house, nearly knocking Syd over on his way. Lucky turned to Bobby, making the motion of keys turning in the ignition, silently asking if Wes was okay to drive.

Bobby shook his head no, then pulled his hand out of his bathing-suit pocket, opening it briefly—just long enough so that Lucky could see he'd already claimed possession of his friend's keys. Bobby made a walking motion with his fingers. Wes would walk back to the base.

On the other side of the deck, Syd helped Lana Quinn clean up the spilled pretzels.

"So. Does the new GF know you're a jerk?"

Lucky turned to see PJ Becker grinning at him, but he knew her words were only half in jest. Which, of course, made them half-serious, as well. This woman *still* hadn't forgotten the way he'd hit on her back when they'd first met. She'd forgiven, sure, but she'd probably never forget. It was one of the things he liked best about her. She'd never, ever let him get away with anything.

"Yeah," he said. "She knows. She likes me anyway." It wasn't entirely a lie. Syd *did* like him. Just not in the way PJ meant.

Senior Chief Harvard Becker's wife gazed at Syd with her gorgeous, liquid-brown eyes—eyes that never missed anything. "You know, O'Donlon, if you're smart enough to have hooked up with someone like Syd Jameson, maybe I seriously underestimated you. She's a good writer—she had a weekly column in the local paper about a year ago, you know. I tried never to miss it. There's a good brain—a thinking brain—in that girl's head." She gave him another brilliant smile and a kiss on the cheek. "Who knows? Maybe you're not such a jerk after all."

As Lucky laughed, PJ went to give her best evil eye to

encourage her to bunk down at the police station until this is over."

Veronica followed his gaze. "You make sure Syd is careful, too."

"Oh, yeah," Lucky said. "Don't worry about that. She's, uh…she's moving in with me."

It was the weirdest thing. It was all part of the pretend girlfriend game, designed to catch the rapist, but as he said the words aloud—words he'd never before uttered, not ever in his entire life—it felt remarkably real. He felt a little embarrassed, a little proud, a little terrified, and a whole hell of a lot of anticipation.

Syd *was* moving in with him. She was going to go home with him tonight. It was true that she was going to sleep in the guest bedroom, but for the first time in God knows how long he wouldn't have to worry about her safety. Maybe, just maybe, he'd get some sleep tonight.

On the other hand, maybe not, considering she was going to be in the next room, and considering he was *still* half-aroused from that incredible kiss.

Veronica's eyes widened, and then filled with tears. She threw her arms around his neck and hugged him. "Oh, Luke, I'm so happy for you!" She pulled back to gaze into his eyes. "I was so certain you were just going to bounce from Heather to Heather for the rest of your life." She raised her voice. "Everyone, Lucky's finally living up to his nickname! He just told me Syd's moving in with him!"

There was a scramble for cans of beer—soda for Frisco and Mia and Tash—as Veronica made a toast. Lucky didn't dare look at Syd directly—he could feel her embarrassment from all the way across the room. And he could feel Frisco's eyes on him, too. His swim buddy and temporary CO was smiling, but there were questions in his eyes. Like,

considering she's supposed to be informed of my team's every move. She called this afternoon, mad as hell about that TV interview. She was ready to wring my neck." He started the engine, switched on the headlights and pulled out into the street, turning around in a neighbor's driveway. "Officially, she's pissed, but unofficially, she hopes this works. She knows we'll keep you as safe—safer— than the police would."

He glanced at her in the dimness of the cab. "I'm going to tell Frisco tomorrow, but I'm going to ask him not to tell Mia. I think Bobby's right. The fewer people who know, the better."

Syd sat as far away from him as she possibly could on the bench seat, trying desperately not to think about the way he'd kissed her. About the way she'd kissed him. At the words he'd said so casually as they left the party: *I'm finally in love....*

Yeah, like that would ever happen. Syd had figured Luke O'Donlon out. He wasn't ever going to fall in love. At least not all the way. He thought he was safe as long as he kept himself surrounded by the beautiful, intelligent, exceptional and *already married* wives of his best friends. He could cruise through life, half in love with Lucy and Veronica and PJ and Mia, never having to worry about getting in too deep. He could have meaningless sexual relationships with self-absorbed, vacuous young women like Heather—again, without risking his heart.

But what if he was wrong? Not about Heather—Syd didn't think for one instant that Luke would ever lose his heart to her. But Lucy McCoy was an entirely different story. As was that outrageously beautiful African American woman she'd met just tonight—PJ Becker. It would be too tragic if Luke actually fell in love with a woman he couldn't have.

"That's not what they were thinking," Luke scoffed.

Yes, it most certainly was. Syd kept her mouth closed.

"After seeing that kiss," he said with a laugh, "they think they *know* why I want to live with you."

That kiss.

For many, many pounding heartbeats, Syd had stood on the front walk of that cute little beach house with her arms wrapped around Luke O'Donlon, her lips locked on his. For many pounding heartbeats, she had dared to imagine that that kiss was real, that it had nothing to do with their game of pretend.

She'd thought she'd seen something warm, something special, deep in his eyes, right before he lowered his mouth to hers.

Okay, face it, she'd thought she'd seen his awareness of his genuine attraction, based on genuine liking and genuine respect.

She'd seen awareness, all right—awareness of the fact that they were being watched through the window. He'd known they were being watched. *That* was why he'd kissed her.

They drove in silence for several long minutes. And then he glanced at her again.

"Maybe you should scoot over here—sit closer to me. If this guy does start following us…"

Syd gave him a look. "Scoot?" she said, trying desperately to keep things light. If she moved next to him, and if he put his arm around her shoulders, she just might forget how to breathe. Unless she could somehow keep him laughing. "I'm sorry, but I never, ever *scoot* anywhere."

Luke laughed. Jackpot. "That's what I love most about you, Sydney, dear. You can pick a fight about *any*thing."

"Can not."

San Felipe," he told her. "It's usually packed this time of night. I figured we'd go get some steamed clams. And maybe after that, we could do a little barhopping."

"I've never been barhopping," she admitted, mostly to fill the pause in the conversation. "I always thought it sounded so exotic."

"Actually, it can be pretty depressing," Luke told her as the light turned green and he focused on the road again, thank God. "I've been barhopping with the other single guys from Alpha Squad. Mostly Bobby and Wes. Although occasionally their buddy Quinn would come along. The Wizard. He's married—you know, to Lana—which never sat quite right with me, because our goal was to cruise the clubs, looking to pick up college girls. But I didn't really know him, didn't really know Lana—I figured it was none of my business."

"God," Syd said. "Did she know?"

Luke shook her head. "No. Quinn used to say that they had an arrangement. He wouldn't tell her and she wouldn't find out. Wes used to get so mad at him. One night he actually broke Quinn's nose."

"Wes is Bobby's swim buddy, right?" Syd thought about the SEAL she'd met for the first time tonight. He was bigger than she'd imagined from the way Luke had described him. Something about him had been disturbingly familiar. When he'd slammed into her on his way out of the party...

"Bob and Wes are the best example of a two-man team I've ever seen," Luke told her, the muscles in his thigh flexing as he braked to make a right turn into a crowded restaurant parking lot. "They're good operators separately, but together—it's like instead of getting two regular guys,

"I'm not wrong," Luke said tightly. "I know this man. You didn't see him at his best tonight, but I know him, all right?"

It wasn't all right, but Syd wisely kept her mouth shut.

allowed to ask any of the SEALs specific questions about their operations, but she *could* pose hypotheticals. And she did, as often as possible.

"What's inside this hypothetical stronghold?" he asked, tossing his keys onto a small table near the front door. "Is this a rescue mission or an info-gathering op?"

"Rescue mission," she decided. "Hostages. There are hostages inside. Hostaged *children*."

He gave her a comically disbelieving look as he moved to the thermostat and adjusted the setting so that the air conditioning switched on. That was good. It was too still in here, too warm. The AC would get the air moving, make it a little less stuffy. A little less...sultry.

"Make it impossibly difficult, why don't you?" he said.

He went into the kitchen, and she followed. "I'm just trying to provide a challenge."

"Okay, great." He opened the refrigerator and scowled at the cluttered shelves. "If we've been sent in to rescue hostaged children, you better believe we've been given a direct order not to fail." He reached in behind a gallon of milk and pulled out a container that looked as if it held iced tea. "Want some?"

Syd nodded, leaning against the door frame. "Thanks."

She watched as he took two tall glasses from a cabinet and filled them with ice.

"So," she said, mostly to fill the silence. "What do you do in that situation?"

He turned to look at her. "We don't fail."

She had to laugh. "You want to be a *little* more specific?"

"I'm inside, right?" he said, pouring the tea over the ice in the glasses. "Alone. But I've got radio contact with my men outside. I guess what I do is, I use stealth and I

dishwasher. Then he picked up his glass, and went back into the living room, gesturing with his head for Syd to follow.

So she followed him. Right over to a wall that was filled with framed photographs. She'd noticed them the last time she was here. Pictures of Luke as a child, his sun-bleached hair even lighter than it was now. Pictures of young Luke with his arms around a chubby, dark-haired little girl. Pictures of Luke with a painfully thin blond woman who had to be his mother. And pictures of young Luke with a dark-haired, dark complexioned man.

He pointed now to the pictures of the man.

"This," he said, "is Isidro Ramos. He's why I joined the SEALs."

Syd looked more closely at the photograph. She could see the warmth in the man's eyes, one arm looped around young Luke's shoulder. She could see the answering adoration on the boy's smiling face. "Who is he?" she asked.

"Was," he told her, sitting down on the couch, taking a sip from his iced tea and stretching his legs out on the coffee table.

Syd knew him well enough by now to know his casualness was entirely feigned. In truth he was on edge. But was it the topic of conversation he was having trouble with—or her presence here?

"Isidro died when I was sixteen," he said. "He was my father."

His…? Syd did a double take. No way could a man that dark have had a son as fair as Luke.

"Not my biological father," he added. "Obviously. But he *was* my father far more than Shaun O'Donlon ever bothered to be."

Syd sat down on the other end of the couch. "And he's why you joined the SEALs?"

"I'm interested," she told him. "A lot can be revealed about a person simply by listening to them talk about their childhood."

"If that's the case, then where did *you* grow up?" he asked.

"New Rochelle, New York. My father is a doctor, my mother was a nurse before she quit to have us. Four kids, I'm the youngest. My brothers and sister are all incredibly rich, incredibly successful, with perfect spouses, perfect wardrobes and perfect tans, cranking out perfect grandkids for my parents right on schedule." She smiled at him. "Note that I don't seem to be on the family track. I'm generally spoken of in hushed tones. The black sheep. Serves them right for giving me a boy's name."

Luke laughed. She really liked making him laugh. The lines around his eyes crinkled in a way that was completely adorable. And his mouth...

She looked down into her tea to avoid staring at his mouth.

"Actually," she confessed, "my family is lovely. They're very nice—if somewhat clueless. And they're quite okay and very supportive about my deviation from the norm. My mother keeps trying to buy me Laura Ashley dresses, though. Every Christmas, without fail. 'Gee, thanks, Mom. In *pink?* Wow, you shouldn't have. No, you *really* shouldn't have,' but next year, the exact same thing."

Syd risked another glance at Luke. He was still laughing.

"So come on, finish up your story. Your father was a jerk. I think I know how it probably goes—he left before you turned two—"

"I wish," Luke said. "But Shaun stayed until I was eight, sucking my mother dry, both emotionally and financially. But the year I turned eight, he inherited a small

at the kitchen table and told us she was going to marry him." Luke laughed, remembering. "He was completely against it. He knew she'd had to get married before, when she was younger. He told her she'd gotten married for the wrong reasons the first time, and that he wasn't going to let her do that again. And she told him that marrying him so that he wouldn't die was the best reason she could imagine. I think she was in love with him, even back then. She convinced him that she was right, they got married, and he moved out of the apartment over the garage and into our house."

His mother had been pretty damn shrewd. She'd known what she wanted, and she'd gone about getting it. She'd known if she could get Isidro into her home, it wouldn't be long before their marriage was consummated. And she'd been right on the money.

It was funny the way life seemed to go in circles, Lucky mused as he gazed at Syd, who was way, *way* down on the other end of the couch, as far away from him as she could possibly sit. Because here he was, playing the same game his mother had played. Pretending that he was acting out of some big-picture necessity, rather than from his own personal need.

Pretending that, oh, yeah, jeez, if he really *had* to, he'd cope with the *inconvenience* of having Sydney around all day and all night.

Yeah, right. Like he didn't hope—the way his mother had hoped with Isidro—that the pressure from being with Syd constantly would trigger some kind of unavoidable and unstoppable sexual explosion. That sooner or later—if not tonight, then maybe tomorrow or the next day—Syd would push open his bedroom door with a crash and announce that she couldn't stand it another minute, that she had to have him right now.

real American. And God!" He laughed. "That November, on election day! He took me and Ellen to the polls with him, so we could watch him vote. And he made us both promise—even though El could barely talk—that we would vote every chance we got."

"So your stepfather is why you became a SEAL."

"Father," he corrected gently. "There was nothing step about him. And, yeah, the things he taught me stuck." Lucky shrugged, knowing that a cynical newspaper journalist probably wouldn't see it the same way he—and Isidro—had. Knowing that she would probably laugh, hoping she wouldn't, wanting to try to explain just the same. "I know there's a lot wrong with this country, but there's also a lot right. I *believe* in America. And I joined the Navy—the SEAL teams in particular—because I wanted to give something back. I wanted to be a part of making sure we remained the land of the free and the home of the brave. And I stayed in the Navy for longer than I'd ever dreamed of because I ended up getting as much as I gave."

She laughed.

He tried to hide his disappointment. "Yeah, I know. It sounds so hokey."

"Oh—" she sat up "—no! I wasn't laughing because of what you said. God, you've just impressed the hell out of me—please don't think I'm laughing at you."

"I have?" Lucky tried to sound casual. "Impressed you? Really?" Yeesh, he sounded like a dork, pathetically fishing for more compliments.

She didn't seem to notice, caught up in her own intensity. Man, when she got serious, she got *serious*. "I was laughing because back when I first met you, I thought I had you all figured out. I thought you were one of those

"Well, yeah," he admitted. "Either jeans or your khakis. I've noticed a certain… repetitiveness to your attire."

"Great," she said. "First I'm an idiot, and then I'm *boring?*"

She was laughing, so he knew she wasn't completely serious, but he still felt the need to try to explain. "That's not what I meant—"

"Quit while you're ahead," she told him. "Just tell me about your sister."

It was nearly 0100 hours, but Lucky wasn't tired. Syd didn't look tired either.

So he told her about his sister, ready and willing to talk all night if she wanted him to.

He wished she wanted more than conversation from him. He wanted to touch her, to take her to his bedroom and make love to her. But he wasn't going to risk destroying this quiet intimacy they shared.

She liked him. He knew that. But this was too new and far too fragile to gamble with.

He wanted to touch her, but he knew he shouldn't. Tonight he was going to have to settle for touching her with his words.

"Blade," Rio Rosetti said. "Or Panther."

"How about Hawk?" Thomas suggested, tongue firmly in cheek.

"Yeah, Hawk's good, too."

Rio was unhappy with his current nickname and was trying to talk his friends into calling him something else.

"Personally, I think we should be developing a kinder, gentler group of SEALs, with kinder, gentler nicknames," Michael Lee said with a completely straight face. "How about Bunny?"

for him to comment, too. Even Michael Lee had lifted his eyes from the computer screen. He laughed. "You guys are kidding, right? You know as well as I do that this is just a ruse to try to trap the rapist. Sure, Syd stayed over, but..." he shrugged, "...nothing happened. I mean, there's really nothing going on between us."

"She *is* wearing one of your shirts," Bobby said.

"Yeah, because last night, in a genius move, I insulted her wardrobe."

He'd fallen asleep on the couch last night and woken to the scent of coffee brewing. He'd thrown off the blanket Syd must've put over him and staggered into the kitchen to find her already showered and dressed—and wearing one of his shirts. It was weird—and a little scary. It was his full-blown morning-after nightmare, in which a woman he barely knew and didn't particularly like would move in and make herself completely at home, right down to stealing from his closet. Except in this case, there had been no night before. *And* in this case, it wasn't a nightmare.

The coffee smelled great, Syd looked amazing in his shirt, and, as she smiled at him, his stomach didn't twist with anxiety. It twisted, all right, but in anticipation.

He liked her, liked having her in his house, liked having her be a part of his morning.

And maybe, if he were really lucky, if he lived up to this nickname of his, he'd wake up tomorrow with her in his bed. Mike handed him three copies of the printed list, and he handed one to Bobby, the others to Thomas and Rio.

Rio was now looking at him as if he were mentally challenged. "Let me get this straight. You had Syd alone. Syd. One of the most incredibly fascinating and sexy women in the world. And she's alone with you, all night. And instead

eye to eye with her breasts. He looked away, his mind instantly blank. What was he just about to say?

Bobby answered for him. "As far as I understand it, parole is for when a prisoner is released early. If he serves out his full sentence, there's usually no parole."

"What's this guy's name?" Syd asked. "Where is he on the list?"

"Owen Finn." Lucky pointed to the list and she leaned even closer to read the small print. She was wearing his deodorant. It smelled different on her. Delicate and femininely fresh.

Damn, he *was* nuts. He should have at least said something to Syd last night. *So, hey, like, what do you say we get it on?* Well, maybe not that. But certainly something in between that and the great big nothing he'd uttered. Because what if this attraction was mutual? What if she'd spent all night wishing they could get physical, too? What could it hurt to be honest?

They were, after all, friends—by her own admission. As his friend, she would appreciate his honesty.

Wouldn't she?

"Finn was convicted of burglary," Syd said, straightening up. "I thought we were looking for someone with a record of sexual assault or some other violent crime."

"Finn," Bobby reported from the Navy Computer's personnel files. "Owen Franklin. Son of a medal of honor winner, entered the U.S. Naval Academy even though his grades weren't quite up to par. Rang out of BUD/S in '96, given a dishonorable discharge four months later, charged and convicted of theft. Yeah, this guy definitely has sticky fingers. No mention of violence, though."

"How about this one?" Thomas pointed to the list, and Syd leaned over Lucky again. "Martin Taus. Charged with four counts of sexual assault but never convicted. Got off

was just an act. But he didn't say anything more, except that he was there to talk, if Lucky wanted someone to talk to. About what, Lucky'd asked. Yeah, he was a little worried about Syd putting herself in danger, but this way at least he could keep an eye on her. Everything was cool. There was nothing to talk about.

"I'll be going over to Luke's in about an hour to set up interior microphones," Bobby said.

"So, I'm going to be alone in the house starting at about seven until...two or three in the morning?" she guessed.

"No, we'll have time before the exercise starts," Lucky told her. "We can have dinner downtown. We'll leave here together at about 1800—six o'clock. After dinner, we'll go to my place, and around 2230, after Bobby and the guys have moved into position, I'll make a big show of kissing you goodbye, and I'll come here. You'll be alone from then until around 0200. About three and a half hours."

Syd nodded. "Maybe if we're lucky, FInCOM will round up most of the suspects on our list before tonight. And if we're *really* lucky, one of them will be our guy."

Lucky nodded, hoping the golden luck for which he'd been nicknamed would, indeed, shine through.

return with Luke's credit card, sitting beneath that perfect, color-streaked sky. The way he was looking at her, the quiet timbre of his voice—his behavior was completely that of an attentive lover. He was remarkably good at playing this part. "What are you thinking about?"

"Kissing you," she admitted.

For an eighth of a second, his guard dropped, his thumb stopped moving and she saw real surprise in his eyes. He opened his mouth to speak, but the waiter returned. And all Luke did was laugh as he gently reclaimed his fingers and signed the bill. He pocketed his receipt and stood, holding out his hand to her.

"Let's walk on the beach."

They went down the wooden steps hand in hand, and when they reached the bottom, he knelt in the sand and took off her sandals, then carried them for her, along with his own shoes. The sand was sensuously cool between her toes.

They walked in silence for about a minute, then Luke cleared his throat. "So, when you were thinking about kissing me, was it a good thought or…?"

"It was more of an amused thought," she admitted. "Like, here I am, with the best-looking man in the state of California, and oh, just in case that's not thrilling enough, he's going to kiss me a few dozen more times before the night is through. You kiss like a dream, you know? Of course you know."

"You're pretty good at it yourself."

"I'm an amateur compared to you. I can't seem to do that thing you do with your eyes. And that little 'I'm going to kiss you now' smile. Only someone with a face like yours can pull that off."

His laughter sounded embarrassed. "Oh, come on. I'm not—"

most emotionally connected yet factual article about a city-wide task force ever written.

She wasn't here simply to kiss this man in the moonlight.

The last of the dusk was fading fast, and the moon was just a sliver in the sky. Syd could hear the party sounds from the Surf Club farther down the beach—the echo of laughter and distant rock and roll.

Luke's face was entirely in shadow. "I like you, Syd," he told her softly. "You make me laugh. But I want to *know* you. I want to know what you want, who you really are. I want to know where you see yourself in fifty years. I want to..." He laughed, and she could've sworn it was self-consciously, that is, if it was possible that Luke O'Donlon could be self-conscious. "I want to know about Kevin Manse. I want to know if you're still in love with him, if you still measure every man you bump into against him."

Syd was so completely surprised, it very nearly qualified as stunned. Kevin *Manse?* What the...? She wished she could see Luke's eyes in the darkness. "What do... *how* do you know about Kevin Manse?"

He cleared his throat. "He, um, came up in some detail when Lana Quinn first hypnotized you."

"*Some* detail...?"

"You, um, flashed back to the first time you, uh, met him."

Syd said a very impolite word. "*Flashed back?* What do you mean, *flashed back?*"

"Um, I guess *relived* is more accurate."

"*Relived?*" Her voice went up several octaves. "What is that supposed to mean?"

"You, um, partly told us what happened, partly talked to Kevin as if he were in the room. You told us you bumped

a shadow against the darkness of the night. "A one-night stand. How many times have *you* done that?"

He answered honestly. "Too many."

"You're probably someone's Kevin Manse," she said. He was silent.

"I'm sorry," she said. "That was harsh."

"But probably true. I've tried to stay away from the eighteen-year-old virgins, though."

"Oh," Syd said. "Well. Then that makes it *all* better."

Luke laughed ruefully. "Man, you are unmerciful."

"I'll cut you down, but not yet—I like seeing you twisting in the wind, baby." Syd laughed. "You want serious? I'll give you the whole pathetic story—that'll really make you squirm. But if you repeat it to *any*one, our friendship is over, do you understand?"

"I'm going to hate this, aren't I?"

"It's pretty hateful." Syd sat up and looked out over the water. "I've never told this to anyone. Not my college roommate, not my sister, not my mother, not anyone. But I'm going to tell you, because we're friends, and maybe you'll learn something from it."

"I feel like I'm approaching a car wreck. I'm horrified at the thought of the carnage, but unable to turn away."

She laughed. "It's not *that* bad."

"No?"

"Well, maybe it was at the time." She hugged her knees close to her chest and sighed. Where to start…? "Kevin was a big football star."

"Yeah," Luke said. "You mentioned that. You said he was a scholar, too. Smart as hell. And probably handsome."

"On a scale from one to ten…" Syd squinted as she thought about it. "A twelve."

"Whoa!"

Lana that Kevin had one of his friends drive you back to your dorm, later that night."

"Yeah," she said. "He said he thought my staying all night would be bad for my reputation. Ha." She rested her chin on her knees, still holding on to herself tightly. "Okay. Next day. Act Two. It's Sunday. There's a big game. And me, I'm a genius. I'm thinking about the fact that thanks to the bottle of Jack Daniel's we put a solid dent in up in Kevin's room, I managed to leave without giving my new soul mate my telephone number. So I spend the morning writing him a note. I think I went through about a hundred drafts before I got it right. 'Dear Kevin, Last night was truly wonderful...'"

She had to swallow to clear away the sudden, aching lump that formed in her throat. God, she was such a sap. All these years later, and Kevin Manse could *still* make her want to cry, damn him.

She felt Luke touch her, his fingers gentle in her hair, light against her back.

"You really don't have to tell me any more of this," he said quietly. "I already feel really bad, and if you want, right now I'll swear to you that I'll never do a one-nighter again. I mean, it's been years since I have anyway, and—"

"I went to the football game," she told him. "With my pathetic little note. And I sat there in the stands and I watched my lover from the night before play a perfect game. After it was over, I tried to get into the stadium locker rooms, but there were security guards who laughed at me when I told them I was Kevin's girlfriend. I didn't get upset. I just smiled. I figured they'd have plenty of time to get to know me—the season was just starting. They told me that Kevin always came out the south entrance after a

hazy sky. "Can I try to find him?" he asked. "Can I track him down and beat the hell out of him?"

Syd managed a shaky laugh.

He wanted to touch her again, to put his arms around her and hold her close, but it seemed like the wrong thing to do, given the circumstances.

"I'm so sorry," he said, and his words seemed so inadequate.

Especially since he'd spent nearly all of dinner planning exactly how he was going to talk Syd into his bed tonight. Late tonight. After 0200. In the small hours of the night, when she would be at her most vulnerable. He'd turn off the microphones, send the rest of his team home. And in the privacy of his living room...

He'd told himself that it would be good for him to be honest with her. To tell her he was attracted, admit that he was having trouble thinking about much else besides the fact that he wanted her. He was planning to move closer and closer as they sat on the couch, closing in on her until she was in his arms. He was planning to kiss her until she lost all sense of direction. He was planning to kiss her until she surrendered.

But in truth, he wasn't really being honest. He was merely calculating that this feigned honesty would get him some.

He hadn't given much thought at all to tomorrow. He hadn't considered Syd's feelings. Or her expectations.

Just like Kevin Manse, he'd thought only about his own immediate gratification. God, he was such a jerk.

Syd drew in a deep breath and let it out in a rush. "We should probably go. It's getting late. You have to head over to the base, and I've...I've got to go tattoo the word *victim* on my forehead, just to be sure our bad guy gets the right idea."

CHAPTER ELEVEN

Syd woke to the shrill sound of the telephone ringing.

The clock on the bedside table in Luke's guest room read 3:52. It was nearly four in the morning. Who could possibly be calling now?

She knew instantly, sitting up, her heart pounding.

The rapist hadn't taken the bait. Instead, some other poor woman had been attacked.

She could hear the low murmur of Luke's voice from the other room.

His voice got louder, and, although she couldn't make out the words, she could pick up his anger loud and clear. No, this wasn't good news, that was for sure.

Luke had come home just after two. He'd been unnaturally quiet, almost pensive, and very, very tired. He'd made a quick circuit of the house, making sure all the doors and windows were securely locked, and then he'd gone into his bedroom and shut the door.

Syd had climbed into the narrow bed in this room that had probably once been Luke's sister's, and had tried to sleep.

Tried and failed. It seemed as if she'd just drifted off when the sound of the phone jerked her back to consciousness.

From the other side of the wall, she heard a crash from Luke's room as something was noisily knocked over. She

outside the entrance to the intensive care unit. "If anyone can get word to Alpha Squad, he can."

Bobby moved briskly off as Mia Francisco pushed open the door and stepped out of ICU.

"I thought I heard your voice." She gave Luke a hug, her eyes red from crying.

"Should you be here?" Luke asked her, putting a hand on her enormous belly.

Mia hugged Syd, too. "How could I not be here?" she said. Her lip trembled. "The doctor says the next few hours are critical. If she makes it through the night—" Her voice broke.

"Oh, God," Syd said. "It's that bad?"

Mia nodded.

"Can I see her?" Luke asked.

Mia nodded again. "She's in room four. There's usually a family-members-only rule with patients in ICU, but with Blue out of the country, the doctors and nurses are letting us sit with her. I called Veronica and Melody. They're both flying in in the morning. And Nell and Becca should be here in about an hour. PJ's already over at the crime scene."

Luke pushed open the door to the intensive care wing, and Syd followed him in.

Nighttime didn't exist in ICU. It was as brightly lit and as filled with busy doctors and nurses as if it were high noon.

Luke stopped outside room four, just looking in. Syd took his hand.

Lucy looked impossibly small and fragile lying in that hospital bed. She was hooked up to all kinds of machines and monitors. Her head was swathed in bandages, her face pale—except for where it was savagely bruised. She had an angry-looking row of stitches above her left eyebrow,

LUCKY STOOD IN BLUE AND Lucy McCoy's second-floor bedroom, grimly taking in the crushed and twisted lamps, the knocked-over rocking chair, the mattress half off its frame, the blood smeared on the sheets and the pale yellow wall, and the broken bay window that had looked out over the McCoys' flower-filled backyard.

Dawn was sending delicate, fairy-like light into the yard and, as he stepped closer to the window, the bits and pieces of broken glass glittered prettily on the grass below.

Syd stood quietly by the door. He'd heard her slip into the bathroom after they'd first arrived and seen the evidence of the violent and bloody fight that had taken place in this very room. He'd heard her get sick. But she'd come out almost right away. Pale and shaking but unwilling to leave.

PJ Becker came into the room, followed by one of the FInCOM agents who'd been assigned to the task force. PJ's recent promotion had pushed her way high up in FInCOM's chain of command, and the agent who was with her looked a little dazed at her presence.

"Dave, you already know Lieutenant O'Donlon and Sydney Jameson. Lieutenant, Dave Sudenberg's one of our top forensics experts," PJ said. "I thought you'd be interested in hearing his take on what happened here last night, since Detective McCoy's not yet able to give us a statement."

Lucky nodded and Dave Sudenberg cleared his throat. "As far as I can tell, the perpetrator entered the premises through a downstairs window," he told them. "He managed to bypass a portion of the security system without shutting the whole thing down, which was good, since the system's lights and alarms later played a large part in saving the detective's life."

There was a real chance Blue would come home to bury his wife.

PJ moved to the window and looked all the way down at the yard below. "Dave thinks her broken collarbone and arm were from the dive she took out the window," she said grimly. "But the broken rib, broken nose, bruised throat and near-fatal head injuries were from your guy."

"We've got enough of his DNA to see if it matches the semen and skin samples he left behind with his other victims," Sudenberg told them. "I've already sent samples to the lab."

"What's it gonna take," Lucky asked, his chest and his throat both feeling so tight he had to push to squeeze his voice out, "to get the police or FInCOM to actually pick up the likely suspects on the list Lucy helped compile?"

"It's getting done, but these things take time," PJ told him as she headed for the door. She motioned for Sudenberg to follow her. "I'll see that you're given updated status reports as they come in."

Lucky nodded. "Thanks."

"See you back at the hospital," PJ said.

LUCKY STOOD IN HIS kitchen, his vision blurring as he stared out the window over the sink.

Lucy had made it through the night but still showed no signs of waking.

Blue could not be reached, not even with the help of Admiral Robinson. The admiral had known where Alpha Squad was though, and had been willing to break radio silence to contact them, but the mountains and rocky terrain were playing havoc with the signal. Lieutenant Mitch Shaw, one of the Admiral's Gray Group operatives, had volunteered to go in after them. To find Blue, to send him back out and to take his place on this critical mission.

fear—God, he was so afraid. It would escape, like water pouring over a dam.

He took a step back from her. "I don't want you doing this anymore. This bait thing. Not after this. No way. All bets are off. You're going to have to stay away from me from now on. I'll make sure Bobby's with you, 24-7."

She kept coming. "Luke. That doesn't make sense. This could well be the only way we'll catch this guy. I *know* you want to catch this guy."

He laughed, and it sounded sharp and brittle. "Understatement of the year."

"Maybe we should both get some sleep. We can talk about this later, after we've had time to think it through."

"There's nothing more to think about," he said. "There's too much that could go wrong. In the time it would take us to get inside the house, even from the backyard, you could be killed. You're smaller than Lucy, Syd. If he hit you the way he hit her—" His voice broke and he had to take a deep breath before he could go on. "I won't let you risk your life that way. The thought of you being alone with that guy even for one second..."

To Lucky's complete horror, the tears he was desperately fighting welled in his eyes, and this time he couldn't force them back. This time they escaped. He wiped at them savagely, but even that didn't stop them from coming.

Ah, God, he was crying. He was standing in front of Syd and crying like a two-year-old.

It was all over. He was completely unmanned.

Except she didn't laugh. She didn't give him one of those "wow, you are both lame *and* stupid" looks that she did so well.

Instead, she put her arms around him and held him

Would he spend the rest of his life haunted by the memory of Lucy's eyes? Would he be forever looking for her smile on a crowded street? Would the scent of her subtle perfume make him turn, searching for her, despite knowing full well that she was gone?

Lucky wasn't ever going to let himself be in that place where Blue was right now. He wasn't ever getting married. Never getting married. It had been his mantra for years as he'd struggled with the concept of commitment, yet now it held special meaning.

He didn't want to walk around feeling the fear that came with loving someone. He didn't want that, damn it!

Except look at him.

He was reduced to this quivering bowl of jelly not simply out of empathy for Blue. A solid part of the emotion that had reduced him to these stupid tears was this god-awful fear that tightened his chest and closed up his throat.

The thought of Syd spending even one single second with the man who had brutalized Lucy made him crazy. The thought of her being beaten into a coma was terrifying.

But the thought of Syd walking out of his life, after they'd caught and convicted the San Felipe Rapist, was nearly as frightening.

He loved her.

No! Dear God, where had *that* thought come from? An overdose of whatever bizarre hormones his emotional outburst had unleashed.

Lucky drew in a deep, shuddering breath and pulled free from Syd's arms. He didn't love her. That was insane. He was Lucky O'Donlon. He didn't *do* love.

He wiped his eyes, wiped his face, reached up for a

She kissed him.

Here in his kitchen, where no one was watching, where no one could see.

It was such a sweet kiss, such a gentle kiss, her lips featherlight against his. It made his knees go even weaker, made him glad he was already sitting down.

She kissed him again, and this time he was ready for her. This time he kissed her, too, catching her mouth with his, careful to be as gentle, tasting the salt of his tears on her lips with the very tip of his tongue.

He heard her sigh and he kissed her again, longer this time, deeper. She opened her mouth to him, slowly, exquisitely meeting his tongue with hers, and Lucky threw it all away. Everything that he'd been trying to convince himself about putting distance between them went right out the window.

To hell with his confusion. He liked confusion. He *loved* confusion. If this was confusion, then damn it, give him more.

He reached for her, and she slid into his arms, her fingers in his hair, on his neck, on his back, her body so supple against him, her breasts so soft.

He'd kissed her before, but never like this. It had never been this real. It had never held this promise, this achingly pure glimpse of attainable paradise.

He kissed her again and again, slowly, lazily losing himself in the soft sweetness of her mouth, deliberately taking his time, purposely not pressuring her for anything more.

These kisses were enough. He wanted her, sure, but even if they only spent the next four hours just kissing, that would be good enough. Kissing her for four hours wouldn't be taking advantage, would it?

But Syd was the one who pushed them over the line.

It wasn't easy to get open, but she had it unfastened and his zipper undone in a matter of seconds.

Lucky's fingers fumbled at the button on her jeans, and she pulled out of his arms to kick off her sandals, to skim her pants down her legs. He did the same with his own pants, kicking off his shoes.

"Where do you keep your condoms?" she asked huskily.

"Bathroom. In the medicine cabinet."

For some reason that surprised her. "Really?" she said. "Not in the top drawer of your bedside table, next to your water bed?"

He had to laugh. "I hate to break it to you, but I don't have a water bed."

"No lava lamp?"

He shook his head, grinning at her like an idiot. "And nary a single black light, either. My apologies. As a bachelor pad, it's definitely lacking."

She took it in stride. "I suppose not having a water bed is better than not having any condoms." She was naked and so incredibly beautiful as she stood there, looking down at him. "As appealing an idea as it is to get it on right here on the kitchen floor, do you suppose if I went into your bedroom via a quick stop in the bathroom, I could convince you to follow me?"

The bedroom. The bedroom suddenly made this all so real. Lucky had to ask. "Syd, are you sure…?"

She gave him her 'I don't believe you' look. "I'm standing here naked, Luke, about to fetch a condom from your bathroom so that you and I can have raw, screaming sex. If that's not an unequivocal yes, I don't know what is."

"Raw, screaming sex," he repeated, his mouth suddenly dry.

"Wildly passionate, deliriously orgasmic, exquisitely

opened herself to him, lifting her hips and pushing his exploring fingers more deeply inside her.

"I think now would be a very good time for you to lose the briefs," she breathed, tugging at his waistband.

He helped her peel them off, and she sighed her approval. He shut his eyes as her hand closed around him.

"I guess you don't scare easily," he murmured.

"I'm terrified," she told him, lowering her head and kissing him.

Her mouth was warm and wet and so soft, and sheer pleasure made fireworks of color explode behind his closed eyes.

And Lucky couldn't wait. He pulled her beneath him, cradling himself between her legs, his body so beyond ready for her that he was trembling.

Condom. Man, he'd nearly forgotten the condom. He reached for it on the bedside table, where she'd put it, tearing open the wrapper as he rolled off her and quickly covered himself.

But he didn't get a chance to roll back on top of her, because Syd straddled him. With one smooth move, she drove him deeply inside her.

If he'd been prone to heart attacks, he'd be a dead man.

Fortunately, his heart was healthy despite the fact it was going at about four hundred beats per minute.

Wild, she'd said. Passionate. Delirious…

Lucky couldn't tell where he ended and Syd began. They moved together, perfectly in sync, kissing, touching, breathing.

Delicious, savage, pounding…

He rolled them both over so that he was on top, so that he had control of their movement. He moved faster and harder and she liked it all, her body straining to meet

CHAPTER TWELVE

"NOTHING'S CHANGED," LUKE SAID, tracing circles around her belly button, head propped up on one elbow as he and Syd lay among his rumpled sheets.

They'd slept for about five hours, and the sun was high in the sky. Luke had put in a call to the hospital—nothing had changed with Lucy's condition, either.

"I really don't want to use you as bait," he continued. "I honestly don't think I can do it, Syd."

His hair was charmingly rumpled, and for the first time since they'd met, he was in need of a shave. It was amazing, really, but not entirely unexpected—even his stubble was golden.

She touched his chin, ran her thumb across his incredible lips. "So what do we do?"

"Pretend to break up."

"Pretend?" she asked, praying that he wouldn't be able to tell that her heart was in her throat. She couldn't bear to look at him.

"I don't want this to end," he told her. "But I need you to be safe."

It was an excuse. Had to be. Because, like he'd said, nothing really had changed. Breaking up with him wouldn't make her any safer.

"Look," she said, pulling away from him and covering herself with the sheet. She tried hard to keep her voice light. "I think it's pretty obvious that neither of us expected

She didn't know what to tell him. "We probably shouldn't have done this, because it's really going to screw up our friendship. You know, I really like you, Luke. I mean, as a friend..."

Oh, brother, could she sound any more stupid? And she was lying, too, by great big omission. Yeah, she really liked him as a friend, but she loved him as a lover, too.

Loved.

L-O-V-E-D.

As in, here, take my heart and crush it into a thousand tiny pieces. As in, here, take my heart and leave me here, emotionally bleeding to death as you move on to bigger and better things. As in, here, take my heart even though you don't really want it.

It was stupid, really. *She* was stupid. She'd realized it when she was having sex with the guy. The fact that she *was* having sex with the guy should have been a dead giveaway that she'd fallen for him in the first place. But, no, she had been too dumb to realize that those warm feelings she felt every time she looked at Luke O'Donlon were far more than feelings of friendship.

She'd gone and let herself fall in love with a Ken doll. Except, Luke wasn't really plastic. He was real, and he was perfect. Well, not *perfect* perfect, but perfect for *her.* Perfect except for the fact that he didn't do serious—he'd warned her about that himself—and that his usual girlfriends had had larger bra sizes back when they were twelve than Syd had now.

Perfect except for the fact that, if she let him, he *would* crush her heart into a thousand tiny pieces. Not intentionally. But it didn't have to be intentional to hurt.

"I like you, too," he told her quietly. "But as more than a friend. *Way* more."

When he said things like that, lying back in his bed,

once, and he thinks he's got the right to tell you what to do! Sleep with a guy once, and suddenly you're in Patronizing City! I'm *not* leaving town, *Luke, baby,* so just forget about it!"

"All right!" His temper snapped, too, and he sat forward, the muscles in his shoulders taut as he pushed himself up. "Great. I'll forget about it. I'll forget about the fact that the thought of you ending up in a hospital bed in a coma like Lucy is making me *freaking crazy!*"

He was serious. He really was scared to death for her. As Syd gazed into his eyes, her anger instantly deflated. She sat on the edge of the bed, wishing she could compromise, but knowing that this was one fight she had to win.

"I'm sorry," she said, reaching for him. "But I can't leave, Luke. This story is too important to me."

"Is it really worth risking your life?"

She touched his hair, his shoulder, traced the definition of the powerful muscles in his arm. "You're a fine one to talk about risking your life and whether a job is worth it."

"I'm trained for it," he said. "You're not. You're a writer."

She met his gaze. "And what if I never wrote anything that I thought was important? What if I always played it safe? I could be very safe, you know, and write copy for the back of cereal boxes. Do you really think that's what I should do for the rest of my life?"

It was hard for him, but he shook his head, no.

"I have a great opportunity here," she told him. "There's a job I really, really want as an editor and staff writer of a magazine I really, *really admire. Think* Magazine."

"I've never heard of it," Luke admitted.

"It's targeted to young women," Syd told him, "as kind

any more than I do." He reached for her, pulling her close, holding her tightly. "Promise me you won't go *any*where by yourself. Promise you'll always make sure someone from the team is watching you."

"I promise," Syd said.

"I'm talking about running down to the convenience store for some milk. It doesn't happen until we catch this guy, do you understand? I'm either right here, right next to you, or Bobby's breathing down your neck."

"I got it," Syd said. "Although, personally, I'd prefer *you* breathing down my neck."

"That can definitely be arranged." He kissed her, hard. "You *will* be safe. I'm going to make *damn* sure of it."

He kissed her again—her throat, her breasts, her stomach, moving even lower, his breath hot against her skin. That wasn't her neck he was breathing down, but Syd didn't bother to tell him. She figured he probably knew.

She closed her eyes, losing herself in the torrents of pleasure that rushed past her, over her, through her. Pleasure and emotion—thick, rich, *deep* emotion that surrounded her completely and made her feel as if she were drowning.

When it came to the things Luke O'Donlon could make her feel, she was in way over her head.

SOUNDS OF LAUGHTER RANG from Lucy McCoy's hospital room.

Hope expanded inside Lucky as he ran the last few steps and pushed open the door and...

He stopped short, and Syd, who was right behind him, bumped into him.

Lucy still lay motionless in her hospital bed, breathing with the help of a respirator.

But she was surrounded by her friends. The room was

please, I know we all thought it would never happen, but our Luke has been smitten at last. Syd's moving in with him."

The noise of all those female voices talking at once as introductions were made and congratulations given—along with hugs and kisses—should have been enough to wake the dead, but Lucy still didn't move.

And Syd was embarrassed. Lucky met her eyes, and knew exactly what she was thinking. The moving in together thing wasn't real. It was part of the girlfriend game. Despite the fact that their relationship had become intimate, he *hadn't* asked her to move in with him.

And she hadn't accepted.

He tried to imagine asking such a thing. How did a man go about it? It wasn't a marriage proposal, so there wasn't any need to get down on your knees, was there? Would you do it casually? While you were making dinner? Or maybe over breakfast? "Hey, babe, by the way…it's occurred to me that as long as you're here all the time…"

It didn't seem very romantic, far more like a convenience than a commitment.

PJ Becker stuck her head in the door. "O'Donlon. About time you graced us with your appearance. Anyone in here given him a sit-rep yet?"

"Situation report," Tasha told Syd. "They talk in code, but don't worry. You'll learn it in no time."

"Well, I found out that Melody wants to set Wes up with her sister," Lucky said to PJ, "but I doubt that's what you meant."

"Mitch left last night," Mitch's wife Becca said quietly. "As soon as Admiral Robinson called. He's going to find Blue, and send him back here, but it's probably going to take some time."

"We've decided to take turns sitting with Lucy,"

looked at Veronica. "Take your time coming over, Ron. Frankie will be fine. In fact, he can just spend the night in the baby's room, if you want."

"Thanks," Veronica said. "That would be great."

Melody turned to Becca. "You don't need a ride, right? You've got your own car…?"

On the other side of the room, Nell stood up and stretched. "I've got to go, too. I'll be back tomorrow, Lucy."

"Whoa," Lucky said, blocking the door. "Wait a minute. Where are you going?"

"Home," they said in unison.

"No, you're not," he said. "There's no way in *hell* I'm letting *any* of you just go home. You're all potential targets. You're not walking out of here without protection."

Melody looked at Veronica. Veronica looked at Nell and Becca. Mia stood up gracefully—no small feat—and they all turned to look at her.

"He's right," she said.

God, it was a logistical nightmare. All these women going in all these different directions….

Melody didn't look convinced. "It's not like I'm alone at home. My sister and the kids are there."

"And *I* certainly don't need protection," PJ added.

"My ranch is *way* out of town," Becca said. "I'm not really worried."

Mutiny. No way was he going to let them mutiny. Lucky bristled, ready to let them know in no uncertain terms that they were *all,* star FInCOM agent PJ Becker included, going to follow the law that he was about to lay down.

But Syd put her hand on his arm.

"*I'm* worried," she said to the other women. She looked down at Lucky, lying there so still and silent in that bed.

CHAPTER THIRTEEN

SYD PACED.

And when she looked at the clock again, it was only six minutes past one—just two minutes later than it had been the *last* time she'd looked.

Luke's house was so silent.

Except, that is, for the booming sound of her pounding heart.

This must be the way it felt to be a worm, stuck on the end of a fishing hook. Or a mouse slipped into a snake trap.

Of course, Luke and Bobby and Thomas and Rio and Mike were hidden in the yard. They were watching all sides of the house, and listening in via strategically placed microphones.

"Damn," she said aloud. "I wish these mikes were two-way. I could use a little heated debate right about now, guys. Fight, flee or surrender. I realized there was an option we haven't discussed—hide. Anyone for *hide?* I'm telling you, those are some really tough choices. Right now it's all I can do to choose between Rocky Road or Fudge Ripple."

The phone rang.

Syd swore. "All right," she said as it rang again. "I know." She wasn't supposed to watch TV or listen to music. Or talk. They couldn't hear potential sounds of

At 1:30 or 2:00 a.m., he'd return through the front door and fall into bed, completely exhausted.

But never too exhausted to make exquisite love to her.

The phone rang. Syd nearly jumped through the roof, then instantly berated herself. It wasn't as if the San Felipe Rapist were going to call her on the phone, was it?

She glanced again at the clock. It was quarter after one in the morning. It had to be Lucky. Or Bobby. Or maybe it was Veronica, calling from the hospital with news about Lucy.

Please, God, let it be good news.

It rang again, and she picked it up. "Hello?"

"Syd." The voice was low and male and unrecognizable.

"I'm sorry," she said briskly. "Who's—"

"Is Lucky there?"

The hair on the back of her neck went up. Dear God, what if it *were* the rapist, calling to make sure she was alone?

"No, sorry." She kept her voice steady. "He's teaching tonight. Who's calling?"

"It's Wes."

Chief Wes Skelly. That information didn't make her feel any better. In fact, it made her even more tense. Wes—who smelled just like the man who'd nearly run her down on the stairs after brutally attacking Gina. Wes—who had the same hair, same build, same accentless voice. Wes, who was—according to Bobby—having a rough year.

How rough, exactly?

Rough enough to completely lose it? Rough enough to turn into a homicidal maniac?

"Are you safe there, all by yourself?" Wes asked. He sounded odd, possibly drunk.

And she *would* need them.

The camera would pull back to show the shadowy shape of a very muscular man with Wes's short hair, with Wes's wide shoulders, creeping across the yard, toward the house.

Bad image. *Bad* image. Syd shook her head, cleared her throat. "Um, Luke, I'm a little spooked, will you please call me?"

Silence.

The phone didn't ring. She stared at it, and it *still* didn't ring.

"Luke, I'm sorry about this, but I'm serious," Syd said. "I just need to know that you're out there and—"

She heard it. A scuffling noise out back.

Flee.

The urge to run was intense, and she scurried for the living room. But the front door was bolted shut—for her own protection—and she didn't have the key. Last night that bolt had made her feel safe. Now it didn't. Now she was trapped.

"I hear a noise outside, guys," she said, praying that she was wrong, that Luke was still listening in. "Out back. Please be listening."

The front windows were painted shut, and the glass looked impossibly thick. How had Lucy managed to break through her bedroom window?

She heard the noise again, closer to the back door this time. "Someone's definitely out there."

Fight.

She turned around in a full circle, looking for something, *any*thing with which to arm herself. Luke didn't have a fireplace, so there were no fireplace pokers. There was nothing, *nothing*. Only a newspaper she could roll up. Perfect—provided the attacker was a bad dog.

knees give out, and she sat down hard, right there in the closet, knocking over fishing poles and lacrosse sticks and God knows what else.

The closet door was yanked open and there was Luke. The panic in his eyes would have been sweet if her relief hadn't morphed instantly into anger.

"What the hell did you think you were doing?" She nearly came out of the closet swinging that bat. "You damn near scared me to *death!*"

"I scared *you?*" He was just as mad as she was. "God, Syd, I came in here and you were gone! I thought—"

"You should have called me, told me you would be here early," she said accusingly.

"It's not *that* early," he countered. "It's nearly 0130. What's early about that?"

It was. The clock on the VCR said 1:27.

"But…" Syd regrouped, thinking fast. Why had she been so frightened? She pointed toward the kitchen. "You came in through the back door. You always come in through the front—which was locked with a deadbolt, you genius! If you *had* been the San Felipe Rapist, I would have been trapped!"

She had him with that one. It stopped him cold and doused his anger. He looked at the lock on the door and then at her. She could see him absorbing the baseball bat that still dangled from her hand. She watched him notice the fact that she was still shaking, notice the tears that were threatening to spill from her eyes.

Damn it, she *wasn't* going to cry in front of him.

"My God," he said. "You don't have a key? Why the hell don't you have a key?"

Syd shook her head, unable to say anything, using all her energy to keep from crying.

Luke *wasn't* lying dead in the backyard. Thank God.

"This is probably nothing," he said to Syd, but she knew he didn't believe that.

The lights were still on in the kitchen. Everything looked completely normal. There were a few dirty dishes in the sink, a newspaper open to the sports page on the kitchen table.

As Syd watched, Luke picked up the telephone and put the receiver to his ear.

He looked at Syd as he hung it up, as he spoke once more to Thomas over his cell phone. "Phone's dead. Stay in position. I'm calling for backup."

A CLEAN CUT.

Probably with a knife, possibly with a scissors.

Lucky sat on his living-room sofa, trying to rub away his massive headache by massaging his forehead.

It wasn't working.

Somehow, someone had gotten close enough to the house tonight to cut the phone wire. Somehow, the son of a bitch had gotten past two experienced Navy SEALs and three bright, young SEAL candidates who had been looking for him.

He hadn't gone inside, but his message had been clear.

He could have.

He'd been right there, just on the other side of a wall from Sydney. If he'd wanted to, he could've gone in, used that knife to kill her as dead as the phone and been gone before Lucky had ever reached the back door.

The thought made him sick to his stomach.

As the FInCOM and police members of the task force filtered through his house, Lucky sat with Syd on the couch, his arm securely around her shoulder—he didn't give a damn who saw.

wanted to establish an alibi and convince everyone that he'd actually been in the men's room for all that time— instead of here at your house, at the exact time your phone wire was cut during a distraction that he knew about."

Lucky shook his head. "No," he said. "Syd, you've got to go with me on this one. It's *not* Wes. It can't be. You've got to trust me."

She gazed at him, looking into his eyes. She'd been scared tonight, badly. When she'd come out of that closet, that was the closest Lucky had ever seen her come to losing it. She was tough, she was strong, she was smart and she was as afraid of all this as he was. And that made her desire to catch this bastard that much crazier. Crazier and completely admirable.

She nodded. "Okay," she said. "If you're that certain… he's off my list. It's not Wes."

She wasn't humoring him, wasn't being patronizing. She was accepting—on faith—something that he believed in absolutely. She trusted him that much. It was a remark- ably good feeling. *Remarkably* good.

Lucky kissed her. Right in front of the task force, in front of Chief Zale.

"Tomorrow," he said, "I'll talk to Wes. See if he wouldn't mind voluntarily giving us a DNA sample, just so we can run it by the lab and then officially take him off the suspect list."

"I don't need you to do that," she said.

"I know." He kissed her again, trying to make light of it despite the tight feeling that was filling his chest from the inside out. "Pissing off Wes Skelly while he's got a killer hangover isn't my idea of fun. But hey, I don't have anything else to do tomorrow."

"Tomorrow," Syd reminded him, "your sister's getting married."

hair and had even put on a little makeup this evening, but she was, at best, interestingly pretty. Passable. Acceptable. But not even remotely close to *incredibly* anything, particularly not beautiful.

Luke actually looked surprised. "You think I'm—" He caught himself, and laughed. "Uh-uh," he said. "Nope. No way. I'm not going to let you pick a fight with me over the fact that I think you look great."

He pulled her close and kissed her, surprising her by giving her a private kiss instead of a public one. It was one of those kisses that melted her bones, turned her to jelly, and left her dizzy, dazed and clinging to him. It was one of those kisses he gave her before he scooped her into his arms and carried her into his bedroom. It was one of those kisses he gave her when he wanted them to stop talking and start communicating in an entirely different manner. It was one of those kisses she could never, ever resist.

"I think you look incredibly beautiful tonight," he murmured into her ear. "Now what *you* do, is *you* say, thank you, Luke."

"Thank you, Luke," she managed.

"Was that so hard?"

He was smiling down at her, with his heavenly blue eyes and his gorgeous face and his sunstreaked hair. *He* was the one who was incredibly beautiful. It seemed impossible that the heated look in his eyes could be real, but it was. He'd somehow pulled her onto the dance floor, and as they moved slowly in time to the music, he was holding her close enough for her to know that that kiss had done the exact opposite of turning *him* to jelly.

He wanted her.

At least for now.

"You two are so perfect together." Gregory's mother, platinum-haired, rail-thin, with a smile as warm as her

There'd been a message this afternoon on her answering machine. *Think* magazine had called from New York. The series of pieces she'd written on women's safety, along with her proposal for an in-depth article on catching serial criminals, had given buoyancy to the résumé she'd sent them months ago. In fact, it had floated right to the top of their pile of editorial candidates' résumés. They wanted her to come for an interview with their publisher and managing editor, Eileen Hess. Ms. Hess was going to be in Phoenix for a few days at a conference. Perhaps it would be more convenient for Syd to meet with her there, rather than flying all the way to New York? It would be more affordable for Syd, too. They were a small magazine, and unfortunately they couldn't afford to pay Syd's airfare.

Syd had called back to let them know that she wouldn't be able to leave California until the San Felipe Rapist was apprehended. She didn't know how long that would be, and if that meant she'd be out of the running for the job, she hoped they'd consider her in the future.

She'd found out they were willing to wait. She could fly to New York next week or even next month. This job was virtually in her pocket, if she wanted it.

If she wanted it.

Of *course* she wanted it.

Didn't she?

Luke kissed her neck, and she knew what she *really* wanted.

She wanted Luke, ready and willing to spend the rest of his life with her.

Talk about pipe dreams.

Her problem was that she had too vivid an imagination. It was far too easy for her to take this make-believe relationship and pretend it was something real.

good news. That Lucy McCoy had come out of her coma, or that they'd found Blue and he was on his way home.

The number on the pager was Frisco's—and so was the voice on the other end of the phone.

"Hey," Frisco said. "You're there. Good news. We caught him."

It was a possibility Lucky hadn't even considered, and he nearly dropped the phone. "Repeat that."

"Martin Taus," Frisco said. "Ex-regular Navy, enlisted, served here at Coronado during the spring and summer of 1996. Discharged in late '96 with lots of little dings against him—nothing big enough to warrant a dishonorable. He served time in Nevada in early '98 for indecent exposure. He's been picked up for sexual assault at least twice before, both times he got off on a technicality. He was brought in early this evening for questioning by the San Felipe PD. He just finished making a videotaped confession about twenty minutes ago."

Syd was watching him, concern in her eyes.

"They caught the rapist," Luke told her, hardly believing it himself.

"Are they sure?" She asked the question exactly as Luke asked Frisco.

"Apparently, he's been pretty specific in describing the attacks," Frisco said. "Chief Zale's getting ready to give a press conference—just in time for the eleven o'clock news. I'm heading over to the police station. Can you meet me there?"

"I'm on my way," Lucky said, and hung up.

Syd wasn't smiling. In fact, she looked extremely skeptical. "Do they actually have evidence, tying this guy to—"

"He confessed," he told her. "Apparently in detail."

to the police station last night. During all this waiting, she'd written a variety of different articles, from features to hard news, on various aspects of the case.

"Don't even *think* about reading over my shoulder," she warned him, her fingers flying over the keyboard, working on her story for *Think* magazine. She'd already sent the hard news story out electronically to the *San Felipe Journal,* and they'd called to tell her it was being picked up by *USA Today.*

"So you buy it, huh?" Luke asked. "You believe this is really our guy and, just like that, it's all over?"

"It *does* seem a little anticlimactic," she had to admit. "But real life isn't always as exciting as the movies. Personally, I prefer it *this* way." She looked up at him. "Are you finally ready to go?"

He sat down wearily next to her at the interview-room table. It had been a long night, and they were both still dressed in their formal clothes despite the fact that it was well after 8:00 a.m. "Yeah, I just wanted to see him," he said. "I just wanted to be in the same room with him for a minute. I knew if I stood there long enough, they'd eventually let me in."

"And?"

"And they did. He was…" Luke shook his head. "I don't think he's our guy."

"Luke, he *confessed.*"

"*I* could confess. That wouldn't make *me* the rapist."

"Did you even *watch* the videotape? It's chilling the way he—"

"Maybe I'm wrong," he countered. "I just…there was something that wasn't right. I was standing there, right next to him, but I couldn't put my finger on it."

"Maybe it's just lack of sleep."

"I know what lack of sleep feels like and no, it's not

under the heading *without Luke*. Everywhere else was exactly the same. New York, San Diego, Chicago. They would all *feel* exactly the same—lonely as hell, at least for a while.

"Wow," Luke said, rubbing his eyes. "I'm stunned. I'm…" He shook his head. "Here I was thinking, I don't know, maybe that we had something here that was worth spending some time on."

Syd couldn't keep from laughing. "Luke. Get real. We both know exactly what we've got going. It's fun, it's great, but it's not serious. You told me yourself—you don't do serious."

"Well…what if I've changed my mind?"

"What if you only *think* you've changed your mind?" she countered gently. "And what if I give up a great career move—something I've worked for and wanted for *years*— and your 'what if' turns out to be wrong?"

He cleared his throat. "I was thinking, um, maybe you really could move in with me."

Syd couldn't believe it. Luke wanted her to move in with him? Mr. I'm-never-serious? For a nanosecond, she let herself believe it was possible.

But then he winced, giving himself away. He didn't really want her to move in with him. He just wasn't used to being the one in a relationship who got dumped. It was a competitive thing. He was grabbing on to anything—no matter how stupid an idea it was in reality—in order to keep her around temporarily, in order to win.

But once he had her, he'd soon tire of her. And she'd move out. Maybe not right away, but eventually. And then she'd be in Coronado without Luke.

The job in New York wouldn't keep her warm at night, but neither would Luke after they'd split up.

"I think," Syd said slowly, "that a decision of that

Lucky jumped, turning to see Veronica standing in the door. He swore. "Ron, are you taking lessons in stealth from the Captain? Jeez, way to give a guy a heart attack."

She came into the room, sat down on the other side of the bed, taking Lucy's other hand. "Hi, Lucy, I'm back." She looked up at Lucky and smiled. "Sorry for eavesdropping."

"Like hell you are."

"So why *don't* you ask Syd to marry you?"

He couldn't answer.

Veronica answered for him. "You're afraid."

Lucky gritted his teeth and answered honestly. "I'm scared she'll turn me down, *and* I'm scared that she won't."

"Well," Veronica said in her crisp British accent. "She'll do neither—and go to New York—unless you do something drastic."

There was a commotion out in the hall, and the door was pushed open. One of the younger nurses blocked the doorway with her body. "I'm sorry, sir, but it might be best if you wait for the doctor to—"

"I talked to the doctor on the phone on my way over here from the airport." The voice from the hallway was soft but pure business, honeyed by a thick south-of-the-Mason-Dixon-Line drawl. "It's *not* best if I wait for the doctor. It's best if I go into that room and see my wife."

Blue McCoy.

Lucky stood up to see Lieutenant Commander Blue McCoy literally pick up the nurse and move her out of his way. And then he was in the room.

"Lucy." He didn't have eyes for anyone but the woman lying in the middle of that hospital bed.

Blue looked exhausted. He hadn't shaved in weeks, but

"I hope so," she told him.

Lucky had spoken to the doctor just a few hours earlier. He turned to tell Joe that but did a quick about-face. Big, bad Joe Cat was crying as he held on tightly to his wife.

"Everything's going to be okay," he heard Veronica tell Joe through her own tears. "Now that Blue's here, now that you're here...everything's going to be okay. I know it."

And Lucky knew then exactly what he wanted. He wanted what Lucy shared with Blue. He wanted what Joe and Veronica had found.

And for the first time in his life, he thought that maybe, just *maybe* he'd found it, too.

Because when Syd was around him, everything *was* okay.

He was definitely going to do it. He was going to ask Syd to marry him.

The door at the end of the corridor opened, and the rest of Alpha Squad came in. Harvard, Cowboy and Crash. And Mitch Shaw was back, too. Lucky walked down to greet them, shooting Mitch a quizzical look.

"By the time I found them," he explained, "they'd completed their mission and were on their way out of the mountains."

"How's Lucy?" Harvard asked. "We don't want to get too close—Blue and Joe were the only ones who had time to shower."

"Lucy's still in a coma," Lucky told them. "It's kind of now-or-never time, as far as coming out of it goes. Her doctors were hoping Blue's voice would help pull her back to our side." He took a step back from them. "Jeez, you guys are ripe." They smelled like a combination of unwashed dog and stale campfire smoke.

Stale smoke...

He looked up and found Harvard, Cowboy, Mitch and Crash all staring at him.

On the other end of the phone, Syd was equally silent.

"Wow," Lucky said. "That didn't come out quite the way I'd hoped it would."

Cowboy started to laugh, but when Harvard elbowed him hard in the chest, he fell instantly silent.

Lucky closed his eyes and turned away. "Syd, will you please come back here so we can talk?"

"Talk." Her voice sounded weak. She cleared her throat. "Yeah, that sounds smart. You're in luck. I'm nearly half-way home."

that was going on last week, because how else would she have known?"

"Luke."

"And Blue goes, 'I've always thought you'd look damn good in a crew cut, Yankee,' and it was all over. There were seven of us here—all SEALs, all crying like babies and—"

"Luke."

"I'm sorry. I'm nervous. I'm talking because I'm nervous, because I'm scared to death that you called me back to tell me to go to hell."

Syd waited for a few seconds to make sure he was finally done. "I called you," she said, glancing into her rearview mirror, "because I've got a little problem. I'm out here, in the middle of nowhere, and I'm…I'm pretty sure that I'm being followed."

LUCKY'S HEART STOPPED. "This is real, right?" he said. "Not just some make-believe scenario game you're playing?"

"It's real. I noticed the car behind me about fifteen miles ago." Over the telephone, Syd's voice sounded very small. "When I slow down, he slows down. When I speed up, he speeds up. And now that I'm thinking about it, I saw this car back at the gas station, last time I stopped."

"Where are you?" he asked. His heart had started up again, but now it was lodged securely in his throat. He stuck his head out of the men's room, braving the noise out in the hospital cafeteria, waving until he caught Frisco's attention. He gestured for his swim buddy to follow him into the men's as Syd answered him.

"Route 78," she was telling him. "Just inside the California state line. I'm about forty miles south of Route 10, heading for Route 8. There's nothing out here, Luke. Not

"He's going to pass me," Syd told Luke, filled with a flash of relief.

The dark sedan was moving faster now, moving up alongside of her.

"God, this was just my imagination," she said. "I'm so sorry, I feel so stupid and—"

The sedan was keeping pace with her. She could see the driver through the window. He was big, broad, built like a football player. His hair was short and brownish blond, worn in a crew cut.

And he had a pair of feature-distorting panty hose over his face.

Syd screamed and hit the gas, dropping the phone as her car surged forward.

"SIT-REP," LUCKY SHOUTED into his cell phone. Damn, she probably didn't remember what sit-rep was. "Syd! What's happening, damn it?"

Joe Cat and Harvard pushed their way into the men's room, their faces grim. Harvard had a map, bless him.

Lucky's voice shook as he briefly outlined the situation, as he took the map from Harvard's hands and opened it. "She's heading south on 78." He swore as he found it on the map. "What the hell is she doing on route 78? Why not 95? Why didn't she cut over to Route 8 closer to Phoenix? Why—" He took a deep breath. "Okay. I want to intercept. Fast. What are my options?" He was praying that he wasn't already too late.

The phone line was still open, and he thought he heard the sound of Syd's car's noisy engine. Please, God...

Joe Cat looked at Harvard. "The Black Hawk that brought us here is probably still on the roof. It had more than enough fuel..."

Harvard kicked into action. "I'll round up the team."

mission that called for full battle dress, we've got enough to outfit a small army."

"If this guy so much as touches Syd…" Lucky couldn't go on.

But Joe Cat knew what he was saying. And he nodded. "It finally happened to you, huh, O'Donlon? This woman got under your skin."

"She's irreplaceable," Lucky admitted.

SYD RODE THE CLUTCH, trying to push a little extra power into her car's top speed. It was working, but for how long?

The temperature gauge was rising. It wasn't going to be long until she was out of time.

She had to get her phone off the floor. It had been at least ten minutes since she'd dropped it—Luke had to be going nuts. She had to talk to him. She had to tell him… what?

That she loved him, that she was sorry, that she wished it might've all turned out differently.

With a herculean effort, she reached for the phone and…

This time her hand connected with it. This time, her fingers scraped along the gritty floor mat. This time, she got it!

But the effort made her swerve, and she fought to control the car with only one hand.

Maybe it would be better if she died in a crash….

The thought was a wild one, and Syd rejected it instantly. That would be surrender of a permanent kind. And she'd never been fond of the surrender or submit solution to any "what if" scenario. If she were going to die, she would die fighting, damn it.

She tucked the phone under her chin and took a deep

her she should cover her head with something, a jacket or something, so she doesn't get cut by the glass. Tell her…" He had to say it. To hell with the fact that everyone was listening in. "Tell Syd I love her."

"HE SAID THAT?" Syd couldn't believe it. "He actually said those words?"

"He said, tell Syd I love her," Frisco repeated.

"Oh, God," Syd said, unsure whether to laugh or cry. "If he actually said that, he thinks I'm going to die, doesn't he?"

Steam started escaping from under the front hood of her car. This was it. "My radiator's going," she told Frisco. "It's funny, all those debates about whether to fight or submit. Who knew I'd actually have to make that choice?"

Luke wanted her to submit. He wanted her to stay in her car, wait for this behemoth to come in after her. But once he did, she wouldn't stand a chance.

But maybe, if she were outside the car, she could use her steering wheel lock as a very literal club. Maybe, if she opened the door and came out swinging…

"Tell Luke I'm sorry," Syd told Frisco. "But I choose *fight*."

Her radiator was sending out clouds of steam, and her car was starting to slow. This was it. The beginning of the end.

"Tell him…I love him, too."

Syd cut the connection and let the phone drop into her lap as the car behind hit her squarely. She had to hold on to the steering wheel with both hands to keep her car in the middle of the road. She had to keep him from moving alongside her and running her off onto the soft shoulder.

Except what would that do, really, but delay the inevitable?

CHAPTER SIXTEEN

"HIS NAME IS OWEN FINN," Lucky reported to Frisco from his kitchen phone. "He was at the Academy, got into BUD/S, but didn't make it through the program. He rang out—it was during the summer of '96. Apparently he was a nutcase. One of those guys who had a million opportunities handed to him on a platter, but he just kept on screwing up. And whenever he did, it was never his fault."

"Yeah," Frisco said. "I know the type. 'I didn't mean to beat my wife until she ended up in the hospital. It wasn't my fault—she got me so mad.'"

"Yeah, right. Four months after he quit BUD/S," Lucky told his friend, "he was charged and convicted of theft. That got him a dishonorable discharge as well as time served. When he got out, as a civilian, he got caught in a burglary attempt, did time in Kentucky as well. I guess he sat there for a few years, stewing on the fact that—in his mind at least—his abysmal record of failure started when he rang out of BUD/S. As soon as he got out of jail, he headed back to Coronado, via a short stop in Texas where he robbed a liquor store. God forbid he should actually *work* to earn money.

"The police psychologist thinks he probably came back here with some kind of vague idea of revenge—an idea that didn't gel until he got here. This psychologist told me and Syd that he thinks Finn got mileage out of being

all-too-public marriage proposal. It figured that Frisco would've heard about it. In fact, Mia was probably standing next to him, tugging on his sleeve, waiting for the word so that she could call Veronica with an update. And Veronica would talk to PJ, and PJ would tell Harvard, who would send out a memo to the rest of Alpha Squad.

The fact that Lucky had actually proposed marriage wasn't being taken lightly by his friends. In fact, it was serious business.

Serious business.

Serious...

"Hang on a sec, can you?" Lucky said into the phone. He set the receiver down on the kitchen table, then went down the hall, and knocked on the closed guest-room door.

"Yeah." Syd sounded impatient. She was writing.

Lucky opened the door and made it quick. "Do you have an estimate for when you'll be done?"

"Two hours," she said. "Go away. Please."

Lucky closed the door, went back into the kitchen and picked up the phone. "Frisco, man, I need your help."

SYD SENT THE ARTICLE electronically, and shut down her laptop computer. She stood up, stretching out her back, knowing that she'd put it off as long as she possibly could.

Luke was out there in his living room, waiting so that they could talk.

To hell with your interview.... Get your butt home and marry me, damn it.

He couldn't have been serious. She *knew* he wasn't serious.

He'd been upset for a variety of reasons. He didn't like the idea of losing her, of losing, period. This marriage

An Important Message from the Editors

Dear Reader,

We hope you enjoyed reading one of our fine novels. If you should like to receive more of these great stories delivered directly to your door, we're offering to send you two more of our books you love so well plus two exciting Mystery Gifts—absolutely FREE!

Please enjoy them with our compliments...

Pam Powers

Peel off Seal and Place Inside...

EDITOR'S
FREE GIFTS
SEAL
THANK YOU

THE EDITOR'S "THANK YOU" FREE GIFTS INCLUDE:

- ▶ 2 Suspense books
- ▶ 2 exciting mystery gifts!

YES! I have placed my Editor's "thank you" Free Gifts seal in the space provided at right. Please send me the 2 FREE books and 2 FREE gifts for which I qualify. I understand that I am under no obligation to purchase anything further, as explained on the back of this card.

PLACE FREE GIFTS SEAL HERE

We want to make sure we offer you the best service suited to your needs. Please answer the following question:
About how many NEW paperback fiction books have you purchased in the past 3 months?

❏ 0-2	❏ 3-6	❏ 7 or more
FC4V	FC47	FC5K

191/391 MDL

FIRST NAME

LAST NAME

ADDRESS

APT.#

CITY

STATE/PROV.

ZIP/POSTAL CODE

to New York. There was a message on my machine. They made me an offer. They want me."

"What about my offer?" Luke asked. "I want you, too."

She searched his eyes, but he still wasn't smiling. There was no sign that he was kidding, no sign that he acknowledged how completely out of character this was. "You seriously expect me to believe that you want to marry me?" She could barely say the words aloud.

"Yes. I need to apologize for the subpar delivery, but—"

"Luke. Marriage is forever. I take that *very* seriously. This isn't some game that we can play until you get bored."

"Do I look like I'm playing a game?" he countered.

She didn't get a chance to answer because the doorbell rang.

"Good," Luke said. "Just in time. Excuse me."

As Syd watched, he opened his door. Thomas King stood there, Rio Rosetti and Michael Lee right behind him. They, like Luke, were wearing their dress uniforms. Their arms were full of...*flowers?*

"Great," Luke said. "Come on in. Just put those down on the table, gentlemen. Perfect."

"Hey, Syd," Thomas said.

"If you don't mind waiting out on the back deck...?" Luke efficiently pushed them toward the kitchen door. "I've got a cooler out there with beer, wine and soda. Help yourselves."

Syd stared at Luke, stared at the flowers. They were gorgeous—all different kinds and colors. The bouquets completely covered the coffee table. "Luke, what is this for?"

"It's for you," he said. "And me."

"Limos R Us," Cowboy announced with a grin. "Three of 'em. White, as ordered."

"Ready to roll, Lieutenant, sir," Harvard added. "Vegas, here we come."

Vegas? As in Las Vegas? Wedding capital of the world?

Syd stood up and looked out the window. Sure enough, three stretch limos, big enough to hold a small army, were idling at the curb. Her heart began to pound, triple time, in her chest. Was it possible Luke truly was serious...?

"Hi, Syd." PJ gave her a hug and a kiss. "You okay after this afternoon?"

Syd didn't have time to answer. PJ disappeared with the others, pushed into the kitchen and out the back door.

"So," Luke said when they were alone once again. "You love me. And I love you. I know this job in New York is good for your career, but you also told me that if you had a chance, if you could find a patron to support you for a year or two, you'd rather quit your day job and write a book." He spread his arms. "Well, here I—"

The doorbell rang.

"Excuse me."

This time it was Frisco and Mia. They came into the living room, followed by an elderly man in a dark suit who was carrying a large briefcase.

"This is George Majors," Frisco told Luke. "He owns that jewelry store over on Ventura."

Luke shook the old man's hand. "This is wonderful," he said. "I really appreciate your coming out here like this. Here, you can set up over here." He pushed aside some of the flowers on the table, pulled Syd down onto the couch.

Mr. Majors opened his briefcase, and inside was a dis-

"I surrender," she whispered, and started to kiss him, but then she pulled back. She was wearing jeans and a T-shirt, and everyone else was dressed for...a *wedding*. "Tonight?" she said. "God, Luke, I don't have a dress!"

The doorbell rang.

It was Joe Cat and Veronica. Mia let them in.

"I have found," Veronica announced, "exactly what Luke asked me to find—the most *exquisite* wedding dress in all of Southern California."

"My God," Syd whispered to Luke. "You thought of everything."

"Damn right," he told her. "I wanted to make sure you knew I was serious. I figured if you saw that all my friends were taking me seriously, then you would, too."

He kissed her—and it was an extremely serious kiss.

"Marry me tonight," he said.

Syd laughed. "At the Igloo of Love? Definitely."

Smiling into his eyes, she knew her life would never be the same. She'd got Lucky. Permanently.

* * * * *

TAYLOR'S TEMPTATION

PROLOGUE

"It was amazing." Rio Rosetti shook his head, still unable to wrap his mind around last night's explosive events. "It was absolutely amazing."

Mike and Thomas sat across from him at the mess hall, their ham and eggs forgotten as they waited for him to continue.

Although neither of them let it show, Rio knew they were both envious as hell that he'd been smack in the middle of all the action, pulling his weight alongside the two legendary chiefs of Alpha Squad, Bobby Taylor and Wes Skelly.

"Hey, Little E., get your gear and strap on your blue-suede swim fins," Chief Skelly had said to Rio just six hours ago. Had it really only been six hours? "Me and Uncle Bobby are gonna show you how it's done."

Twin sons of different mothers. That's what Bobby and Wes were often called. Of *very* different mothers. The two men looked nothing alike. Chief Taylor was huge. In fact, the man was a total animal. Rio wasn't sure, because the air got kind of hazy way up by the top of Bobby Taylor's head, but he thought the chief stood at least six and a half feet tall, maybe even more. And he was nearly as wide. He had shoulders like a football player's protective padding, and, also like a football player, the man was remarkably fast. It was pretty freaky, actually, that a guy that big could achieve the kind of speed he did.

His size wasn't the only thing that set him apart from

Bobby had been doing a stint as a BUD/S instructor in Coronado, and he'd taken Rio, along with Mike Lee and Thomas King, under his extremely large wing. Which wasn't to say he coddled them. No way. In fact, by marking them as the head of a class filled with smart, confident, determined men, he'd demanded more from them. He'd driven them harder than the others, accepted no excuses, asked nothing less than their personal best—each and every time.

They'd done all they could to deliver, and—no doubt due to Bobby's quiet influence with Captain Joe Catalan-otto—won themselves coveted spots in the best SEAL team in the Navy.

Rewind to six hours ago, to last night's operation. SEAL Team Ten's Alpha Squad had been called in to assist a FInCOM/DEA task force.

A particularly nasty South American drug lord had parked his luxury yacht a very short, very cocky distance outside of U.S. waters. The Finks and the DEA agents couldn't or maybe just didn't want to for some reason— Rio wasn't sure which and it didn't really matter to him— snatch the bad dude up until he crossed that invisible line into U.S. territory.

And that was where the SEALs were to come in.

Lieutenant Lucky O'Donlon was in charge of the op— mostly because he'd come up with a particularly devi-ous plan that had tickled Captain Joe Cat's dark sense of humor. The lieutenant had decided that a small team of SEALs would swim out to the yacht—named *Swiss Chocolate,* a stupid-ass name for a boat—board it covertly, gain access to the bridge and do a little creative work on their computerized navigational system.

As in making the yacht's captain think they were head-ing south when they were really heading northwest.

Bad dude would give the order to head back toward

He was Thomas. Not Tommy. Not even Tom. *Thomas.* Not one member of Team Ten ever called him anything else.

Thomas had won the team's respect. Unlike Rio, who somehow, despite his hope for a nickname like Panther or Hawk, had been given the handle Elvis. Or even worse, Little Elvis or Little E.

Holy Chrysler. As if Elvis wasn't embarrassing enough.

"We took a rubber duck out toward the *Swiss Chocolate,*" Rio told Thomas and Mike. "Swam the rest of the way in." The swift ride in the little inflatable boat through the darkness of the ocean had made his heart pound. Knowing they were going to board a heavily guarded yacht and gain access to her bridge without anyone seeing them had a lot to do with it. But he was also worried.

What if he blew it?

Bobby apparently could read Rio's mind almost as easily as he read Wes Skelly's, because he'd touched Rio's shoulder—just a brief squeeze of reassurance—before they'd crept out of the water and onto the yacht.

"The damn thing was lit up like a Christmas tree and crawling with guards," Rio continued. "They all dressed alike and carried these cute little Uzi's. It was almost like their boss got off on pretending he had his own little army. But they weren't any kind of army. Not even close. They were really just street kids in expensive uniforms. They didn't know how to stand watch, didn't know what to look for. I swear to God, you guys, we moved right past them. They didn't have a clue we were there—not with all the noise they were making and the lights shining in their eyes. It was so easy it was a joke."

"If it were a joke," Mike Lee asked, "then what's Chief Taylor doing in the hospital?"

Rio shook his head. "No, that part wasn't a joke." Someone on board the yacht had decided to move the

thought humanly possible. He could scan the images that scrolled past on the screen at remarkable speeds, too.

"It took him less than three minutes to do whatever it was he had to do," he continued, "and then we were out of there—off the bridge. Lucky and Spaceman were in the water, giving us the all-clear." He shook his head, remembering how close they'd been to slipping silently away into the night. "And then all these babes in bikinis came running up on deck, heading straight for us. It was the absolute worst luck—if we'd been anywhere else on the vessel, the diversion would've been perfect. We would've been completely invisible. I mean, if you're an inexperienced guard are you going to be watching to see who's crawling around in the shadows or are you going to pay attention to the beach bunnies in the thong bikinis? But someone decided to go for a swim off the starboard side—right where we were hiding. These heavy-duty searchlights came on, probably just so the guys on board could watch the women in the water, but wham, there we were. Lit up. There was no place to hide—and nowhere to go but over the side."

"Bobby picked me up and threw me overboard," Rio admitted. He must not have been moving fast enough— he was still kicking himself for that. "I didn't see what happened next, but according to Wes, Bobby stepped in front of him and blocked him from the bullets that started flying while they both went into the water. That was when Bobby caught a few—one in his shoulder, another in the top of his thigh. He was the one who was hurt, but he pulled both me and Wes down, under the water—out of sight and out of range."

Sirens went on. Rio had been able to hear them along with the tearing sound of the guards' assault weapons and the screams from the women, even as he was pulled underwater.

much longer before a helo came to evac Bobby to the hospital.

"He's going to be okay," he told both Thomas and Mike again. That was the first thing he'd said about their beloved chief's injuries, before they'd even sat down to breakfast. "The leg wound wasn't all that bad, and the bullet that went into his shoulder somehow managed to miss the bone. He'll be off the active-duty list for a few weeks, maybe a month, but after that…" Rio grinned. "Chief Bobby Taylor will be back. You can count on that."

"You want me to take leave and go to Boston," Bobby didn't really enjoy making Wes squirm, but he needed his best friend to see just how absurd this sounded, "because you and Colleen got into another argument." He still didn't turn it into a question. He just let it quietly hang there.

"No, Bobby," Wes said, the urgency in his voice turned up to high. "You don't get it. She's signed on with some kind of bleeding-heart, touchy-feely volunteer organization, and next she and her touchy-feely friends are flying out to flippin' Tulgeria." He said it again, louder, as if it were unprintable, then followed it up by a string of words that truly were.

Bobby could see that Wes was beyond upset. This wasn't just another ridiculous argument. This was serious.

"She's going to provide earthquake relief," Wes continued. "That's lovely. That's wonderful, I told her. Be Mother Teresa. Be Florence Nightingale. Have your goody two-shoes permanently glued to your feet. But stay *way* the hell away from Tulgeria! Tulgeria—the flippin' terrorist capital of the world!"

"Wes—"

"I tried to get leave," Wes told him. "I was just in the captain's office, but with you still down and H. out with food poisoning, I'm mission essential."

"I'm there," Bobby said. "I'm on the next flight to Boston."

Wes was willing to give up Alpha Squad's current assignment—something he was really looking forward to, something involving plenty of C-4 explosives—to go to Boston. That meant that Colleen wasn't just pushing her brother's buttons. That meant she was serious about this. That she really was planning to travel to a part of the world where Bobby himself didn't feel safe. And he wasn't a freshly pretty, generously endowed, long-legged—*very*

her, so she kept her temper, kept it cool and clean. "I'm well aware that you don't like—"

"'Don't like' doesn't have anything to do with it," the man at the front of the gang—John Morrison—cut her off. "We don't want your center here, we don't want *you* here." He looked at the kids, who'd stopped washing Mrs. O'Brien's car and stood watching the exchange, wide-eyed and dripping with water and suds. "You, Sean Sullivan. Does your father know you're down here with *her?* With the hippie chick?"

"Keep going, guys," Colleen told the kids, giving them what she hoped was a reassuring smile. *Hippie chick.* Sheesh. "Mrs. O'Brien doesn't have all day. And there's a line, remember. This car wash team has a rep for doing a good job—swiftly and efficiently. Let's not lose any customers over a little distraction."

She turned back to John Morrison and his gang. And they *were* a gang, despite the fact that they were all in their late thirties and early forties and led by a respectable local businessman. Well, on second thought, calling Morrison *respectable* was probably a little too generous.

"Yes, Mr. Sullivan does know where his son is," she told them levelly. "The St. Margaret's Junior High Youth Group is helping raise money for the Tulgeria Earthquake Relief Fund. All of the money from this car wash is going to help people who've lost their homes and nearly all of their possessions. I don't see how even *you* could have a problem with that."

Morrison bristled.

And Colleen silently berated herself. Despite her efforts, her antagonism and anger toward these Neanderthals had leaked out.

"Why don't you go back to wherever it was you came from?" he told her harshly. "Get the hell out of our neigh-

these children get hurt. She would do whatever she had to do, including trying again to make friends with these dirt wads.

"I apologize for losing my temper. Shantel," she called to one of the girls, her eyes still on Morrison and his goons. "Run inside and see if Father Timothy's coming out with more of that lemonade soon. Tell him to bring six extra paper cups for Mr. Morrison and his friends. I think we could probably all use some cooling off."

Maybe that would work. Kill them with kindness. Drown them with lemonade.

The twelve-year-old ran swiftly for the church door.

"How about it, guys?" Colleen forced herself to smile at the men, praying that this time it would work. "Some lemonade?"

Morrison's expression didn't change, and she knew that this was where he was going to step forward, inform her he didn't want any of their lemonade—expletive deleted—and challenge her to just try washing out his mouth. He'd then imply—ridiculously, and solely because of her pro bono legal work for the HIV Testing and AIDS Education Center that was struggling to establish a foothold in this narrow-minded but desperately needy corner of the city—that she was a lesbian and offer to "cure her" in fifteen unforgettable minutes in the closest back alley.

It would almost be funny. Except for the fact that Morrison was dead serious. He'd made similar disgusting threats to her before.

But now, to her surprise, John Morrison didn't say another word. He just looked long and hard at the group of eleven- and twelve-year-olds standing behind her, then did an about face, muttering something unprintable.

It was amazing. Just like that, he and his boys were walking away.

But then he looked at her and smiled, and warmth seeped back into his dark-brown eyes.

He had the world's most beautiful eyes.

"Hey, Colleen," he said in his matter-of-fact, no worries, easygoing voice. "How's it going?"

He held out his arms to her, and in a flash she was running across the asphalt and hugging him. He smelled faintly of cigarette smoke—no doubt thanks to her brother, Mr. Just-One-More-Cigarette-Before-I-Quit—and coffee. He was warm and huge and solid and one of very few men in the world who could actually make her feel if not quite petite then pretty darn close.

As long as she'd wished him here, she should have wished for more. Like for him to have shown up with a million-dollar lottery win in his pocket. Or—better yet—a diamond ring and a promise of his undying love.

Yes, she'd had a wild crush on this man for close to ten years now. And just once she wanted him to take her into his arms like this and kiss her senseless, instead of giving her a brotherly noogie on the top of her head as he released her.

Over the past few years she'd imagined she'd seen appreciation in his eyes as he'd looked at her. And once or twice she could've sworn she'd actually seen heat—but only when he thought both she and Wes weren't looking. Bobby was attracted to her. Or at the very least she wished he were. But even if he were, there was no way in hell he'd ever act on that attraction—not with Wes watching his every move and breathing down his neck.

Colleen hugged him tightly. She had only two chances each visit to get this close to him—once during hello and once during goodbye—and she always made sure to take full advantage.

But this time he winced. "Easy."

Oh, God, he'd been hurt. She pulled back to look up

He nodded, regarding her steadily. "It didn't feel like 'nothing.'"

"Nothing *you* have to worry about," she countered. "I'm doing some pro bono legal work for the AIDS Education Center, and not everyone is happy about it. That's what litigation's all about. Where's Wes? Parking the car?"

"Actually, he's—"

"I know why you're here. You came to try to talk me out of going to Tulgeria. Wes probably came to forbid me from going. Hah. As if he could." She picked up her sponge and rinsed it in a bucket. "I'm not going to listen to either of you, so you might as well just save your breath, turn around and go back to California. I'm not fifteen anymore, in case you haven't noticed."

"Hey, I've noticed," Bobby said. He smiled. "But Wes needs a little work in that area."

"You know, my living room is completely filled with boxes," Colleen told him. "Donations of supplies and clothing. I don't have any room for you guys. I mean, I guess you can throw sleeping bags on the floor of my bedroom, but I swear to God, if Wes snores, I'm kicking him out into the street."

"No," Bobby said. "That's okay. I made hotel reservations. This week is kind of my vacation, and—"

"Where *is* Wes?" Colleen asked, shading her eyes and looking down the busy city street. "Parking the car in Kuwait?"

"Actually." Bobby cleared his throat. "Yeah."

She looked at him.

"Wes is out on an op," he told her. "It's not quite Kuwait, but…"

"He asked *you* to come to Boston," Colleen realized. "For him. He asked you to play big brother and talk me out of going to Tulgeria, didn't he? I don't believe it. And you *agreed?* You jerk!"

He looked away, clearly embarrassed, and she realized suddenly that her brother wasn't here.

Wes wasn't here.

Bobby was in town *without Wes.* And without Wes, if she played it right, the rules of this game they'd been playing for the past decade could change.

Radically.

Oh, my goodness.

"Look." She cleared her throat. "You're here, so…let's make the best of this. When's your return flight?"

He smiled ruefully. "I figured I'd need the full week to talk you out of going."

He was here for a whole week. Thank you, Lord. "You're not going to talk me out of anything, but you cling to that thought if it helps you," she told him.

"I will." He laughed. "It's good to see you, Colleen."

"It's good to see you, too. Look, as long as there's only one of you, I can probably make room in my apartment—"

He laughed again. "Thanks, but I don't think that would be a very good idea."

"Why waste good money on a hotel room?" she asked. "After all, you're practically my brother."

"No," Bobby said emphatically. "I'm not."

There was something in his tone that made her bold. Colleen looked at him then in a way she'd never dared let herself look at him before. She let her gaze move down his broad chest, taking in the outline of his muscles, admiring the trim line of his waist and hips. She looked all the way down his long legs and then all the way back up again. She lingered a moment on his beautiful mouth, on his full, gracefully shaped lips, before gazing back into his eyes.

She'd shocked him with that obvious once-over. Well,

CHAPTER TWO

WES WOULD KILL HIM if he found out.

No doubt about it.

If Wes knew even *half* the thoughts that were steam-rolling through Bobby's head about his sister, Colleen, Bobby would be a dead man.

Lord have mercy on his soul, the woman was hot. She was also funny and smart. Smart enough to have figured out the ultimate way to get back at him for showing up here as her brother's mouthpiece.

If she were planning to go anywhere besides Tulgeria, Bobby would have turned around. He would have headed for the airport and caught the next flight out of Boston.

Because Colleen was right. He and Wes had absolutely no business telling her what she should and shouldn't do. She was twenty-three years old—old enough to make her own decisions.

Except both Bobby and Wes had been to Tulgeria, and Colleen hadn't. No doubt she'd heard stories about the warring factions of terrorists that roamed the dirt-poor countryside. But she hadn't heard Bobby and Wes's stories. She didn't know what they'd seen, with their own eyes.

At least not yet.

But she would before the week was out.

And he'd take the opportunity to find out what that run-in with the local chapter of the KKK had been about, too.

Apparently, like her brother, Wes, trouble followed

over TV and magazines, looking more like malnourished 12-year-old boys. No, Colleen Skelly was a woman—with a capital *W.* She was the kind of woman that a real man could wrap his arms around and really get a grip on. She actually had hips and breasts—and not only was that the understatement of the century, but it was the thought that would send him to hell, directly to hell. 'Do not pass Go, do not collect two hundred dollars,' do not live another minute longer.

If Wes ever found out that Bobby spent any amount of time at all thinking about Colleen's breasts, well, that would be it. The end. Game over.

But right now Wes—being more than three thousand miles away—wasn't Bobby's problem.

No, Bobby's problem was that somehow *Colleen* had realized that he was spending far too much time thinking about her breasts.

She'd figured out that he was completely and mindlessly in lust with her.

And Wesley wasn't around to save him. Or beat him senseless.

Of course, it was possible that she was just toying with him, just messing with his mind. *Look at what you can't have, you big loser.*

After all, she was dating some lawyer. Wasn't that what Wes had said? And these days, wasn't *dating* just a euphemism for *in a relationship with?* And that was really just a polite way of saying that they were sleeping together, lucky son of a bitch.

Colleen glanced up from her conversation with the station-wagon mom and caught him looking at her butt.

Help.

He'd known that this was going to be a mistake back in California—the second the plea for help had left Wes's lips. Bobby should have admitted it, right there and then.

trusting himself around Colleen Skelly someplace dark and cool and mysterious.

She touched him, reaching up to brush something off his sleeve, and he jumped about a mile straight up.

Colleen laughed. "Whoa. What's with you?"

I want to sink back with you on your brightly colored bedspread, undress you with my teeth and lose myself in your laughter, your eyes and the sweet heat of your body.

Not necessarily in that order.

Bobby shrugged, forced a smile. "Sorry."

"So how 'bout it? You want to get Chinese?"

"Oh," he said, stepping back a bit and shifting around to pick up his seabag and swing it over his shoulder, glad he had something with which to occupy his hands. "I don't know. I should probably go try to find my hotel. It's the Sheraton, just outside of Harvard Square?"

"You're sure I can't talk you into spending the night with me?"

It was possible that she had no idea how suggestive it was when she asked a question like that, combined with a smile like that.

On the other hand, she probably knew damn well what she was doing to him. She was, after all, a Skelly.

He laughed. It was either that or cry. *Evasive maneuvers, Mr. Sulu.* "Why don't we just plan to have lunch tomorrow?"

Lunch was good. Lunch was safe. It was businesslike and well lit.

"Hmm. I'm working straight through lunch tomorrow," she told him. "I'm going to be driving the truck all day, picking up donations to take to Tulgeria. But I'd love to have breakfast with you."

This time it wasn't so much the words but the way she said it, lowering her voice and smiling slightly.

could to figure out a way to keep him from getting out when they arrived at his hotel.

She'd been pretty obvious so far, and she wondered just how blatant she was going to have to be. She laughed aloud as she imagined herself laying it all on the table, bringing it down to the barest bottom line, asking him if he wanted to get with her, using the rudest, least-elegant language she knew.

"So…what are you going to do tonight?" she asked him instead.

He glanced at her warily, as if he were somehow able to read her mind and knew what she really wanted to ask him.

"Your hair's getting really long," she interrupted him before he could even start to answer. "Do you ever wear it down?"

"Not too often," he told her.

Say it. Just say it. "Not even in bed?"

He hesitated only briefly. "No, I usually sleep with it braided or at least pulled back. Otherwise it takes forever to untangle in the morning."

She hadn't meant while he slept. She knew from the way he wasn't looking at her that he was well aware of what she had meant.

"I guess from your hair that you're still doing the covert stuff, huh?" she asked. "Oops, sorry. Don't answer that." She rolled her eyes. "Not that you would."

Bobby laughed. He had a great laugh, a low-pitched rumble that was always accompanied by the most gorgeous smile and extremely attractive laughter lines around his eyes. "I think it's fine if I say yes," he told her. "And you're right—the long hair makes it kind of obvious, anyway."

"So is Wes out on a training op or is it the real thing this time?" she asked.

hooked up with someone new. Or gotten back together with what's-her-name. Kyra Something.

"Wes told me you and Kyra called it quits." There was absolutely no point in sitting here wondering. So what if she came across as obvious? She was tired of guessing. Did she have a chance here, or didn't she? Inquiring minds wanted to know.

"Um," Bobby said. "Yeah, well… She, uh, found someone who wasn't gone all the time. She's actually getting married in October."

"Oh, yikes." Colleen made a face at him. "The *M* word." Wes always sounded as if he were on the verge of a panic attack when that word came up.

But Bobby just smiled. "Yeah, I think she called to tell me about it because she was looking for a counteroffer, but I just couldn't do it. We had a lot of fun, but…" He shook his head. "I wasn't about to leave the teams for her, you know, and that's what she wanted." He was quiet for a moment. "She deserved way more than I could give her, anyway."

"And you deserve more than someone who'll ask you to change your whole life for them," Colleen countered.

He looked startled at that, as if he'd never considered such a thing, as if he'd viewed himself as the bad guy in the relationship—the primary reason for its failure.

Kyra Whomever was an idiot.

"How about you?" he asked. "Wes said you were dating some lawyer."

Oh, my God. Was it possible that Bobby was doing a little fishing of his own?

"No," she said, trying to sound casual. "Nope. That's funny, but… Oh, I know what he was thinking. I told him I went to Connecticut with Charlie Johannsen. Wes must've thought…" She had to laugh. "Charlie's longtime

was all she could talk about. But people's priorities changed. It wasn't going to be easy to sell it, but she refused to let it be the end of her world—a world that was so much wider now, extending all the way to Tulgeria and beyond.

She made herself smile at him. "I am. Law school's expensive."

"Colleen, if you need a loan—"

"I've got a loan. Believe me I've got *many* loans. I've got loans to pay off loans. I've got—"

"It took you five years to rebuild this car. To find authentic parts and—"

"And now someone's going to pay top dollar for a very shiny, very well-maintained vintage Mustang that handles remarkably badly in the snow. I live in Cambridge, Massachusetts. I don't need a car—especially not one that skids if you so much as whisper the word *ice*. My apartment's two minutes from the T, and frankly, I have better things to spend my money on than parking tickets and gasoline."

"Okay," he said. "Okay. I have an idea. I've got some money saved. I'll lend you what you need—interest free— and we can take the next week and drive this car back to your parents' house in Oklahoma, garage it there. Then in a few years when you graduate—"

"Nice try," Colleen told him. "But my travel itinerary has me going to Tulgeria next Thursday. Oklahoma's not exactly in the flight path."

"Think about it this way—if you don't go to Tulgeria, you get to keep your car and have an interest-free loan."

She took advantage of another red light to turn and look at him. "Are you attempting to bribe me?"

He didn't hesitate. "Absolutely."

She had to laugh. "You really want me to stay home?

CHAPTER THREE

DARK, COOL AND MYSTERIOUS.

Somehow, despite his best intentions, Bobby had ended up sitting across from Colleen in a restaurant that was decidedly dark, cool and mysterious.

The food *was* great. Colleen had been right about that, too.

Although she didn't seem to be eating too much.

The meeting with the buyer had gone well. The man had accepted her price for the car—no haggling.

It turned out that that meeting had been held in the well-lit office of a reputable escrow agent, complete with security guard. Colleen had known damn well there was absolutely no danger from psycho killers or anyone else.

Still, Bobby had been glad that he was there while the buyer handed over a certified check and she handed over the title and keys to the Mustang.

She'd smiled and even laughed, but it was brittle, and he'd wanted to touch her. But he hadn't. He knew that he couldn't. Even just a hand on her shoulder would have been too intimate. And if she'd leaned back into him, he would have put his arms around her. And if he'd done that there in the office, he would have done it again, later, when they were alone, and there was no telling where that might lead.

No, strike that. Bobby knew damn well it would lead to him kissing her. And that could and would lead to a full

She was quiet by then, too. It was unusual to be around a Skelly who wasn't constantly talking.

"Are you okay?" he asked.

She looked up at him, and he realized that there were tears in her eyes. She shook her head. But then she forced a smile. "I'm just being stupid," she said before the smile wavered and disappeared. "I'm sorry."

She pushed herself out of the booth and would have rushed past him, toward the rest rooms at the back of the restaurant, if he hadn't reached out and grabbed her hand. He slid out of the bench seat, too, still holding on to her. It took him only a second to pull more than enough dollars to cover the bill out of his pocket and toss it onto the table.

This place had a rear exit. He'd automatically noted it when they'd first came in—years of practice in preparing an escape route—and he led her to it now, pushing open the door.

They had to go up a few steps, but then they were outside, on a side street. It was just a stone's throw to Brattle Street, but they were still far enough from the circus-like atmosphere of Harvard Square on a summer night to have a sense of distance and seclusion from the crowds.

"I'm sorry," Colleen said again, trying to wipe away her tears before they even fell. "I'm stupid—it's just a stupid car."

Bobby had something very close to an out-of-body experience. He saw himself standing there, in the shadows, next to her. Helplessly, with a sense of total doom, he watched himself reach for her, pull her close and enfold her in his arms.

Oh, dear Lord, she was so soft. And she held him tightly, her arms around his waist, her face buried in his shoulder as she quietly tried not to cry.

The deal she'd just made gave her twenty-four hours to change her mind.

"It's not too late," he reminded her. He reminded himself, too. He could gently release her, take one step back, then two. He could—without touching her again—lead her back to the lights and crowd in Harvard Square. And then he'd never even have to mention anything to Wes. Because nothing would have happened.

But he didn't move. He told himself he would be okay, that he could handle this—as long as he didn't look into her eyes.

"No, I'm selling it," she told him, pulling back slightly to look up at him, wiping her nose on a tissue she'd taken from her shoulder pack. "I've made up my mind. I need this money. I loved that car, but I love going to law school, too. I love the work I do, I love being able to make a difference."

She was looking at him so earnestly he forgot about not looking into her eyes until it was too late. Until the earnest look morphed into something else, something loaded with longing and spiked with desire.

Her gaze dropped to his mouth, and her lips parted slightly, and when she looked once again into his eyes, he knew. She wanted to kiss him nearly as much as he wanted to kiss her.

Don't do this. Don't...

He could feel his heart pounding, hear the roar of his blood surging through his body, drowning out the sounds of the city night, blocking out all reason and harsh reality.

He couldn't not kiss her. How could he keep from kissing her when he needed to kiss her as much as he needed to fill his lungs with air?

But she didn't give him a chance to lean down toward her. She stood on her tiptoes and brushed her mouth across

moment he was afraid he might actually have embarrassed himself beyond recovery.

From just a kiss.

But he hadn't. Not yet, anyway. Still, he couldn't take it anymore, not another second longer, and he crushed her to him, filling his hands with the softness of her body, sweeping his tongue into her mouth.

She didn't seem to mind. In fact, her pack fell to the ground, and she kissed him back enthusiastically, welcoming the ferocity of his kisses, winding her arms around his neck, pressing herself even more tightly against him.

It was the heaven he'd dreamed of all these years.

Bobby kissed her, again and again—deep, explosively hungry kisses that she fired right back at him. She opened herself to him, wrapping one of her legs around his, moaning her pleasure as he filled his hand with her breast.

He caught himself glancing up, scanning a nearby narrow alleyway between two buildings, estimating whether it was dark enough for them to slip inside, dark enough for him to unzip his shorts and pull up her skirt, dark enough for him to take her, right there, beneath someone's kitchen window, with her legs around his waist and her back against the roughness of the brick wall.

He'd pulled her halfway into the alley before reality came screaming through.

Wes's sister. This was Wes's *sister*.

He had his tongue in Wes's sister's mouth. One hand was filled with the softness of Wes's sister's derriere as he pressed her hips hard against his arousal. His other hand was up Wes's sister's shirt.

Had he completely lost his mind?

Yes.

Bobby pulled back, breathing hard.

That was almost worse, because now he had to look at her. She was breathing hard, too, her breasts rising

"What, have you taken some kind of vow of abstinence?"

Somehow he managed to smile at her. "Sort of."

Just like that she understood. He saw the realization dawn in her eyes and flare rapidly into anger. "Wesley," she said. "This is about my brother, isn't it?"

Bobby knew enough not to lie to her. "He's my best friend."

She was furious. "What did he do? Warn you to stay away from me? Did he tell you not to touch me? Did he tell you not to—"

"No. He warned me not even to *think* about it." Wes had said it jokingly, one night on liberty when they'd each had five or six too many beers. Wes hadn't really believed it was a warning he'd needed to give his best friend.

Colleen bristled. "Well, you know what? Wes can't tell *me* what to think, and *I've* been thinking about it. For a long time."

Bobby gazed at her. Suddenly it was hard to breathe again. A long time. "Really?"

She nodded, her anger subdued, as if she were suddenly shy. She looked everywhere but in his eyes. "Yeah. Wasn't that kind of obvious from the way I jumped you?"

"I thought I jumped you."

Colleen looked at him then, hope in her eyes. "Please come home with me. I really want you to—I want to make love to you, Bobby. You're only here for a week—let's not waste a minute."

Oh, God, she'd said it. Bobby couldn't bear to look at her, so he closed his eyes. "Colleen, I promised Wes I'd look out for you. That I'd take care of you."

"Perfect." She bent down to pick up her bag. "Take care of me. Please."

Oh, man. He laughed because, despite his agony, he

CHAPTER FOUR

COLLEEN HAD PRINTED OUT the email late last night, and she now held it tightly in her hand as she approached Bobby.

He was exactly where he'd said he would be when he'd called—sitting on the grassy slope along the Charles River, looking out at the water, sipping coffee through a hot cup with a plastic lid.

He saw her coming and got to his feet. "Thanks for meeting me," he called.

He was so serious—no easygoing smile on his face. Or maybe he was nervous. It was hard to be sure. Unlike Wes, who twitched and bounced off the walls at twice his normal frenetic speed when he was nervous, Bobby showed no outward sign.

He didn't fiddle with his coffee cup. He just held it serenely. He'd gotten them both large cups, but in his hand, large looked small.

Colleen was going to have to hold hers with both hands.

He didn't tap his foot. He didn't nervously clench his teeth. He didn't chew his lip.

He just stood there and breathed as he solemnly watched her approach.

He'd called at 6:30 this morning. She'd just barely fallen asleep after a night spent mostly tossing and turning—and analyzing everything she'd done and said last night, trying to figure out what she'd done wrong.

sternly, "you could have told me at least a *little* about what happened. You could have told me you were shot instead of letting me think you'd hurt yourself in some normal way—like pulling a muscle playing basketball."

He handed her the piece of paper. "I didn't think it was useful information," he admitted. "I mean, what good is telling you that a bunch of bad guys with guns tried to kill your brother a few weeks ago? Does knowing that really help you in any way?"

"Yes, because *not* knowing hurts. You don't need to protect me from the truth," Colleen told him fiercely. "I'm not a little girl anymore." She rolled her eyes. "I thought we cleared *that* up last night."

Last night. When some extremely passionate kisses had nearly led to getting it on right out in the open, in an alley not far from Harvard Square.

"I got coffee and muffins," Bobby said, deftly changing the subject. "Do you have time to sit and talk?"

Colleen watched as he lowered himself back onto the grass. Gingerly. Why hadn't she noticed that last night? She was *so* self-absorbed. "Yes. Great. Let's talk. You can start by telling me how many times you were shot and exactly where."

He glanced at her as she sat down beside him, amusement in his dark eyes. "Trust Wes to be melodramatic. I took a round in the upper leg that bled kind of heavily. It's fine now—no problem." He pulled up the baggy leg of his shorts to reveal a deeply tanned, enormously muscular thigh. There was a fresh pink scar up high on his leg. Where it would really hurt a whole lot to be shot. Where there were major veins—or were they arteries?—which, if opened, could easily cause a man to bleed to death very quickly.

Wes hadn't been melodramatic at all. Colleen couldn't

"It is to me," she returned. "And I'm betting it's a pretty big deal to my brother, too."

"It's really only a big deal to him because I'm winning," Bobby admitted.

At first his words didn't make sense. And then they made too much sense. "You guys keep score?" she asked in disbelief. "You have some kind of contest going...?"

Amusement danced in his eyes. "Twelve to five and a half. My favor."

"Five and a *half?*" she echoed.

"He got a half point for getting me back to the boat in one piece this last time," he explained. "He couldn't get a full point because it was partially his fault I needed his help in the first place."

He was laughing at her. Oh, he wasn't actually laughing aloud, but Colleen knew that, inside, he was silently chortling away.

"You know," she said with a completely straight face, "it seems only fair that if you save someone's life that many times, you ought to be able to have wild sex with that person's sister, guilt free."

Bobby choked on his coffee. Served him right.

"So what are you doing tonight?" Colleen asked, still in that same innocent voice.

He coughed even harder, trying to get the liquid out of his lungs.

"'Be nice to him,'" she read aloud from Wes's email. She held it out for him to see. "See, it says it right there."

"That's *not* what Wes meant," Bobby managed to gasp.

"How do you know?"

"I *know.*"

"Are you okay?" she asked.

His eyes were tearing, and he still seemed to have trouble breathing. "You're killing me."

wouldn't change things between them. Her friendship was very important to him.

"I really care about you," he told her. "But I have to be honest. What happened last night was, well, it was a mistake."

Yup. She'd definitely heard it before. She could have written it out for him on a three-by-five-card. Saved him some time.

"I know that I said last night that I couldn't...that we couldn't...because of *Wes* and, well, I need you to know that there's more to it than that."

Yeah, she'd suspected that.

"I can't possibly be what you really want," he said quietly.

Now *that* was different. She'd never heard that before.

"I'm not..." He started to continue, but then he shook his head and got back on track. "You mean too much to me. I can't take advantage of you, I *can't*. I'm ten years older than you, and—Colleen, I knew you when you were thirteen—that's just too weird. It would be crazy, it wouldn't go anywhere. It couldn't. *I* couldn't. We're too different and..." He swore softly, vehemently. "I really am sorry."

He looked about as miserable as she was feeling. Except he probably wasn't embarrassed to death. What had she been thinking, to throw herself at him like that last night?

She closed her eyes, feeling very young and very foolish—as well as ancient beyond her years. How could this be happening again? What was it about her that made men only want to be her friend?

She supposed she should be thankful. This time she got the "let's stay friends" speech *before* she'd gone to bed with the guy. That had been the lowest of a number of

He'd been on the verge of telling her the truth—that he hadn't slept at all last night, that he'd spent the night alternately congratulating himself for doing the right thing and cursing himself for being an idiot.

Last night she made it clear that she wanted him. And Lord knows that the last thing he honestly wanted was to stay mere friends with her. In truth, he wanted to get naked with her—and stay naked for the entire rest of this week.

But he knew he wasn't the kind of man Colleen Skelly needed. She needed someone who would be there for her. Someone who came home every night without fail. Someone who could take care of her the way she deserved to be taken care of.

Someone who wanted more than a week of hot sex.

He didn't want another long-distance relationship. He couldn't take it. He'd just gotten out of one of those, and it wasn't much fun.

And would be even less fun with Colleen Skelly—because after Wes found out that Bobby was playing around with his sister, Wes would come after him with his diving knife.

Well, maybe not, but certainly he and Wes would argue. And *Colleen* and Wes would argue. And that was an awful lot of pain, considering Bobby would spend most of his time three thousand miles away from her, him missing her with every breath he took, her missing him, too.

No, hurting Colleen was bad, but telling her the truth would hurt them both even more in the long run.

up with for Bobby to search her out so desperately. Wes had to have been injured. Or—please, God, no—dead.

Colleen flashed hot and then cold. "Oh, no," she said. "What happened? How bad is it?"

Bobby stared at her. "Then you haven't heard? I was ready to yell at you because I thought you knew. I thought you went out to make these pickups, anyway."

"Just tell me he's not dead," she begged him. She'd lived through one dead brother—it was an experience she never wanted to repeat. "I can take anything as long as he's not dead."

His expression became one of even more perplexity as he climbed into the air-conditioned cab and closed the door. "He?" he asked. "It was a woman who was attacked. She's in ICU, in a coma, at Mass General."

A woman? At Mass General Hospital...? Now it was Colleen's turn to stare at him stupidly. "You didn't track me down because Wes is hurt?"

"Wes?" Bobby shook his head as he leaned forward to turn the air conditioner fan to high. "No, I'm sure he's fine. The mission was probably only a training op. He wouldn't have been able to send email if it were the real thing."

"Then what's going on?" Colleen's relief was mixed with irritation. He had a lot of nerve, coming after her like this and scaring her to death.

"Andrea Barker," he explained. "One of the chief administrators of the AIDS Education Center. She was found badly beaten—barely breathing—outside of her home in Newton. I saw it in the paper."

Colleen nodded. "Yeah," she said. "Yeah, I heard about that this morning. That's really awful. I don't know her that well—we talked on the phone only once. I've mostly met with her assistant when dealing with the center."

"So you *did* know she's in the hospital." Something

deliberately, and if I know it, then the police know it, too. The burglar story is probably just something they threw out to the press, to make the real perpetrator think he's home-free."

"You don't know that for sure."

"Yes," he said. "You're right. I don't know it absolutely. But I'm 99 percent sure. Sure enough to be afraid that, as the legal representative to the AIDS Education Center, you could be the next target. Sure enough to know that the last thing you should be doing today is driving a truck around all by yourself."

He clenched his teeth, the muscles jumping in his jaw as he glared at her. That spark of anger made his eyes cold, as if she were talking to a stranger.

Well, maybe she was.

"Oh. Right." Colleen let her voice get louder with her growing anger. What did he care what happened to her? She was just an idiot who'd embarrassed both of them last night. She was just his *friend.* No, not even. The real truth was that she was just some pain-in-the-butt sister of a friend. "I'm supposed to lock myself in my apartment because there *might* be people who don't like what I do? Sorry, that's not going to happen."

"I spoke to some people," Bobby told her. "They seem to think this John Morrison who threatened you yesterday could be a real danger."

"Some people?" she asked. "Which people? If you talked to Mindy in the center's main office—well, she's afraid of her own shadow. And Charlie Johannsen is no—"

"I dare you," Bobby said, "to look me in the eye and tell me that you're not just a little bit afraid of this man."

She looked at him. Looked away. "Okay. So maybe I am a *little*—"

"And yet you came out here, anyway. By yourself."

or maybe even fear. Is he going to say something rude? Is he going take it a step further and follow you? Or is he just going to look at you and maybe whistle, and let you see from his eyes that he's thinking about you in ways that you don't want him to be thinking about you?

"And each time that happens," Colleen told him, "it's no less specific—or potentially unreal—than John Morrison's threats."

Bobby was silent, just sitting there, looking out the window.

"I'm so sorry," he finally said. "What kind of world do we live in?" He laughed, but it wasn't laughter that had anything to do with humor. It was a burst of frustrated air. "The really embarrassing part is that I've been that guy. Not the one who actually says those things, I'd never do that. But I'm the one who looks and even whistles. I never really thought something like that might frighten a woman. I mean, that was *never* my intention."

"Think next time," she told him.

"Someone really said that to you?" He gave her a side-long glance. "In those words?"

She nodded, meeting his gaze. "Pretty rude, huh?"

"I wish I'd been there," he told her. "I would've put him in the hospital."

He said it so matter-of-factly, but she knew it wasn't just an idle threat. "If you had been there," she pointed out, "he wouldn't have said it."

"Maybe Wes is right." Bobby smiled at her ruefully. "Maybe you *should* have a twenty-four-hour armed escort, watching your every move."

"Oh, no," Colleen groaned. "Don't *you* start with that, too. Look, I've got a can of pepper spray in my purse and a whistle on my key ring. I know you don't think so, but I'm about as safe as I can be. I've been

at her, and it was the exact same way he'd looked at her last night, right before he'd pulled her close and kissed the hell out of her. There was hunger in his eyes. Heat and need and *desire*.

He looked away quickly, as if he didn't want her to see those things. Colleen looked away, too, her mind and heart both racing.

He was lying. He'd lied this morning, too. He didn't want them to stay just friends any more than *she* did.

He hadn't given her the "let's stay friends" speech because he had an aversion to women like her, women who actually had hips and thighs and weighed more than ninety pounds, wet. He hadn't made that speech because he found her unattractive, because she didn't turn him on.

On the contrary...

With a sudden clarity that should have been accompanied by angelic voices and a brilliant light, Colleen knew.

She *knew*. Bobby had said there was more to it, but there wasn't. This was about Wes.

It was Wesley who had gotten in the way of her and Bobby Taylor, as surely as if he were sitting right there between them, stinking of stale cigarette smoke, in the cab of this truck.

But she wasn't going to call Bobby on that—no way. She was going to play—and win—this game, secure that she knew the cards he was holding in his hand.

Bobby wasn't going to know what hit him.

She glanced at him again as she pulled out of the parking lot. "So you really think Andrea's attack had something to do with her being an AIDS activist?" she asked.

He glanced at her, too, and this time he managed to keep his eyes mostly expressionless. But it was back there—a little flame of desire. Now that she knew what to look for, she couldn't help but see it. "I think until she

looking wounded. She was relaxed and cheerful. He would even dare to call her happy.

Bobby didn't know how that had happened, but he wasn't about to complain.

"You don't have to braid it," he said. "A ponytail's good enough. And all I really need help with is tying it back. I can brush it myself."

He reached for the brush, but she pulled it back, away from him.

"I'll braid it," she said.

"If you really want to." He let her win. What harm could it do? Ever since he'd gotten injured, he'd had to ask for help with his hair. This morning he'd gone into a beauty salon not far from his hotel, tempted to cut it all off.

Back in California, he'd gotten help with his hair each day. Wes stopped by and braided it for him. Or Mia Francisco—the lieutenant commander's wife. Even the captain—Joe Cat—had helped him out once or twice.

He shifted slightly in the seat so Colleen had access to the back of his head, reaching up with his good arm to take out the elastic.

She ran both the brush and her fingers gently through his hair. And Bobby knew immediately that there was a major difference between Colleen braiding his hair and Wes braiding his hair. They were both Skellys, sure, but that was where all similarities ended.

"You have such beautiful hair," Colleen murmured, and he felt himself start to sweat.

This was a bad idea. A very, very bad idea. What could he possibly have been thinking? He closed his eyes as she brushed his hair back, gathering it at his neck with her other hand. And then she was done brushing, and she just used her hands. Her fingers felt cool against his forehead as she made sure she got the last stray locks off his face.

you who are completely ripped. Hey, did you pack your uniform?"

She thought he was good-looking and *ripped*. Bobby had to smile. He liked that she thought of him that way, even though he wasn't sure it was completely true. He was a little too big, too solid to get the kind of muscle definition that someone like Lucky O'Donlon had.

Now, there was a man who was truly ripped. Of course, Lucky wasn't here right now as a comparison, which was just as well. Even though he was married, women were still drawn to him like flies to honey.

"Hello," Colleen said. "Did you fall asleep?"

"No," Bobby said. "Sorry." She'd asked him something. "Um..."

"Your uniform?"

"Oh," he said. "No. No, I'm not supposed to wear a uniform while my hair's long—unless there's some kind of formal affair that I can't get out of attending."

"No this one's not formal," she told him. "It's casual—a bon voyage party at the local VFW the night before we leave. But there will be VIPs there—senators and the mayor and... I just thought it would be cool for them to meet a real Navy SEAL."

"Ah," he said. She was almost done braiding his hair, and he was simultaneously relieved and disappointed. "You want me to be a circus attraction."

She laughed. "Absolutely. I want you to stand around and look mysterious and dangerous. You'd be the hit of the party." She reached over his shoulder, her arm warm against his slightly damp, air-conditioner-chilled T-shirt. "I need the elastic."

He tried to hand it to her, and they both fumbled. It dropped into his lap. He grabbed it quickly—God forbid she reach for it there—and held it out on his open palm for her to take.

Bobby laughed as Colleen climbed down from the cab of the truck. "Hey," he said, sliding across the seat and keeping her from closing the door by sticking out his foot. "I'm glad we're still friends."

"You know, I've been thinking about this friend thing," she said, standing there, hands on her hips, looking up at him. "I think we should be the kind of friends who have wild sex three or four times a day."

She shot him a smile and turned toward the seniors center.

Bobby sat there, staring after her, watching the sunlight on her hair and the gentle swaying of her hips as she walked away.

She was kidding.

Wasn't she?

God, maybe she wasn't.

"Help," he said to no one in particular as he followed her inside.

She wasn't quite sure she liked it.

She was scared, yes. She didn't want Bobby charging in, a one-man assault team, to find John Morrison and his gang in her living room. At the same time, if John Morrison and his gang *were* in her apartment, she didn't want to run away and lose the opportunity to have them all arrested.

"Put me down," she ordered him. They could go downstairs, call the police from Mr. Gheary's apartment.

To her surprise he did put her down, none too gently pushing her away from him. As she struggled to regain her balance, she realized he was charging up the last few stairs toward her apartment door. Toward a man who was coming out.

Wearing an unbelievably loud plaid shirt.

"Bobby, don't!"

She wasn't the only one shouting.

The owner of that shirt was shouting, too, shrieking, really, in pure terror.

It was Kenneth. Bobby had him against the entryway wall, his face pressed against the faded wallpaper, his armed twisted up behind his back.

"Bobby, *stop!* He's a friend of mine," Colleen shouted, taking the stairs two at a time, just as the door to her apartment opened wide, revealing the equally wide eyes of Ashley and her brother, Clark. She did a double take. Ashley's blue-haired brother, Clark.

"What are you doing here?" she asked Ashley, who was supposed to be spending the entire summer working at her father's law firm in New York.

"I escaped from Scarsdale," Ashley said faintly, staring at Bobby, who still had Kenneth pinned, his feet completely off the ground. "Clark and Kenneth came and broke me out."

That explained the blue hair. Nineteen-year-old Clark

everything—too tall, too stacked, too blunt, too funny, too into having a good time wherever she went. Laughter spilled out of her constantly. Her eyes were never the same color from one minute to the next, but they were always, *always* welcoming and warm.

Desire knifed through him so sharply he had to clench his fists.

"Forgive my brother," Ashley continued. "He's terminally stupid."

He yanked his gaze away from Colleen, aware he'd been staring at her with his tongue nearly hanging out. God, he couldn't let her catch him looking at her that way. If she knew the truth…

Who was he kidding? She'd probably already guessed the truth. And now she was trying to drive him slowly insane with all those deep looks and the seemingly innocently casual way she touched him damn near constantly in passing. A hand on his arm, on his knee. Fingers cool against his face as she fixed a stray lock of his hair. Brushing against him with her shoulder. Sitting so close that their thighs touched.

And the things she said to him! She thought they should be the kind of friends who had sex three or four times a day. She'd only been teasing. She liked being outrageous— saying things like that and trying to shake him up.

That one had worked.

"I'm a chief petty officer," Bobby explained to the kid with blue hair, working to keep up with the conversation. That kid's name was Clark. He was Ashley's brother— no doubt about that. He had the same perfectly sculpted nose and chin, slightly differently shaped eyes that were a warmer shade of gray. "I'm in the Navy."

"Whoa, dude," Clark said. "With long hair like that?" He laughed. "Hey, maybe they'll take me, huh?"

"Bobby's a—" Colleen cut herself off, and Bobby knew

have found any. I don't get headaches. Did you look in the bathroom?"

"I'm feeling much better," Ashley interrupted. Bobby had just met her, but even he could tell that she was lying. "We're going out."

"But what about that letter you were going to write to Dad?"

"It can wait." Ashley motioned toward the door with her head, making big eyes at her brother. "This is Bobby Taylor. Wes's friend?" Clark stared at her blankly, as only a younger brother can stare at an older sister. "The Navy SEAL…?"

"Oh," Clark said. "*Oh*. Right." He looked at Bobby. "You're a SEAL, huh? Cool."

Colleen's smile was rueful and apologetic. "Sorry," she told Bobby. "I tried."

Clark grinned at Kenneth. "Dude! You were almost killed by a Navy SEAL! You should definitely tell the girls at that party tonight. I bet one of 'em will go home with you."

"Ashley, you really don't have to go anywhere," Colleen said to her friend. "You look wiped. What happened? What'd your father do now?"

Ashley just shook her head.

"What's a Navy SEAL?" Kenneth asked. "And do you suppose if he actually *had* killed me then Jennifer Reilly might want to marry me? I mean, if you think she might go home with me if he *almost* killed me…."

"Oh, no way!" Clark countered. "I wasn't thinking Jenn Reilly, dude! Set your sights lower, man. Think B or C tier. Think Stacy Thurmond or Candy Fremont."

"You rank the women you know into *tiers?*" Colleen was outraged. "Get out of my house, scumball!"

"Whoa," Clark said, backing up and tripping over one

he'd just admitted that he had an A list. And that would make him little better than...what had she called Clark? A scumball.

"That came out really wrong," he told her quickly as her eyes started to narrow.

Clark, the genius, stepped up to the plate. "See? All guys have lists. It's a guy thing," he protested, not old enough to know that all either of them could do now was grovel, apologize and pray for forgiveness. "It doesn't mean anything."

"Bobby, strangle him, strangle his strange, plaid-clothed little friend," Colleen ordered him, "and then strangle yourself."

"What I *meant* to say," Bobby told her, moving close enough to catch her chin with his hand, so she now had to look up into his eyes, "was that I find you as beautiful on the outside as you are on the inside."

The searchlight clicked back on, and the rest of the world faded. Colleen was looking at him, her eyes wide, her lips slightly parted. She was the only other person in the entire universe. No one and nothing else existed. He couldn't even seem to move his hand away from the soft smoothness of her face.

"Strangle me?" Bobby heard Kenneth protest, his voice faint, as if coming from a great distance. "Why strangle *me?* I don't put anyone into tiers, thank you very much."

"Yeah, because you can't see past Jenn Reilly," Clark countered, also from somewhere way back there, beyond Colleen's eyes and Colleen's lips. "For you, Jenn's got her own gigantic tier—and everyone else is invisible. You and Jenn are *so* not going to happen, man. Even if hell froze over, she would walk right past you and date Frosty the Snowman. And then she would call you later to tell you how it went because you guys are *friends*. Sheesh. Don't

Bobby cleared his throat experimentally. A few more times and he'd have his voice back. Provided he didn't look at Colleen again.

"Not that there's anything wrong with being gay," Kenneth added hastily, glancing at Bobby. "We should probably make sure we're not offending a gay Navy SEAL here—an extremely big, extremely tall gay Navy SEAL. Although I still am not quite certain as to exactly what a Navy SEAL might be."

Clark looked at Bobby with new interest. "Whoa. It never even occurred to me. *Are* you gay?"

For the first time in a good long number of minutes, there was complete and total silence. They were all looking at him. *Colleen* was looking at him, frowning slightly, speculation in her eyes.

Oh, great. Now she thought he'd told her he only wanted to be friends because he was—

He looked at her, wavering, unable to decide what to say. Should he just shut up and let her think whatever she thought, hoping that it would make her keep her distance?

Colleen found her voice. "Congratulations, Clark, you've managed to reach new heights of rudeness. Bobby, don't answer him—your sexual orientation is no one's business but your own."

"I'm straight," he admitted.

"I'm sure you are," Colleen said a little too heartily, implying that she suspected otherwise.

He laughed again. "Why would I lie?"

"I believe you," she said. "Absolutely." She winked at him. "Don't ask, don't tell. We'll just pretend Clark didn't ask."

Suddenly this wasn't funny anymore, and he laughed in disbelief. "What do you want me to do…?" Prove it? He stopped himself from saying those words. Oh, God.

Besides the fact that you SEALs frequently kill people—usually with your bare hands—and that you're known for being exceedingly rough in bed?"

Bobby started to laugh. He couldn't help it. And then Colleen was laughing, too, with the others just staring at them as if they were crazy.

She was so alive, so full of light and joy. And in less than a week she was going to get on an airplane and fly to a dangerous place where she could well be killed. And, Lord, what a loss to the world that would be. The thought was sobering.

"Please don't go," he said to her.

Somehow she knew he was talking about the trip to Tulgeria. She stopped laughing, too. "I have to."

"No, you don't. Colleen, you have no idea what it's like there."

"Yes, I do."

Ashley pulled her brother and Kenneth toward the door. "Coll, we're going to go out for a—"

"No, you're not." Colleen didn't look away from Bobby. "Kick Thing A and Thing B out onto the street, but if you're getting one of your headaches, you're not going anywhere but to bed."

"Well then, I'll be in my room," Ashley said quietly. "Come on, children. Let's leave Aunt Colleen alone."

"*Hasta la vista*, baby." Clark nodded to Bobby. "Dude."

"Thanks again for not killing me," Kenneth said cheerfully.

They went out the door, and Ashley faded quietly down the hallway.

Leaving him alone in the living room with Colleen.

"I should go, too." That would definitely be the smart thing. As opposed to kissing her. Which would definitely

each other with swords—these big machete-style things, with these curved, razor-sharp blades.

"No one is safe there." He said it again, hoping she was listening. "No one is safe."

She looked pale, but her gaze didn't waver. "I have to go. You tell me these things, and I have to go more than ever."

"More than half of these terrorists are zealots." He leaned across the table, willing her to hear him, to *really* hear him. "The other half are in it for the black market— for buying and selling anything. Including Americans. *Especially* Americans. Collecting ransom is probably the most lucrative business in Tulgeria today. How much would *your* parents pay to get you back?"

"Bobby, I know you think—"

He cut her off. "Our government has a rule—no negotiating with terrorists. But civilians in the private sector… Well, they can give it a go—pay the ransom and gamble that they'll actually get their loved one back. Truth is, they usually don't. Colleen, please listen to me. *They usually don't get the hostages back.*"

Colleen gazed at him searchingly. "I've heard rumors of mass slaughters of Tulgerian civilians in retaliation by the local government."

Bobby hesitated, then told her the truth. "I've heard those rumors, too."

"Is it true?"

He sighed. "Look, I know you don't want to hear this, but if you go there you might die. *That's* what you should be worrying about right now. Not—"

"*Is* it true?"

God, she was magnificent. Leaning across the table toward him, palms down on the faded formica top, shoulders set for a fight, her eyes blazing, her hair on fire.

"I can guarantee you that the U.S. has special forces

CHAPTER SEVEN

THE PHOTOGRAPHS WERE IN her bedroom. Colleen grabbed the envelope from her dresser, stopping to knock softly on Ashley's door on her way back to the kitchen.

"Come in."

The room was barely lit, with the shades all pulled down. Ash was at her computer, and despite the dim lighting, Colleen could see that her eyes were red and swollen. She'd been crying.

"How's the headache?" Colleen asked.

"Pretty bad."

"Try to sleep."

Ashley shook her head. "I can't. I have to write this."

"Write what?"

"A brief. To my father. That's the only way he'll ever pay attention to me—if I write him a legal brief. Isn't that pathetic?"

Colleen sighed. It *was* pathetic. Everything about Ashley's relationship with her father was pathetic. She'd actually gotten caller-ID boxes for all of their telephones, so they'd know not to answer when Mr. DeWitt called. Colleen loved it when her own father called.

"Why don't you do it later?" she said to her friend. "After the headache's gone."

Ashley's headaches were notoriously awful. She'd been to the doctor, and although they weren't migraines, they were similar in many ways. Brought on by tension and stress, the doctor had said.

Although if he *did* happen to fall in love with her… No, she couldn't let herself think that way. That path was fraught with the perils of disappointment and frustration. All she wanted was to have fun, she reminded herself again, wishing the words hadn't sounded so hollow when she'd said them aloud.

"He's probably wondering what happened to you," Ashley pointed out.

Colleen went out the door, stopping to look at her friend, her hand on the knob. "I'll be back in about thirty minutes to get your full report on Scarsdale and your dear old dad."

"That's really not necessary—"

"I know you," Colleen said. "You're not going to sleep until we talk, so we're going to talk."

BOBBY HEARD THE DOOR SHUT, heard Colleen coming back down the hall to the kitchen.

He'd heard the soft murmur of voices as she'd stopped to speak to her roommate.

The soundproofing in this old place was virtually nonexistent.

That meant that grabbing her when she came back into the room, and having hot, noisy sex right there, on top of the kitchen table was definitely not an option.

Oh, man, he had to get out of here.

He stood up, but Colleen came into the room, blocking his escape route.

"Sit," she ordered. "Just for a few more minutes. I want to show you something."

She took a photograph out of an envelope and slid it across the table toward him. It was a picture of a small girl, staring solemnly into the camera. She had enormous eyes—probably because she was so skinny. She was all narrow shoulders, with a pointy chin, dressed in ill-fitting

orphanage, St. Christof's, deep inside Tulgeria's so-called war zone," she told him, "which also happens to be the part of the country that sustained the most damage from the earthquake. My Children's Aid group has been corresponding—for over two years—with the nuns who run St. Christof's. We've been trying to find a legal loophole so we can get those children out of Tulgeria. These are unwanted children, Bobby. Most are of mixed heritage—and nobody wants them. The terrible irony is that we have lists of families here in the U.S. who want them desperately—who are dying to adopt. But the government won't let them go. They won't pay to feed them, yet they won't give them up."

The pictures showed the bleakness of the orphanage. Boarded-up windows, peeling paint, bombed-out walls. These children were living in a shell of a former house. In all of the pictures, the nuns—some clad in old-fashioned habits, some dressed in American jeans and sneakers— were always smiling, but Bobby could see the lines of strain and pain around their eyes and mouths.

"When this earthquake happened," Colleen continued, still in that same soft, even voice, "we jumped at the chance to actually go in there." She looked Bobby squarely in the eyes. "Bringing relief aid and supplies to the quake victims is just our cover. We're really going in to try to get those children moved out of the war zone, to a safer location. Best-case scenario would be to bring them back to the States with us, but we know the chances of that happening are slim to none."

Bobby looked at her. "I can go," he said. "Colleen, I'll do this for you. I'll go instead of you."

Yes, that would work. He could get some of the other men in Alpha Squad to come along. Rio Rosetti, Thomas King and Mike Lee were all young and foolish. They'd jump at the chance to spend a week's vacation in the number-one most dangerous hot spot in the world. And

late to call tonight. The admiral and his wife, Zoe, had twins. Max and Sam.

The twins were pure energy in human form—as Bobby well knew. He baby-sat them once when the admiral and his wife were out in California, when their regular sitter had canceled at the last minute. Max and Sam were miniature versions of their father. They both had his striking-blue eyes and world-famous smile.

Jake would've just finished reading them a story and putting them to bed. Bobby knew he would then go in search of his wife, maybe make them both a cup of herbal tea and rub her shoulders or feet....

"I'll call him tomorrow morning," Bobby said.

Colleen smiled. She didn't believe he was tight enough with an admiral to be able to give the man a call. "Well, it would be nice if you could go, but I'm not going to hold my breath." She gathered up the pictures and put them back in the envelope.

"How many people are going?" he asked. "You know, in your group?"

"About twelve."

Twelve unprepared, untrained civilians running around loose.... Bobby didn't swear—at least not aloud.

"Most of them will actually be distributing supplies to the quake victims. They'll be hooking up with the Red Cross volunteers who are already in place in the country," she continued. "Of the twelve, there are five of us who'll be concentrating on getting those children moved."

Five was a much better, much more compact number. Five people could be whisked out of sight and removed from danger far more easily than twelve.

"Who's meeting you at the airport?" he asked.

"We've rented a bus and made arrangements to be picked up by the driver," she told him.

A bus. Oh, *man*. "How many guards?"

"I may not be there," he said. "But I'm sure as hell going to try."

Colleen smiled. "You know, every time someone says that they'll *try,* I think of that scene in *The Empire Strikes Back* with Luke Skywalker and Yoda. You know, the one where Yoda says, 'Try not. Do or do not.'"

"Yeah, I know that scene," Bobby told her. "And I'm sorry, but—"

She reached across the table and touched his hand. "No, don't apologize. I didn't mean to sound as if I were accusing you of anything. See, the truth is I've fought so many losing battles for so many years that I really appreciate someone who tries. In fact, a try is all I ever ask for anymore. It may not work out, but at least you know you gave it a shot, right?"

She wasn't talking about him coming to Tulgeria. She was talking about the way he'd kissed her. And the way he'd pushed her away, refusing to see where that kiss might lead. Refusing even to try.

Bobby wasn't sure what to say. He felt like the worst kind of coward. Too scared even to try.

Even when her hand was on top of his, her fingers so cool against the heat of his skin. Even when he wished with all of his heart that she would leave her hand right there for a decade or two.

But Colleen took her hand away as she stood. He watched as she placed the envelope with the pictures on the cluttered surface of a built-in desk in the corner of the room.

"You know, I've met most of the people who want to adopt these kids," she told him. "They're really wonderful. You look into their eyes, and you can see that they already love these children just from seeing their pictures, from reading their letters." Her voice wavered. "It just breaks

She lowered her eyes as if she were suddenly shy. "I always have, you know."

She spoke barely loud enough for him to hear her, but he did. He heard. His ears were working perfectly. It was his lungs that were having trouble functioning.

"So now you know," she said quietly. When she looked up at him, her smile was rueful. "How's that for a powerful rebuttal to the 'I just want to be friends' speech?"

He couldn't respond. He didn't have any idea at all of what to say. She wanted him. She always had. He felt like laughing and crying. He felt like grabbing her, right there in the kitchen. He felt like running—as hard and as fast and as far as he possibly could.

"I figure either I'm right, and you didn't mean what you said this morning," she told him. "Or I'm wrong, and I'm a complete idiot who deserves humiliation and rejection twice in two days."

Bobby kept his mouth shut, wishing he *were* the kind of man who could just run for the door—and keep running when he hit the street. But he knew that he wasn't going to get out of there without saying *some*thing.

He just wasn't sure what that something should be. Tell the truth and admit he hadn't meant what he'd said? That was one hell of a bad idea. If he did that, she'd smile and move closer and closer and...

And he'd wake up in her bed.

And then Wes would kill him.

Bobby was starting to think he could maybe handle death. It would be worth it for a chance at a night with Colleen.

What he would never be able to live with was the look of betrayal in his best friend's eyes. He clamped his mouth shut.

"I know I act as if it's otherwise," Colleen continued, turning away from him and fiddling with half a dozen

She'd pretty much been flashing hot and cold by then herself—alternately clapping herself on the back for her bravery and deriding herself for pure stupidity.

What if she *were* completely wrong? What if she were completely misinterpreting everything she'd seen in his eyes? What if he hadn't really been looking at her with barely concealed longing and desire? What if it had just been a bad case of indigestion?

"I had to try," Colleen told Ashley—and herself as well.

Ash was sitting cross-legged on her bed, hugging her beat-up, raggedy stuffed bear—the one she'd been given when she was three and had chicken pox. The one she still slept with despite the fact that she'd just turned twenty-four.

It was ironic. Colleen's friend had everything. Money. A beautiful face. A slim, perfect body. Weight that didn't fluctuate wildly given her moods. A 4.0 grade point average. Impeccable taste.

Of course, Colleen had something Ashley didn't have. And Colleen wouldn't have traded that one thing for Ashley's looks and body, even if her friend had thrown in all the gold in Ft. Knox, too.

Not a chance.

Because Colleen had parents who supported her, 100 percent. She knew, without a doubt, that no matter what she did, her mom and dad were behind her.

Unlike Mr. DeWitt, who criticized Ashley nonstop.

Colleen couldn't imagine what it had been like growing up in that house. She could picture Ash as a little girl, desperately trying to please her father and never quite succeeding.

"Ashley, what's this? A Father's Day gift? A ceramic bowl? You made it yourself on the wheel in pottery class? Oh, well, next time you'll do much better, won't you?"

He called me in the middle of the night and told me he had to see me. Right then. So he came over to the house and we went into the garden and… He was really upset and he told me he was in love with me. He said he'd fallen for me, and he told me that he had to come clean before it went any further, that he couldn't live with himself any longer."

"But that's good," Colleen countered. "Isn't it? He was honest when it mattered the most."

"Colleen, he accepted a position where the job description included tricking the boss's daughter into marrying him." Ashley was still aghast at the idea. "What kind of person would do that?"

"One who maybe saw your picture?" Colleen suggested.

Ashley stared at her as if she were in league with Satan.

"I'm not saying it's a good thing," she added quickly. "But how bad could the guy be if he really did fall in love with you?"

"Did he?" Ashley asked darkly. "Or is he just saying that he did? Is this confession just another lie?"

Oh, ick. Colleen hadn't thought of it that way. But Ash was right. If *she* were trying to con someone into marrying her, she'd pretend to be in love with them, confess everything and beg for forgiveness. That would save her butt in the event that the truth ever did surface after the wedding.

"He slept with me, Colleen," Ashley said miserably. "And my father was *paying* him."

"Yeah," Colleen said, "I don't think your father was paying him to do that, though."

"It feels that way." Ashley was one of those women who still looked beautiful when she cried. "You know the really stupid thing?"

Colleen shook her head. "No."

CHAPTER EIGHT

"WAIT," BOBBY SAID. "Zoe, no, if he's taking a day off, don't..." Bother him. But Zoe Robinson had already put him on hold.

"Hey, Chief!" Admiral Jake Robinson sounded cheerful and relaxed. "What's up? Zo tells me you're calling from Boston?"

"Uh, yes, sir," Bobby said. "But, sir, this can wait until tomorrow, because—"

"How's the shoulder?" the admiral interrupted. Admirals were allowed to interrupt whenever they wanted.

"Much better, sir," Bobby lied. It was exactly like Admiral Robinson to have made certain he'd be informed about the injuries of anyone on the SEAL teams—and to remember what he'd been told.

"These things take time." It was also like Robinson to see through Bobby's lie. "Slow and steady, Taylor. Don't push it too hard."

"Aye, sir. Admiral, I had no idea that your secretary would patch me through here, to your home."

"Well, you called to talk to me, didn't you?"

"Yes, sir, but you're an *admiral,* sir, and—"

"Ah." Robinson laughed. "You wanted it to be harder to reach me, huh? Well, if you need me to, I'll call Dottie in my office and tell her to put you on hold for a half an hour."

Bobby had to laugh, too. "No, thank you. I'm just... surprised."

Wonderful. Beautiful. Amazingly sexy. Intelligent. *Perfect.* "She's special, sir. Actually, she reminds me of Zoe in a lot of ways. She's tough, but not really—it's just a screen she hides behind, if you know what I mean."

"Oh, yes. I do." The admiral laughed softly. "Oh, boy. So, I know it's none of my business, but does Wes know that you've got a thing for his sister?"

Bobby closed his eyes. Damn, he'd given himself away. There was no point in denying it. Not to Jake. The man may have been an admiral, but he was also Bobby's friend. "No, he doesn't."

"Hmm. Does *she* know?"

Good question. "Not really."

"Damn."

"I mean, she's incredible, Jake, and I think—no, I *know* she's looking for a fling. She's made that more than clear but I can't do it, and I'm…"

"Dying," Jake supplied the word. "Been there, done that. If she really is anything like Zoe, you don't stand a chance." He laughed. "Colleen Skelly, huh? With a name like that, I'm picturing a tiny red head, kind of built like her brother—compact. Skinny. With a smart mouth and a temper."

"She's a redhead," Bobby said. "And you're right about the mouth and the temper, but she's tall. She might even be taller than Wes. And she's not skinny. She's…" Stacked. Built like a brick house. Lush. Voluptuous. All those descriptions felt either disrespectful or as if he were exchanging locker-room confidences. "Statuesque," he finally came up with.

"Taller than Wes, huh? That must tick him off."

"She takes after their father, and he's built more like their mother's side of the family. It ticks Colleen off, too. She's gorgeous, but she doesn't think so."

"Genetics. It's proof that Mother Nature exists," Jake

established rapport with the civilians," Jake cut him off. "But I'll let it be your choice, Bobby. If you don't want to go—"

"Oh, no sir, I *want* to go." It was a no-brainer. He wanted to be there, himself, to make sure Colleen stayed safe.

Yes, it would have been easier to toss the entire problem into Admiral Robinson's capable hands and retreat, swiftly and immediately, to California. But Wes would be back in three days. Bobby could handle keeping his distance from Colleen for three days.

Couldn't he?

"Good," Jake said. "I'll get the ball rolling."

"Thank you, sir."

"Before you go, Chief, want some unsolicited advice?"

Bobby hesitated. "I'm not sure, sir."

The admiral laughed—a rich burst of genuine amusement. "Wrong answer, Taylor. This is one of those times that you're supposed to 'Aye, aye, sir' me, simply because I'm an admiral and you're not."

"Aye, aye, sir."

"Trust your heart, Chief. You've got a good one, and when the time comes, well, I'm confident you'll know what to do."

"Thank you, sir."

"See you in a few days. Thanks again for the call."

Bobby hung up the phone and lay back on his hotel room bed, staring up the ceiling.

When the time comes, you'll know what to do.

He already knew what he had to do.

He had to stay away from Colleen Skelly, who thought— God help them both—that she wanted him.

What did she know? She was ridiculously young. She had no clue how hard it was to sustain a relationship over

Colleen gave up on them and looked at Bobby, who nodded. "I took care of it," he said.

It was no surprise. He was dependable. Smart. Sexier than a man had the right to be at ten in the morning.

Their eyes met only briefly before he looked away— still it was enough to send a wave of heat through her. Shame. Embarrassment. Mortification. What exactly had she said to him last night? *I want you.* In broad daylight, she couldn't believe her audacity. What had she been thinking?

Still, he was here. He'd shown up bright and early this morning, hot cup of coffee in hand, to help lug all of the boxes of emergency supplies out of her living room and into the Relief Aid truck.

He'd said hardly anything to her. In fact, he'd only said, "Hi," and then got to work with Clark and Kenneth, hauling boxes down the entryway stairs and out to the truck. Bad shoulder or not, he could carry two at once without even breaking a sweat.

Colleen had spent the past ninety minutes analyzing that "Hi," as she'd built wall upon wall of boxes in the back of the truck. He'd sounded happy, hadn't he? Glad to see her? Well, if not glad to see her, he'd sounded neutral. Which was to say that at least he hadn't sounded *un*happy to see her. And that was a good thing.

Wasn't it?

Everything she'd said to him last night echoed in her head and made her stomach churn.

Any minute now they were going to be alone in the truck. Any minute now he was going to give her the friends speech, part two. Not that she'd ever been persistent and/or stupid enough before to have heard a part-two speech. But she had a good imagination. She knew what was coming. He would use the word *flattered* in reference to last night's no-holds-barred, bottom-line statement. He knew that after Clark and Kenneth got out of the truck, Bobby wasn't going to let her get close enough to braid his hair ever again—not after what she'd said to him last night.

"Sorry," she said, her voice low. "I guess I must have embarrassed you to death last night."

"You scared me to death," he admitted, his voice pitched for her ears only. "Don't get me wrong, Colleen, I'm flattered. I really am. But this is one of those situations where what I want to do is completely different from what I should do. And should's got to win."

She looked up at him and found her face inches from his. A very small number of inches. Possibly two. Possibly fewer. The realization almost knocked what he'd just said out of her mind. Almost.

What he wanted *to do,* he'd said. True, he'd used the word *flattered* as she'd expected, but the rest of what he was saying was...

Colleen stared at that mouth, at those eyes, at the perfect chin and nose that were close enough for her to lean forward, if she wanted to, and kiss.

Oh, she wanted to.

And he'd just all but told her, beneath all those ridiculous *shoulds,* that he wanted her, too. She'd won. She'd *won!*

Look at me, she willed him, but he seemed intent upon reading the truck's odometer. *Kiss me.*

"I spoke to Admiral Robinson, who greenlighted U.S. military protection for your trip," he continued. "He wants me to remain in place as liaison with your group, and, well—" his gaze flicked in her direction "—I agreed. I'm here. I know what's going on. I have to stick around, even though I know you'd rather I go away."

"Whoa, Bobby." She put her hand on his knee. "I don't *want* you to go anywhere."

couldn't bear looking at her, and shook his head slightly. "I know," he said. "Believe me, I know."

When he opened his eyes, he looked at her, briefly meeting her gaze again. He was sitting close—close enough for her to see that his eyes truly were completely, remarkably brown. There were no other flecks of color, no imperfections, no inconsistencies.

But far more hypnotizing than the pure, bottomless color was the brief glimpse of frustration and longing he let her see. Either on purpose or accidentally, it didn't matter which.

It took her breath away.

"I need about three more inches of seat before I can close this door," Clark announced. He shifted left in a move reminiscent of a football player's offensive drive, making Kenneth yelp and ramming Bobby tightly against Colleen.

Completely against Colleen. His muscular thigh was wedged against her softer one. He had nowhere to put his shoulder or his arm, and even though he tried to angle himself, that only made it worse. Suddenly she was practically sitting in the man's lap.

"There," Clark added with satisfaction as he closed the truck door. "I'm ready, dudes. Let's go."

Just drive. Colleen knew the smartest thing to do was to just drive. If traffic was light, it would take about fifteen minutes to reach Kenmore Square. Then Clark and Kenneth would get out, and she and Bobby wouldn't have to touch each other ever again.

She could feel him steaming, radiating heat from the summer day, from the work he'd just done, and he shifted, trying to move away, but he only succeeded in making her aware that they both wore shorts, and that his bare skin was pressed against hers.

Oh, my *God*.

Colleen pulled back the same instant that Bobby released her.

He was breathing hard and staring at her, with a wild look in his eyes she'd never seen before. Not on him, anyway, the King of Cool.

"This is how you help?" he asked incredulously.

"Yes," she said. She couldn't breathe, either, and having him look at her that way wasn't helping. "I mean, no. I mean—"

"Gee, I'm sorry," Kenneth said brightly. "We've got to be going. Clark, *move* it."

"Clark, don't go anywhere," Colleen ordered, opening the door. "Bobby's going to drive. I'm coming around to sit on the other side."

She got out of the truck's cab, holding onto the door for a second while she waited for the jelly in her legs to turn back to bone.

She could feel Bobby watching her as she crossed around the front of the truck. She saw Clark lean forward, across Kenneth, and say something to him.

"Are you sure, man?" Clark was saying to Bobby as she opened the door.

"Yes," Bobby said with a definiteness that made her want to cry. Clark had no doubt asked if Bobby wanted the two of them to make themselves scarce. But Bobby didn't want them to leave. He didn't want to be alone with Colleen until he absolutely had to.

Well, she'd really messed *that* up.

As Bobby put the truck in gear, she leaned forward and said, across Clark and Kenneth, "I wasn't trying to make it worse for you. That was supposed to be like, I don't know, I guess a…a kind of a kiss goodbye."

He looked at her and it was a look of such total incomprehension, she tried to explain.

CHAPTER NINE

THERE WERE PROTESTORS. On the sidewalk. In front of the AIDS Education Center. With signs saying NIMBY. Not In My Back Yard.

Bobby, following Colleen's directions, had taken a detour after letting Clark and Kenneth out near Kenmore Square. Colleen had something to drop at the center—some papers or a file having to do with the ongoing court battle with the neighborhood zoning board.

She'd been filling up the silence in the truck in typical Skelly fashion, by telling Bobby about how she'd gotten involved doing legal work for the center, through a student program at her law school.

Although she'd yet to pass the bar exam, there was such a shortage of lawyers willing to do pro bono work like this—to virtually work for free for desperately cash-poor nonprofit organizations—student volunteers were allowed to do a great deal of the work.

And Colleen had always been ready to step forward and volunteer.

Bobby could remember when she was thirteen—the year he'd first met her. She was just a little kid. A tomboy—with skinned knees and ragged cutoff jeans and badly cut red hair. She was a volunteer even back then, a member of some kind of local environmental club, always going out on neighborhood improvement hikes, which was just a fancy name for cleaning up roadside trash.

Once, he and Wes had had to drive her to the hospital

to, angry at himself, as well, for kissing her back, "but if you think I'm going to sit here and watch while you face down an angry mob—"

"It's not an angry mob," she countered. "I don't see John Morrison, although you better believe he's behind this."

He had to stop for the light, and she opened the door and slipped down from the cab.

"Colleen!" Disbelief and something else, something darker that lurched in his stomach and spread fingers of ice through his blood, made his voice crack. Several of those signs were made with two-by-fours. Swung as a weapon, they could break a person's skull.

She heard his yelp, he knew she had, but she only waved at him as she moved gracefully across the street.

Fear. That cold dark feeling sliding through his veins was fear.

He'd learned to master his own personal fear. Sky diving, swimming in shark-infested waters, working with explosives that, with one stupid mistake, could tear a man into hamburger. He'd taken hold of that fear and controlled it with the knowledge that he was as highly skilled as a human being could be. He could deal with anything that came along—anything, that is, that was in his control. As for those things outside of his control, he'd developed a zen-like deal with the powers that be. He'd live life to its fullest, and when it was his turn to go, when he no longer had any other options, well then, he'd go—no regrets, no remorse, no panic.

He wasn't, however, without panic when it came to watching Colleen head into danger.

There was a lull in the traffic, so he ran the light, pulling as close to the line of parked cars in front of the building as possible. Putting on his flashers, he left the truck

As if she truly believed he would ever actually raise a hand against her or any other woman.

No, he'd never fight her. But there were other ways to win.

Bobby picked her up. He tossed her over his good shoulder, her stomach pressed against him, her head and arms dangling down his back. It was laughably easy to do, but once he got her there, she didn't stay still. She wriggled and kicked and howled and punched ineffectively at his butt and the backs of his legs. She was a big woman, and he wrenched his bad shoulder holding her in place, but it wasn't that that slowed him.

No, what made him falter was the fact that her T-shirt had gapped and he was holding her in place on his shoulder with his hand against the smooth bare skin of her back. He was holding her legs in place—keeping her from kicking him—with a hand against the silkiness of her upper thighs.

He was touching her in places he shouldn't be touching her. Places he'd been dying to touch her for years. But he didn't put her down. He just kept carrying her down the sidewalk, back toward the truck that was double parked in front of the center.

His hair was completely down, loose around his face, and she caught some of it with one of her flailing hands. Caught and yanked, hard enough to make his eyes tear.

"Ouch! God!" That was it. As soon as he got back to his room, he was shaving his head.

"Let! Me! Go!"

"You dared me," he reminded her, swearing again as she gave his hair another pull.

"I didn't think you were man enough to actually do it!"

Oh, ouch. That stung far worse than getting his hair pulled.

She ran her fingers quickly through her hair, and as she did, she gave him a look and a smile that was just a little too smug, as if she'd won and he'd lost.

He forced himself to stop thinking about her belly button and glared at her. "This is just some kind of game to you, isn't it?"

"No," she said, glaring back, "this is my life. I'm a woman, not a child, and I don't need to ask *any*one's permission before I 'so much as lift my finger,' thank you very much."

"So you just do whatever you want. You just walk around, doing whatever you want, *kissing* whoever you want, whenever you want—" Bobby shut himself up. What the hell did that have to do with this?

Everything.

She'd scared him, yes, by not telling him why she was so confident the protestors didn't pose a threat, and that fear had morphed into anger. And he'd also been angry, sure, that she'd completely ignored his warning.

But, really, most of his anger came from that kiss she'd given him, less than an hour ago, in front of her apartment building.

That incredible kiss that had completely turned him upside down and inside out and...

And made him want far more than he could take.

Worse and worse, now that he'd blurted it out, she knew where his anger had come from, too.

"I'm sorry," she said quietly, reaching up to push his hair back from his face.

He stepped away from her, unable to bear the softness of her touch, praying for a miracle, praying for Wes suddenly to appear. His personal guardian angel, walking down the sidewalk, toward them, with that unmistakable Skelly swagger.

Colleen had mercy on him, and didn't stand there,

instead of throwing cinder blocks through the front windows again."

"Again?" Bobby walked her more swiftly toward the truck, wanting her safely inside the cab and out of this wretched neighborhood. "He did that before?"

"Twice," she told him. "Of course, he got neighborhood kids to do the dirty work, so we can't prove he was behind it. You know, I find it a little ironic that the man owns a bar. And his place is not some upscale hangout...it's a dive. People go there to get seriously tanked or to connect with one of the girls from the local 'escort service,' which is really just a euphemism for Hookers R Us. I'm sure Morrison gets a cut of whatever money exchanges hands in his back room, the sleaze, and *we're* a threat to the neighborhood...? What's he afraid of?"

"Where's his bar?" Bobby asked.

She gave him an address that meant nothing to him. But with a map he'd find it easily enough.

He handed her the keys. "Call Rene on the cell phone and tell her you're on your way."

She tried to swallow her surprise. "You're not coming?"

He shook his head, unable to meet her eyes for more than the briefest fraction of a second.

"Oh," she said.

It was the way she said it, as if trying to hide her disappointment that made him try to explain. "I need to take some time to..." What? Hide from her? Yes. Run away? Absolutely. Pray that he'd last another two and a half days until Wes arrived?

"Look, it's all right," she said. "You don't need to—"

"You're driving me crazy," he told her. "Every time I turn around, I find myself kissing you. I can't seem to be able to stop."

"You're the only one of us who sees that as a bad thing."

didn't say another word as she climbed into the truck from the passenger's side, as she slid behind the wheel and started the big engine.

As he watched, she maneuvered the truck onto the street and, with a cloud of exhaust, drove away.

Two and a half more days.

How the hell was he going to survive?

hadn't slept in about a week. "Sorry, someone was coming out, so I came in."

"You mean, you sneaked in."

He gave up on the smile. "You must be Colleen, Ash's roommate. I'm Brad—the idiot who should be taken out and shot."

Colleen looked into his Paul-Newman-blue eyes and saw his pain. This was a man who was used to getting everything he wanted through his good looks and charisma. He was used to being Mr. Special, to winning, to being envied by half of the world and wanted by the other half.

But he'd blown it, big-time, with Ashley, and right now he hated himself.

She shut the door to remove the chain. When she opened it again, she stepped back to let him inside. He was wearing a dark business suit that was rumpled to the point of ruin—as if he'd had it on during that entire week he hadn't been sleeping.

He needed a shave, too.

"She's really not here," Colleen told him as he followed her into the living room. "She went to visit her aunt on Martha's Vineyard. Don't bother asking, because I don't know the details. Her aunt rents a different house each summer. I think it's in Edgartown this year, but I'm not sure."

"But she *was* here. God, I can smell her perfume." He sat down, heavily, on the sofa, and for one awful moment Colleen was certain that he was going to start to cry.

Somehow he managed not to. If this was an act, he deserved an Oscar.

"Do you know when she'll be back?" he asked.

Colleen shook her head. "No."

"Is this your place or hers?" He was looking around the living room, taking in the watercolors on the walls, the

BOBBY STARED AT THE phone as it rang, knowing it was Colleen on the other end. Had to be. Who else would call him here? Maybe Wes, who had called earlier and left a message.

It rang again.

Bobby quickly did the math, figuring out the time difference…. No, it definitely wasn't Wes. Had to be Colleen.

A third time. Once more and the voice mail system would click on.

He reached for it as it began to ring that final time, silently cursing himself. "Taylor."

"Hi, it's me."

"Yeah," he said. "I figured."

"And yet you picked it up, anyway. How brave of you."

"What's happening?" he asked, trying to pretend that everything was fine, that he hadn't kissed her—again—and then spent the entire afternoon and evening wishing he was kissing her again.

"Nothing," Colleen said. "I was just wondering what you were up to all day."

"This and that." Mostly things he didn't want to tell her. That when he wasn't busy lusting after her, he'd been checking out John Morrison, for one. From what Bobby could tell from the locals, Morrison was mostly pathetic. Although, in his experience, pathetic men could be dangerous, too. Mostly to people they perceived to be weaker than they were. Like women. "Is your door locked?"

Colleen lowered her voice seductively. "Is yours?"

Oh, God. "This isn't a joke, Colleen," he said, working hard to keep his voice even. Calm. It wasn't easy. Inside he was ready to fly off the handle, to shout at her again. "A woman you work with was attacked—"

"Yes, my door is locked," she said. "But if someone

give you. I can't handle another long-distance relationship right now. I can't do that to myself."

"I'll take the days," she said. "Day. Make it singular if you want. Just once. Bobby—"

"I can't do that to you." But oh, sweet heaven, he wanted to. He *could* be at her place in five minutes. Less. One kiss, and he'd have her clothes off. Two, and... Oh, *man*.

"I want to know what it's like." Her voice was husky, intimate across the phone line, as if she were whispering in his ear, her breath hot against him. "Just once. No strings, Bobby. Come on..."

Yeah, no strings—except for the noose Wes would tie around his neck when he found out.

Wes, who'd left a message for Bobby on his hotel voice mail...

"Hey, Bobby! Word is Alpha Squad's heading back to Little Creek in a few days to assist Admiral Robinson's Gray Group in Tulgeria as part of some kind of civilian protection gig. Did you set that up, man? Let me guess. Leenie dug in her heels, so you called the Jakester. Brilliant move, my friend. It would be perfect—if Spaceman wasn't being such a total jerk out here on my end.

"He's making all this noise about finally getting to meet Colleen. Remember that picture you had of her? It was a few months ago. I don't know where you got it, but Spaceman saw it and wouldn't stop asking about her. Where does she go to school? How old is she? Yada-yada-yada, on and on about her hair, her eyes, her smile. Give me a break! As if I'd ever let a SEAL within twenty-five feet of her—not even an officer and alleged gentleman like Spaceman, no way. Look, I'll call you when we get into Little Creek. In the meantime, stick close to her, all right? Put the fear of God or the U.S. Navy into any of those college jerks sniffing around her, trying to get too

before you go to bed, right? If I touched you," her voice dropped another notch, "your skin would be clean and cool and smooth.

"And your hair's down—it's probably still a little damp, too. If I were there, I'd brush it out for you. I'd kneel behind you on the bed and—"

"If you were here," Bobby said, interrupting her, his voice rough to his own ears, "you wouldn't be brushing my hair."

"What would I be doing?" she shot back at him.

Images bombarded him. Colleen, flashing him her killer smile just before she lowered her head and took him into her mouth. Colleen, lying back on his bed, hair spread on his pillows, breasts peaked with desire, waiting for him, welcoming him as he came to her. Colleen, head back as she straddled him, as he filled her, hard and fast and deep and—

Reality intervened. Phone sex. Dear sweet heaven. What was she doing to him? Beneath the towel—yes, she was right about the towel he wore around his waist—he was completely aroused.

"What would you be doing? You'd be calling a cab to take you home," he told her.

"No, I wouldn't. I'd kiss you," she countered, "and you'd pick me up and carry me to your bed."

"No, I wouldn't," he lied. "Colleen, I have…I really have to go now. Really."

"Your towel would drop to the floor," she said, and he couldn't make himself hang up the phone, both dreading and dying to hear what she would say next. "And after you put me down, you'd let me look at you." She drew in a breath, and it caught—a soft little gasp that made him ache from wanting her. "I think you're the most beautiful man I've ever seen."

small. "I'm afraid you won't...like me." She was serious. She honestly thought—

"Are you kidding? I love your body," Bobby told her. "I dream about you wearing that nightgown. I dream about—"

Oh, my God. What was he doing?

"Oh, tell me," she breathed. "Please, Bobby, tell me what you dream."

"What do you think I dream?" he asked harshly, angry at her, angry at himself, knowing he still wasn't man enough to hang up the phone and end this, even though he knew damn well that he should. "I dream exactly what you're describing right now. You in my bed." His voice caught on his words. "Ready for me."

"I am," she told him. "Ready for you. Completely. You're still watching, so I...I touch myself—where I'm dying for you to touch me."

She made a noise that outdid all of the other noises she'd been making, and Bobby nearly started to cry. Oh, man, he couldn't do this. This was Wes's sister on the other end of this phone. This was wrong.

He turned his back to the mirror, unable to look at his reflection.

"Please," she gasped, "oh, please, tell me what you dream when you dream about me."

Oh, *man*. "Where did you learn to do this?" He had to know.

"I didn't," she said breathlessly. "I'm making it up as I go along. You want to know what I dream about you?"

No. Yes. It didn't matter. She didn't wait for him to answer.

"My fantasy is that the doorbell rings, and you're there when I answer it. You don't say anything. You just come inside and lock the door behind you. You just look at me and I know. This is it. You want me.

watch your face, Colleen." He dragged out her name, taking his time with it, loving the way it felt in his mouth, on his tongue. *Colleen.* "So I can look into your eyes, your beautiful eyes. Oh, I love looking into your eyes, Colleen, while you…"

"Oh, yes," she gasped. "Oh, Bobby, oh—"

Oh, *man.*

you want to know the truth, this isn't the first time I've let my fantasies of you and me push me over the edge—"

"Oh, my God, don't tell me that!"

"Sorry." Colleen made herself stop talking. She was making this worse, telling him secrets that made her blush when she stopped to think about it. But his feelings of guilt were completely unwarranted.

"I've got to leave," he told her, his voice uncharacteristically unsteady. "I have to get out of here. I've decided— I'm going down to Little Creek early. I'll be back in a few days, with the rest of Alpha Squad."

With Wes.

One step forward, two steps back.

"I'd appreciate it if you didn't go into detail with my brother about—"

"I'm going to tell him that I didn't touch you. Much. But that I wanted to."

"Because it's not like I make a habit of doing that— phone sex, I mean. And since you obviously didn't like it, I'm not going to—"

"No," he interrupted her. "You know, if I'm Guilt Man, then you're Miss Low Self-Esteem. How could you even think I didn't like it? I loved it. Every excruciating minute. You are unbelievably hot, and you completely killed me. If you got one of those 900 numbers, you could make a fortune, but you damn well better not."

"You loved it, but you don't want to do it again?"

Bobby was silent on the other end of the line, and Colleen waited, heart in her throat.

"It's not enough," he finally said.

"Come over," she said, hearing her desire coat her voice. "Please. It's not too late to—"

"I can't."

"I don't understand why not. If you want me, and I want

that mess of what you want and I want and Wes wants. Boom. What happens upon impact? You get lucky, I get lucky, which would probably be transcendental—no, not probably, *definitely*. So that's great…or is it? Because all I can see, besides the immediate gratification of us both getting off, is a boatload of pain.

"I risk getting too…I don't know, *attached* to someone who lives three thousand miles away from me.

"I risk my relationship with your brother.…

"You risk your relationship with your brother.…

"You risk losing any opportunities that might be out there of actually meeting someone special, because you're messing around with me."

Maybe you're the special one. Colleen didn't dare say it aloud. He obviously didn't think so.

"I've got a flight into Norfolk that leaves Logan just after 1500 hours," he said quietly. "I'm going into the Relief Aid office in the morning. I've got a meeting set up at 1100 hours to talk about the security we're going to be providing in Tulgeria—and what we expect from your group in terms of following the rules we set up. I figured you'd want to sit in on that."

"Yeah," Colleen said. "I'll be there." And how weird was *that* going to be—meeting his eyes for the first time since they'd…since she'd… She took a deep breath. "I'll borrow a truck, after, and give you a lift to the airport."

"That's okay. I'll take the T." He spoke quickly.

"What, are you afraid I'm going to jump you, right there in the truck, in the airport's short-term parking lot?"

"No," he said. He laughed, but it was grim instead of amused. "I'm afraid I'm going to jump you. From here on in, Colleen, we don't go anywhere alone."

"But—"

"I'm sorry. I don't trust myself around you."

"Bobby—"

Oh, Christ. "Does Colleen know?"

Susan nodded. "She was here when the news came in. But she went home. Her little girl—the one she'd been writing to—was on the list of children who were killed."

Analena. Oh, God. Bobby closed his eyes.

"She was very upset," Susan told him. "Understandably."

He straightened up and started for the door. He knew damn well that Colleen's apartment was the last place he should go, but it was the one place in the world where he absolutely needed to be right now. To hell with his rules.

To hell with everything.

"Bobby," Susan called after him. "She told me you're leaving for Virginia in a few hours. Try to talk her into coming back here when you go. She really shouldn't be alone."

COLLEEN LET THE DOORBELL ring the same way she'd let the phone ring.

She didn't want to talk to anyone, didn't want to see anyone, didn't want to have to try to explain how a little girl she'd never met could have owned such an enormous piece of her heart.

She didn't want to do anything but lie here, on her bed, in her room, with the shades pulled down, and cry over the injustice of a world in which orphanages were bombed during a war that really didn't exist.

Yet, at the same time, the last thing she wanted was to be alone. Back when she was a kid, when her world fell apart and she needed a shoulder to cry on, she'd gone to her brother Ethan. He was closest in age to her—the one Skelly kid who didn't have that infamous knee-jerk temper and that smart-mouthed impatience.

that usually lingered on his shirt and even in his hair had finally been washed away.

But it was late. If he was going to get to Logan in time to catch his flight to Norfolk… "You have to leave soon," she told him, trying to be strong, wiping her face and lifting her head to look into his eyes.

For a man who could make one mean war face when he wanted to, he had the softest, most gentle eyes. "No." He shook his head slightly. "I don't."

Colleen couldn't help it. Fresh tears welled, and she shook from trying so hard not to cry.

"It's okay," he told her. "Go on and cry. I've got you, sweet. I'm here. I'll be here for as long as you need me."

She clung to him.

And he just held her and held her and held her.

As she fell asleep, still held tightly in his arms, his fingers running gently through her hair, her last thought was to wonder hazily what he was going to say when he found out that she could well need him forever.

BOBBY WOKE UP SLOWLY. He knew even before he opened his eyes that, like Dorothy, he wasn't in Kansas anymore. Wherever he was, it wasn't his apartment on the base, and he most certainly wasn't alone.

It came to him in a flash. Massachusetts. Colleen Skelly.

She was lying against him, on top of him, beneath him, her leg thrown across his, his thigh pressed tight between her legs. Her head was on his shoulder, his arms beneath her and around her, the softness of her breasts against his chest, her hand tucked up alongside his neck.

They were both still fully dressed, but Bobby knew with an acceptance of his fate—it was actually quite calming and peaceful, all things considered—that after she awoke, they wouldn't keep their clothes on for long.

have time for an instant family—not now while I'm in law school. I don't have time for a husband, let alone a child. And yet…"

She shook her head. "When I saw her pictures and read her letters… Oh, Bobby, she was so alive. I didn't even get a chance to know her, but I wanted to—God, I wanted to!"

"If you had met her, you would have fallen completely in love with her." He smiled. "I know you pretty well. And she would've loved you, too. And you would have somehow made it work," he told her. "It wouldn't have been easy, but there are some things you just have to do, you know? So you do it, and it all works out. I'm sorry you won't get that chance with Analena."

She lifted her head to look at him. "You don't think I'm being ridiculous?"

"I would never think of you as ridiculous," he told her quietly. "Generous, yes. Warm. Giving. Loving, caring…"

Something shifted. There was a sudden something in her eyes that clued him in to the fact that, like him, she was suddenly acutely, intensely aware of every inch of him that was in contact with every inch of her.

"Sexy as hell," he whispered. "But never ridiculous."

Her gaze dropped to his mouth. He saw it coming. She was going to kiss him, and his fate would be sealed.

He met her halfway, wanting to take a proactive part in this, wanting to do more than simply be unable to resist the temptation.

Her lips were soft, her mouth almost unbearably sweet. It was a slow, languorous kiss—as if they both knew that from here on in, there was no turning back, no need to rush.

He kissed her again, longer this time, deeper—just in

her—about that—did to him. He pulled her chin back so that she had to look into his eyes, as he answered her with just as much soul-baring honesty. "Maybe someday you'll let me watch."

Someday. The word hung between them. It implied that there was going to be more than just tonight.

"You don't do long-distance relationships," she reminded him.

"No," he corrected her. "I don't *want* to do it that way. I have in the past, and I've hated it. It's so hard to—"

"I don't want to be something that's hard," she told him. "I don't want to be an obligation that turns into something you dread dealing with."

He steeled himself, preparing to pull away from her, out of her arms. "Then maybe I should go, before—"

"Maybe we should just make love and not worry about tomorrow," she countered.

She kissed him, and it was dizzying. He kissed her back hungrily, possessively—all sense of laziness gone. He wanted her, now. He needed her.

Now.

Her hands were in his hair, freeing it completely from the ponytail that had already halfway fallen out. She kissed him even harder, angling her head to give him better access to her mouth—or maybe to give herself better access to *his* mouth.

Could she really do this?

Make love to him tonight and only tonight?

Her legs tightened around his thigh, and he stopped thinking. He kissed her again and again, loving the taste of her, the feel of her in his arms. He reached between them, sliding his hand up under her shirt to fill his hand with her breast.

She pulled back from him to tug at his T-shirt. She wanted it off, and it was easier simply to give

any harder, any hotter, but just the thought of her wearing something like that, just because he liked it—just for him—heated him up another notch.

She would do it, too. After he made her realize that he truly worshiped her body, that he found her unbelievably beautiful and sexy, she would be just as adventurous about that as she was with everything else.

Phone sex. Sweet heaven.

Phone sex was all about words. About saying what he wanted, about saying how he felt.

He hadn't been very good at it—not like Colleen. Unlike her, words weren't his strong suit. But he had to do it again now. He had to use words to reassure her, to let her know just how beautiful he thought she was.

He could do it with body language, with his eyes, with his mouth and his hands. He could show her, by the way he made love to her, but even then, he knew she wouldn't completely believe him.

No, if he wanted to dissolve that edge of tension that tightened her shoulders, he had to do it with words.

Or did he? Maybe he could do a combination of both show *and* tell.

"I think you're spectacular," he told her. "You're incredible and gorgeous and…"

And he was doing this wrong. She wasn't buying any of it.

He touched her, reaching up beneath her shirt to caress her. He had the show part down. He wanted to taste her, and he realized with a flash that instead of trying to make up compliments filled with meaningless adjectives, he should just say what he wanted, say how he felt. He should just open his mouth and speak his very thoughts.

"I want to taste you right here," he told her as he touched her. "I want to feel you in my mouth."

He tugged her shirt up just a little, watching her face,

answer. He just took one of her own exploring hands, and pressed it against him.

"You are *so* sexy, that happens to me every time I see you," he whispered, looking into her eyes to let her see the intense pleasure that shot through him at her touch. "Every time I *think* of you."

She was breathing hard, and he pulled her to him and kissed her again, reaching between them to help her rid him of his briefs.

Her fingers closed around him, and he would have told her how much he liked that, but words failed him, and all he could do was groan.

She seemed to understand and answered him in kind as he slipped his hand between her legs. She was so slick and soft and hot, he could feel himself teetering on the edge of his self-control. He needed a condom. *Now.*

But when he spoke, all he could manage to say was her name.

Again she understood. "Top drawer. Bedside table."

He lunged for it, found it. An unopened, cellophane-wrapped box. He both loved and hated the fact that the box was unopened. Growling with frustration, he tried to rip the damned thing in half.

Colleen took it from his hands and opened it quickly, laughing at the way he fumbled the little wrapped package, getting in the way, touching and kissing him as he tried to cover himself.

Slow down. She'd told him herself that she hadn't had much experience. He didn't want to be too rough, didn't want to hurt her or scare her or...

She pulled him back with her onto the bed in a move that Xena the Warrior Princess would have been in awe of. And she told him, in extremely precise language, exactly what she wanted.

How could he refuse?

just been shot all over again—funny, he hadn't felt even a twinge until now and—

Colleen was crying.

"Oh, my God," he said, shifting off her, pulling her so that she was in his arms. "Did I hurt you? Did I...?"

"No!" she said, kissing him. "No, it's just...that was so perfect, it doesn't seem fair. Why should I be so lucky to be able to share something so special with you?"

"I'm sorry," he said, kissing her hair, holding her close. He knew she was thinking about Analena.

"Will you stay with me?" she asked. "All night?"

"I'm right here," he said. "I'm not going anywhere."

"Thank you." Colleen closed her eyes, her head against his chest, her skin still damp from their lovemaking.

Bobby lay naked in Colleen's bed, holding her close, breathing in her sweet scent, desperately trying to fend off the harsh reality that was crashing down around him.

He'd just made love with Colleen Skelly.

No, he'd just had *sex* with Colleen Skelly. He'd just got it on with Wes's little sister. He'd put it to her. Nailed her. Scored. That was the way Wes was going to see it—not sweetly disguised with pretty words like *making love*.

Last night he'd had phone sex with Colleen. Tonight he'd done the real deal.

Just one night, she wanted. Just one time. Just to find out what it would be like.

Would she stick to that? Give him breakfast in the morning, shake his hand and thank him for the fun experience and send him on his way?

Bobby wasn't sure whether to hope so or hope not. He already wanted too much. He wanted— No, he couldn't even think it.

Maybe, if they only made love this once, Wes would understand that it was an attraction so powerful—more powerful than both of them—that couldn't be denied.

CHAPTER TWELVE

COLLEEN WOKE UP ALONE IN HER BED.

It was barely even dawn, and her first thought was that she'd dreamed it. All of it. Everything that had happened yesterday and last night—it was all one giant combination nightmare and raging hot fantasy.

But Bobby's T-shirt and briefs were still on her floor. Unless he'd left her apartment wearing only his shorts, he hadn't gone far.

She could smell coffee brewing, and she climbed out of bed.

Muscles she didn't even know existed protested— further proof that last night hadn't been a dream. It was a good ache, combined with a warmth that seemed to spread through her as she remembered Bobby's whispered words as he'd… As they'd…

Who knew that such a taciturn man would be able to express himself so eloquently?

But even more eloquent than his words was the expressiveness of his face, the depth of emotion and expressions of sheer pleasure he didn't try to hide from her as they made love.

They'd made love.

The thought didn't fill her with laughter and song as she'd imagined it would.

Yes, it had been great. Making love to Bobby had been more wonderful than she'd ever dared to dream. More special and soul shattering than she'd imagined. But it

Bobby greeted her with a smile and an already-poured cup of coffee. "I hope I didn't wake you," he said, turning back to the stove where both oatmeal and eggs were cooking, "but I didn't have dinner last night, and I woke up pretty hungry."

As if on cue, her stomach growled.

He shot her another smile. "You, too, I guess."

God, he was gorgeous. He'd showered, and he was wearing only his cargo shorts, low on his hips. With his chest bare and his hair down loose around his shoulders, he looked as if he should be adorning the front of one of those romance novels where the kidnapped white girl finds powerful and lasting love with the exotically handsome Indian warrior.

The timer buzzed, and as Colleen watched, the Indian warrior look-alike in her kitchen used her pink-flowered oven mitts to pull something that looked remarkably like a coffee cake out of her oven.

It was. He'd baked a *coffee cake*. From scratch. He smiled at her again as he put it carefully on a cooling rack.

He'd set her kitchen table, too, poured her a glass of cranberry juice. She sat down as he served them both a generous helping of eggs and bowls of oatmeal.

It was delicious. All of it. She wasn't normally a fan of oatmeal, but somehow he'd made it light and flavorful instead of thick and gluey.

"What's on your schedule for today?" he asked, as if he normally sat across from her at breakfast and inquired about her day after a night of hot sex.

She had to think about it. "I have to drop a tuition check at the law school before noon. There's probably going to be some kind of memorial service for—"

She broke off abruptly.

"You okay?" he asked softly, concern in his eyes.

She looked back at him, trying to see him the same way. He was darkly handsome, with bold features that told of his Native American heritage. He was handsome and smart and reliable. He was honest and sincere and funny and kind. And impossibly buff with a body that was at least a two thousand on a scale from one to ten.

"Why aren't you married?" she asked him. He was also ten years older than she was. It seemed impossible that some smart woman hadn't grabbed him up. Yet, here he was. Eating breakfast in her kitchen after spending the night in her bed. "Both you and Wes," she added, to make the question seem a little less as if she were wondering how to sign up for the role of *wife*.

He paused only slightly as he ate his oatmeal. "Marriage has never been part of my short-term plan. Wes's either. The responsibility of a wife and a family... It's pretty intense. We've both seen some of the guys really struggle with it." He smiled. "It's also hard to get married when the women you fall in love with don't fall in love with you." He laughed softly. "Harder still when they're married to someone else."

Colleen's heart was in her throat. "You're in love with someone who's married...?"

He glanced up at her, a flash of dark eyes. "No, I was thinking of...a friend." He made his voice lighter, teasing. "Hey, what kind of man do you think I am, anyway? If I could be in love with someone else while I messed around with you...?"

Relief made her giddy. "Well, I'm in love with Mel Gibson and *I* messed around with you last night."

He laughed, pushing his plate away from the edge of the table. He'd eaten both the pile of eggs and the mound of oatmeal and now he glanced over at the coffee cake, taking a sip of his cooling coffee.

"Is that really what we did last night?" Colleen asked

know. And he quit after the third try. He told me he thought we should just be friends."

"Oh, God." Bobby winced.

"I thought it had to be my fault—that there was something wrong with me." Colleen had never told all of this to anyone. Not even Ashley, who had heard a decidedly watered-down version of the story. "I spent a few years doing the nun thing. And then, about a year and a half ago…" She couldn't believe she was actually telling him this, her very deepest secrets. But she wanted to. She needed him to understand. "I bought this book, a kind of a self-help guide for sexually challenged women—I guess that's a PC term for frigid these days. And I discovered fairly early on that the problem probably wasn't entirely mine."

"So, you haven't—" Bobby was looking at her as if he were trying to see inside her head. "I mean, between last night and the jerk, you haven't…?"

"There's been no one else. Just me and the book," she told him, wishing she could read his mind, too. Was this freaking him out, or did he like the fact that he'd essentially been her first real lover? "Trying desperately to learn how to be normal."

"Yeah, I don't know," Bobby shook his head. "It's probably hopeless. Because I *am* somewhat legendary. And it's a real shame, but if you want to have any kind of satisfying sex life, you're just going to have to spend the rest of your life making love to me."

Colleen stared at him.

"That was a joke," he said quickly. "I'm kidding. Colleen, last night I didn't do anything special. I mean, it was *all* special, but you were right there with me, the entire time. Except…"

"What?" She searched his face.

"Well, without having been there, it's hard to know for

She didn't adjust it, didn't pull it closed. She just moved closer, so that she was standing beside him. Close enough that she was invading his personal space.

But she didn't touch him. Didn't even speak. She just waited for him to turn his head and look up at her.

He did just that. Looked at her. Looked away again. Swallowed hard. "Colleen, I think—"

Now was definitely not the time for thinking. She sat on his lap, straddling him, forcing him to look at her. Her robe was completely open now, the belt having slipped its loose knot.

He was breathing hard—and trying not to. "I thought we decided this was going to be a one-night thing. Just to get it out of our systems."

"Am I out of your system?" she asked, knowing full well that she wasn't.

"No, and if I'm not careful, you're going to get under my skin," he admitted. "Colleen, please don't do this to me. I spent the night convincing myself that as long as we didn't make love again, I'd be okay. And I know it's a long shot, but even your brother might understand that something like this could happen between us—once."

His words would have swayed her—if he hadn't touched her, his hands on her thighs, just lightly, as if he couldn't stop himself, couldn't resist.

She shrugged her robe off her shoulders, and it fell to the floor behind her, and then there she was. Naked, in the middle of her kitchen, with daylight streaming in the windows, warming her skin, bathing her in golden sunshine.

Bobby's breath caught in his throat, and as he looked at her, she felt beautiful. She saw herself as if through his eyes, and she *was* beautiful.

It felt unbelievably good.

She shifted forward, pressing herself against him,

She must've made some kind of noise of frustration and despair, because he stood up. He just lifted himself from the chair, with her in his arms, with his body still buried deeply inside her. Even deeper now that he was standing.

Colleen gasped, and then had to laugh as he carried her—effortlessly, as if she weighed nothing—across the room, her arms around his neck, her legs now locked around his waist. He didn't stop until he'd pressed her up against the wall by the refrigerator. The muscles in his chest and arms stood out, making him seem twice as big. Making her seem almost small.

Still... "Don't hurt your shoulder," she told him.

"What shoulder?" he asked hoarsely, and kissed her.

It was so impossibly macho, the way he held her, her back against the wall, the way he possessed her so completely with his mouth. His kiss was far from gentle, and that was so exciting, it was almost ridiculous. Still, there was no denying that she found it sexy beyond belief, to be pinned here, like this, as he kissed her so proprietarily.

She was expecting more roughness, expecting sex that was hard and fast and wild, but instead he began a long, lingering withdrawal, then an equally deliberate penetration that filled her maddeningly slowly.

It was sexier than she could have dreamed possible—this man holding her like this, taking his time to take her completely. On his terms.

He kissed her face, her throat, her neck as if he owned her.

And he did.

She felt her release begin before she was ready for it, before he'd even begun that slow, sensuous slide inside of her for the third heart-stopping time. She didn't want this to end, and she tried to stop herself, to hold him still for a moment, but she was powerless.

CHAPTER THIRTEEN

BOBBY WAS FLOATING.

He was in that place halfway between sleep and consciousness, his face buried in Colleen's sweet-smelling hair, his body still cradled between the softness of her legs.

So much for willpower. So much for resolving not to make love to her again. So much for hoping that Wes would forgive him for one little, single transgression.

Ah, but how he'd loved making love to her again. And no red-blooded, heterosexual man could've resisted the temptation of Colleen Skelly, naked, on his lap.

And really, deep in his heart, he knew it didn't matter. Wes was going to go ape over the fact that Bobby had slept with Colleen. Realistically, how much worse could it be to have slept with her twice? What difference could it possibly make?

To Wes? None. Probably. Hopefully.

But the difference it made to Bobby was enormous.

As enormous as the difference between heaven and hell.

Speaking of heaven, he was still inside of her, he realized, forcing himself to return to earth. Falling asleep immediately after sex was not a smart move when using condoms as the sole method of birth control. Because condoms could leak.

He should have pulled out of her twenty minutes ago.

rect what could well be the biggest, most life-changing mistake either one of them had ever made.

"Probably not," he admitted. "Although…"

"I'll take one right now, if you want me to. I'm not sure where I am in my cycle. I've never really been regular." She was sitting there, unconcerned about her nakedness, looking to him for suggestions and options and his opinion, with complete and total trust.

That kind of trust was an incredible turn-on, and he felt his body respond. How could that be? The disbelief and cold fear that had surged through his veins at his discovery should have brought about an opposite physical response—more similar to the response one had from swimming in an icy lake.

And his mental reaction to a broken condom should have included not even *thinking* about having sex for the next three weeks without shaking with fear.

But there was Colleen, sitting next to him on her bed, all bare breasts and blue-green eyes and quiet, steadfast trust.

Right now she needed him to be honest about this. There was no quick fix. No miraculous solutions. "I think it's probably too late to do anything but pray."

She nodded. "That's what I figured."

"I'm sorry."

"It's not your fault," she said.

He shook his head. "It's not about fault—it's about responsibility, and I *am* responsible."

"Well, I am, too. You were coerced."

Bobby smiled, thinking of the way she'd sat on his lap, intending to seduce him, wondering if she had even the slightest clue that his last hope of resisting her had vanished the moment she'd appeared in the kitchen wearing only that robe.

"Mmmrph!"

"Sorry!"

Thanking the Lord—not for the first time today—that Ashley was still on the Vineyard, Colleen flew down the hallway stark naked and slapped on the bathroom light. One glance in the mirror and she knew she had to take a shower. Her hair was wild. And her face still held the satisfied look of a woman who'd kept her lover very busy all morning long.

She couldn't do anything about the face, but the hair she could fix with a fast shower.

She turned on the shower and climbed in before the water had a chance to heat up, singing a few operatic high notes in an attempt to counteract the cold.

"You all right?" Bobby had followed her in. Of course, she'd left the bathroom door wide open.

She peeked out from behind the shower curtain. He was as naked as she was, standing in front of the commode with that utterly masculine, wide-spread stance.

"I have to take a tuition check to my law school," she told him, quickly rinsing her hair, loving the fact that he was comfortable enough to be in the bathroom with her, feeling as if they'd crossed some kind of invisible, unspoken line. They were lovers now—not just two people who had given in to temptation and made love once. "The deadline's noon today, and like a total idiot, I pushed it off until the last minute." Literally.

"I'll come with you."

She turned off the water and pulled back the curtain, grabbing her towel and drying herself as she rushed back to her bedroom. "I can't wait for you," she called to him. "I'm literally forty-five seconds from walking out the door."

She stepped into clean underwear and pulled her blue dress—easy and loose fitting, perfect for days she was

He kissed her, pulling her into his arms, his hand coming up to cup her breast as if he couldn't not touch her.

Colleen felt herself start to dissolve into a puddle of heat. What would happen if she didn't get that check to the office on time?

She might have to pay a penalty. Or she'd get bumped from the admissions list. There were so many students wait-listed, the admissions office could afford to play hardball. Reluctantly, she pulled back from Bobby.

"I'll hurry," she told him.

"Good," he said, still touching her, looking at her as if she were the one standing naked in front of him, lowering his head to kiss her breast before he let her go. "I'll be here."

He wasn't in love with her. He was in lust.

And that was exactly what she'd wanted, she reminded herself as she ran down the stairs.

Except, now that she had it, it wasn't enough.

THE PHONE WAS RINGING as Bobby stepped out of Colleen's shower.

He grabbed a towel and wrapped it around himself as he went dripping into the kitchen. "'Lo?"

He heard the sound of an open phone line, as if someone were there but silent. Then, "Bobby?"

It was Wes. No, not just "It was Wes," but "Oh, God, it was Wes."

"Hey!" Bobby said, trying desperately to sound normal—as opposed to sounding like a man who was standing nearly naked not two feet from the spot where mere hours earlier he'd pinned Wes's sister to the wall as they'd... As he'd...

"What are you doing at Colleen's place?" Wes sounded

Bobby told Wes. "She sold the Mustang because she was having trouble making ends meet."

Wes swore loudly. "I can't believe she sold that car. I would've lent her money. Why didn't she ask me for money?"

"I offered to do the same. She didn't want it from either one of us."

"That's stupid. Let me talk to the stupid girl, will you?"

"Actually," Bobby told Wes, "it's not stupid at all." And she wasn't a girl. She was a woman. A gorgeous, vibrant, independent, sexy woman. "She wants to do this her way. By herself. And then when she graduates, and passes the bar exam, she'll know—*she* did this. Herself. I don't blame her, man."

"Yeah, yeah, right, just put her on the phone."

Bobby took a deep breath, praying that Wes wouldn't think it was weird—him being in Colleen's apartment when she wasn't home. "She's not here. She had to go over to the law school for something and—"

"Leave her a message then. Tell her to call me." Wes rattled off a phone number that Bobby dutifully wrote on a scrap of paper. But he then folded it up, intending to put it into his pocket as soon as he was wearing something that had a pocket. No way was he going to risk Colleen calling Wes back before he himself had a chance to speak to him.

"Put it in gear," Wes ordered. "You're needed for this meeting. If Colleen's going to be stupid and insist on going to Tulgeria, we need to do this right. If you get down here tonight, we'll get started planning this op a full twelve hours earlier than if we wait to have this meeting in the morning. I want those extra twelve hours. This is Colleen's safety—her *life*—we're talking about here."

"I'm there," Bobby said. "I'll be on that flight."

CHAPTER FOURTEEN

WHEN COLLEEN GOT HOME, Clark and Kenneth were sitting in her living room, playing cards.

"Hey," Clark said. "Where's your TV?"

"I don't have a TV," she told him. "What are you doing here? Is Ashley back?"

"Nah. Mr. Platonic called us," Clark answered. "He didn't want you coming home to an empty apartment."

"He had to go someplace called Little Creek," Kenneth volunteered. "He left a note on your bed. I didn't let Clark read it."

Bobby had gone to Little Creek. He'd finally run away, leaving the two stooges behind as baby-sitters.

"Thanks," she said. "I'm home now. You don't have to hang here."

"We don't mind," Clark said. "You actually have food in your kitchen and—"

"Please, I need you to go," Colleen told them. "I'm sorry." She had no idea what Bobby had written in that note that was in her bedroom. She couldn't deal with reading it while they were in her living room.

And she couldn't deal with not reading it another second longer.

"It's cool," Clark said. "I was betting we wouldn't get the warmest welcome, since you're one of those liberated, I-can-take-care-of-myself babes and—"

She heard the door close as Kenneth dragged Clark out.

Colleen took her backpack into her bedroom. Bobby

if she had no doubt that he would be back in her bed in a matter of a day or two. And as if her world wouldn't end if he didn't come back.

The phone rang, and she rolled to the edge of her bed, lying on her stomach to look at the caller ID box, hoping... *Yes.* It was Bobby. Had to be. The area code and exchange was from Little Creek. She knew those numbers well—Wes had been stationed there when he'd first joined the Navy. Back before he'd even met Bobby Taylor.

Bobby must've just arrived, and he was calling her first thing. Maybe this wasn't just about sex for him....

Colleen picked up the phone, keeping her voice light, even though her heart was in her throat. "Too bad you had to leave. I spent the entire T ride imagining all the different ways we were going to make love again this afternoon."

The words that came out of the phone were deafening and colorful. The voice wasn't Bobby's. It was her brother's. "I don't know who you think I am, Colleen, but you better tell me who you thought you were talking to so that I can kill him."

"Wes," she said weakly. Oh, no!

"This is great. This is just great. Just what I want to hear coming out of the mouth of my little sister."

Her temper sparked. "Excuse me, I'm *not* little. I haven't been little for a long time. I'm twenty-three years old, thank you very much, and yes, you want to know the truth? I'm in a relationship that's intensely physical and *enormously* satisfying. I spent last night and most of the morning having wild sex."

Wes shouted. "Oh, my *God!* Don't tell me that! I don't want to hear that!"

"If I were Sean or...or..." She didn't want to say Ethan. Mentioning their dead brother was like stomping with both

"Wait," he said. "I'm calling for a reason."

"No kidding? A reason besides sibling harassment?"

"Yeah. I have to go pick up Bobby at the airport, but before I leave, I need info on your contacts in the Tulgerian government. Admiral Robinson is going to run a quick check on everyone involved." Wes paused. "Didn't you get my message to call me?" he asked. "When I spoke to Bobby just before noon, I told him to leave a message for you and—"

Silence.

Big, long silence.

Colleen could almost hear the wheels in Wes's head turning as he put two and two together.

Colleen had spent—in her own words—"most of the morning having wild sex" with her mysterious lover.

Her brother had spoken to Bobby earlier. In Colleen's apartment. Just before noon. As in the "just before noon" that occurred at the very end of a morning filled with wild sex.

"Tell me I'm wrong," Wes said very, very quietly— never a good sign. "Tell me it's not Bobby Taylor. Tell me my best friend didn't betray me."

Colleen couldn't keep quiet at that. "*Betray* you? Oh, my God, Wesley, that's absurd. What's between me and Bobby has nothing to do with you at all!"

"I'm right?" Wes lost it. "I *am* right! How could he *do* that, that son of a—I'm gonna kill him!"

Oh, *damn!* "Wes! Listen to me! It was *my* fault. I—"

But her brother had already hung up.

Oh, dear Lord, this was going to be bad. Wes was going to pick up Bobby from the airport and...

Colleen checked her caller-ID box and tried to call Wes back.

THE FLIGHT TO NORFOLK was just long enough to set Bobby completely on edge. He'd had enough time to buy

she leaned forward to kiss him, as she pressed her body against him, as their legs tangled and...

Help.

He wanted her with every breath.

God, why couldn't he have felt this way about Kyra?

Because even back then, he was in love with Colleen.

Man, where had *that* thought come from? Love. God. This was already way too complicated without screwing it up by putting love into the picture.

In a matter of minutes Bobby was going to be hip deep in a conversation with Wes that he was dreading with every ounce of his being. And Wes was going to warn him away from Colleen. *Don't go near her any more.* He could hear the words already.

If he were smart, he'd heed his friend.

If he weren't smart, if he kept thinking with his body instead of his brain, he was going to get in too deep. Before he even blinked, he would find himself in a long-distance relationship, God help him. And then it would be a year from now, and he'd be on the phone with Colleen again, having to tell her—again—that he wasn't going to make it out for the weekend, and she would tell him that was okay—

again—but in truth, he'd know that she was trying not to cry.

He didn't want to make her cry—but that didn't mean he was in love with her.

And the fact that he wanted to be with her constantly, the fact that he missed her desperately even now, mere hours after having been in bed with her, well, that was just his body's healthy response to great sex. It was natural, having had some, to want more.

Bobby squeezed his eyes shut. Oh, God, he wanted more.

It wouldn't be too hard to talk Colleen into giving a

tan and revealed the barbwire tattoo on his upper arm. His hair was long and messy. The longer it got, the lighter it looked as it was bleached by the sun, as the reddish highlights were brought out.

Bobby and Wes had been virtually inseparable for nearly eleven years—even though they'd hated each other's guts at the outset of BUD/S training, when they'd been assigned together as swim buddies. That was something not many people knew. But Wes had earned Bobby's respect through the grueling training sessions—the same way Bobby earned Wes's. It took them a while, but once they recognized that they were made from the same unbreakable fabric, they'd started working together.

It was a case of one plus one equaling three. As a team, they were unstoppable. And so they became allies.

And when Wes's little brother Ethan had died, they'd taken their partnership a step forward and become friends. Real friends. Over the past decade that bond had strengthened to the point where it seemed indestructible.

But years of working with explosives had taught Bobby that indestructibility was a myth. There was no such thing.

And there was a very good chance that over the next few minutes, he was going to destroy ten years of friendship with just a few small words.

I slept with your sister.

"Hey," Wes said in greeting. "You look tired."

Bobby shrugged. "I'm okay. You?"

Wes pushed himself off the wall. "Please tell me you didn't check your luggage."

They started walking, following the stream of humanity away from the gate. "I didn't. I didn't bring it. There was no time to go back to the hotel. I just left it there."

"Bummer," Wes said. "Paying for a room when you don't even sleep there. That's pretty stupid."

Wes stopped walking. "Aw, come on, Bobby, you can do better than that. You've *been* with her? You could say *slept with,* but of course you didn't sleep much, did you, dirt wad? How about..." He used the crudest possible expression. "Yeah, that works. *That's* what you did, huh? You *son* of a..." He was shouting now.

Bobby stood there. Stunned. Wes had known. Somehow he'd already known. And Bobby had been too self-absorbed to realize it.

"I sent you there to take *care* of her," Wes continued. "And *this* is what you do? How could you do this to me?"

"It wasn't about you," Bobby tried to explain. "It was about me and— Wes, I've been crazy about her for years."

"Oh, this is fine," Wes had gone beyond full volume and into overload. "For *years,* and this is the first I hear of it? What, were you just waiting for a chance to get her alone, scumbag?" He shoved Bobby, both hands against his chest.

Bobby let himself get shoved. He could have planted himself and absorbed it, but he didn't. "No. Believe me I tried to stay away from her, but...I couldn't do it. As weird as it sounds, she got it into her head that she wanted me, and hell, you know how she gets. I didn't stand a chance."

Wes was in his face. "You're ten years older than she is, and you're trying to tell me that *she* seduced *you?*"

"It's not that simple. You've got to believe—" Bobby cut himself off. "Look, you're right. It *is* my fault. I'm more experienced. She offered, and God, I wanted her, and I didn't do the right thing. For *you.*"

"Ho, *that's* great!" Wes was pacing now, a tightly wound bundle of energy, ready to blow. "Meaning you did the right thing for Colleen, is that what you're saying?

him in the exact place that would knock him over, take him down onto his back on the concrete. After years of training together, Wes knew his weak spots well.

"Hey!" The shout echoed against the concrete ceilings and walls as Wes hit him with a flurry of punches. "Hey, Skelly, back off!"

The voice belonged to Lucky O'Donlon. An SUV pulled up with a screech of tires, and O'Donlon and Crash Hawken were suddenly there, in the airport parking garage, pulling Wes off him.

And the three newest members of Alpha Squad, Rio Rosetti, Mike Lee and Thomas King climbed out of the back, helping Bobby to his feet.

"You okay, Chief?" Rio asked, his Italian street-punk attitude completely overridden by wide-eyed concern. The kid had some kind of hero worship thing going for both Bobby and Wes. If this little altercation didn't cure him of it forever, Bobby didn't know what would.

He nodded at Rio. "Yeah." His nose was bleeding. By some miracle it wasn't broken. It should have been. Wes had hit him hard enough.

"Here, Chief." Mike handed him a handkerchief.

"Thanks."

Crash and Lucky were both holding on tightly to Wes, who was sputtering—and ready to go another round if they released him.

"You want to explain what this is all about?" Crash was the senior officer present. He rarely used his officer voice—he rarely spoke at all—but when he did, he was obeyed instantly. To put it mildly.

But Wes wouldn't have listened to the president of the United States at this moment, and Bobby didn't want to explain any of this to anyone. "No, sir," he said stiffly, politely. "With all due respect, sir…"

"We got a call from your sister, Skelly," Lucky

ing him away from Lucky and Crash, with Rio, Mike and Thomas clinging to him like monkeys.

He pulled back his arm, ready to throw another brain-shaking punch when another voice, a new voice, rang out.

"Stop this. *Right. Now.*"

It was the senior chief.

Another truck had pulled up.

Bobby froze, and that was all the other SEALs needed. Lucky and Crash pulled Wes out of his grip and safely out of range, and then, God, Senior Chief Harvard Becker was there, standing in between him and Wes.

"Thank you for coming, Senior," Crash said quietly. He looked at Bobby. "I answered the phone when Colleen called. She didn't say as much, but I correctly guessed the cause of the, uh, tension between you and Skelly. I anticipated that the senior's presence would be helpful."

Wes's nose was broken, and as Bobby watched— not without some grim satisfaction—he leaned forward slightly, his face averted as he bled onto the concrete floor.

Lucky stepped closer to Harvard. He was speaking to him quietly, no doubt filling him in. Telling him that Bobby slept with Wes's sister.

God, this was so unfair to Colleen. She was going to Tulgeria with this very group of men. Who would all look at her differently, knowing that she and Bobby had...

Damn it, why couldn't Wes have agreed to talk this problem out...privately? Why had he turned this into a fist fight and, as a result, made Bobby's intimate relationship with Colleen public knowledge?

"So what do you want to do?" Harvard asked, hands on his hips as he looked from Bobby to Wes, his shaved head gleaming in the dim garage light. "You children want to move this somewhere so you can continue to beat

"YOU'RE GOING TO have to marry her."

Bobby sat back in his chair, his breath all but knocked out of him. "What? Wes, that's insane."

Wes Skelly sat across the table from him in the conference room on base that Harvard had appropriated and made into a temporary office. He was still furious. Bobby had never seen him stay so angry for such a long time.

It was possible Wes was going to be angry at Bobby forever.

He leaned forward now, glaring. "What's *insane* is for you to go all the way to Cambridge to *help* me and end up messing around with my sister. What's *insane* is that we're even having this conversation in the first place— that you couldn't keep your pants zipped. You got yourself into this situation. You play the game—you pay when you lose. And you lost big-time, buddy, when that condom broke."

"And I'm willing to take responsibility if necessary—"

"If necessary?" Wes laughed. "*Now* who's insane? You really think Colleen's going to marry you if she *has* to? No way. Not Colleen. She's too stubborn, too much of an idealist. No, you have to go back to Boston tomorrow morning. First thing. And make her think you *want* to marry her. Get her to say yes *now*—before she does one of those home tests. Otherwise, she's going to be knocked up and refusing to take your phone calls. And boy, won't *that* be fun."

Bobby shook his head. It was aching, and his face was throbbing where Wes's fists had connected with it—which was just about everywhere. He suspected Wes's nose hurt far worse; yet, both of their physical pain combined was nothing compared to the apprehension that was starting to churn in his stomach. Ask Colleen to marry him. God.

CHAPTER FIFTEEN

COLLEEN CAME HOME FROM the Tulgerian children's memorial service at St. Margaret's to find Ashley home and no new messages on the answering machine. Bobby had called last night, while she was at a Relief Aid meeting, so at least she knew he'd survived his altercation with her brother. Still, she was dying to speak to him.

Dying to be with him again.

"Any calls?" she called to Ashley, who was in her room.

"No."

"When did you get back?" Colleen asked, going to her roommate's bedroom door and finding her...*packing?*

"I'm not back," Ashley said, wiping her eyes and her nose with her sleeve. She had been crying but she forced an overly bright smile. "I'm only here temporarily and I'm not telling you where I'm going because you might tell someone."

Colleen sighed. "I guess Brad found you."

"I guess you would be the person who told him where I was...?"

"I'm sorry, but he seemed sincerely broken up over your disappearing act."

"You mean broken up over losing his chances to inherit my share of DeWitt and Klein," Ashley countered, savagely throwing clothes into the open suitcase on her bed. "How could you even *think* I'd consider getting back together

"No, *you* have a great backbone. I'm really good at borrowing yours when I need it," Ashley countered. She pushed her hair back from her face, attempting to put several escaped tendrils neatly back into place. "I have to do this, Colleen. I've got a cab waiting...."

Colleen hugged her friend. "Call me," she said, pulling back to look into Ashley's face. Her friend's normally perfect complexion was sallow, and she had dark circles beneath her eyes. This Brad thing had truly damaged her. "Whenever you get where you're going, when you've had a little more time to think about this—call me, Ash. You can always change your mind and come back. But if you don't—well, I'll come out to visit and cheer while you dance on the bar."

Ashley smiled even though her eyes filled with tears. "See, everything's okay with you. Why couldn't *you* be my father?"

Colleen had teared up, too, but she still had to laugh. "Aside from the obvious biological problems, I'm not ready to be anyone's parent. I'm having a tough enough time right now keeping my own life straightened out."

And yet, she could well be pregnant. Right now. Right this moment, a baby could be sparking to life inside her. In nine months she could be someone's mother. Someone very small who looked an awful lot like Bobby Taylor.

And somehow that thought wasn't quite so terrifying as she'd expected it to be.

She heard an echo of Bobby's deep voice, soft and rumbly, close to her ear. *There are some things you just have to do, you know? So you do it, and it all works out.*

If she were pregnant, despite what she'd just told Ashley, she would make it work out. Somehow.

She gave her friend one more hug. "You liked law

Leaving Colleen face-to-face with the flowers that Bobby had brought. For *her*.

She had to smile. It was silly and sweet and a complete surprise. She left the door ajar and went into the kitchen to find a vase. She was filling it with water when Bobby returned.

He looked nice, as if he'd taken special care with his appearance. He was wearing Dockers instead of his usual jeans, a polo shirt with a collar in a muted shade of green. His hair was neatly braided. Someone had helped him with that.

"Sorry I didn't call you last night. The meeting didn't end until well after midnight. And then I was up early, catching a flight back here."

He was nervous. She could see it in his eyes, in the tension in his shoulders—but only because she knew him so very well. Anyone else would see a completely relaxed, easygoing man, standing in her kitchen, dwarfing the refrigerator.

"Thanks for the flowers," she said. "I love them."

He smiled. "Good. I didn't think you were the roses type, and they, well, they reminded me of you."

"What?" she said. "Big and flashy?"

His smile widened. "Yeah."

Colleen laughed as she turned to give him a disbelieving look. Their eyes met and held, and just like that the heat was back, full force.

"I missed you," she whispered.

"I missed you, too."

"Kinda hard for you to take off my clothes when you're way over there."

He yanked his gaze away, cleared his throat. "Yeah, well. Hmmm. I think we need to talk before..." He cleared his throat. "You want to go out, take a walk? Get some coffee?"

could see inside her head, inside her very heart and soul, as if he saw her completely, as a whole, unique, special person.

"Marry me."

Colleen nearly dropped her glass. *What?*

But she'd heard him correctly. He reached into his pocket and took out a jeweler's box. A *ring* box. He opened it and handed it to her—it was a diamond in a gorgeously simple setting, perfect for accenting the size of the stone. Which was enormous. It had to have cost him three months' pay.

She couldn't breathe. She couldn't speak. She couldn't move. Bobby Taylor wanted to marry her.

"Please," he said quietly. "I should have said, *please* marry me."

The sky was remarkably blue, and the air was fresh and sweet. On the street below, a woman shouted for someone named Lenny. A car horn honked. A bus roared past.

Bobby Taylor wanted to *marry* her.

And yes, *yes,* she wanted to marry him, too. *Marry* him! The thought was dizzying, terrifying, but it came with a burst of happiness that was so strong, she laughed aloud.

Colleen looked up at him then, into the almost palpable warmth of his eyes. He was waiting for her answer.

But she was waiting, too, she realized. This was where he would tell her that he loved her.

Except he didn't. He didn't say anything. He just sat there, watching her, slightly nervous, slightly…detached? As if he were waiting for her to say no.

Colleen looked hard into his eyes. He was sitting there, waiting, as if he expected her to turn him down.

As if he didn't really want her to marry him.

As if…

Her happiness fizzled, and she handed him the ring

knew she was dangerously close to crying. "I can't decide if that makes you a really good friend or a total chump."

She headed for the door to the stairs, praying she would make it into her apartment before her tears escaped. "I should get back to work."

God, she was a fool. If he'd been just a little more disingenuous, if he'd lied and told her he loved her, she would have given herself away. She would have thrown her arms around his neck and told him yes. Yes, she'd marry him, yes, she loved him, too.

She loved him so much...but there was no *too*.

"Colleen, wait."

Oh, damn, he was chasing her down the stairs. He caught her at her apartment door as she fumbled her key in the lock, as her vision blurred from her tears.

She pushed open the door, and he followed. She tried to turn away, but it was too late.

"I'm so sorry," he said hoarsely, engulfing her in his arms. "Please believe me—the last thing I wanted to do was upset you like this."

He was so solid, so huge, and his arms gave her the illusion of safety. Of being home.

He swore softly. "I didn't mean to make you cry, Colleen."

She just held him tightly, wanting them both just to pretend this hadn't happened. He hadn't asked her to marry him, she hadn't discovered just how much she truly loved him. Yeah, that would be easy to forget. He could return the ring to the jeweler's, but she didn't have a clue what she was going to do with her heart.

She did, however, know exactly what to do with her body. Yes, she was going to take advantage of every second she had with this man.

She pushed the door closed behind them and, wrap-

setting yourself up as a potential sniper target. Think drabs—browns, greens, beiges. I also don't want you to bring anything clingy—wear loose overshirts, okay? Long sleeves, long skirts—and you know this already. Right." Bobby laughed, disgusted with himself. "Sorry."

She kissed him again. "I love that you care."

"I do," he said, holding her gaze, wishing there was some way to convey just how much.

But the door buzzer rang, and Colleen gently extracted herself from his arms. She slipped on her robe. Man, he loved that robe. He sat up. "Maybe you should let me get the door."

But she was already out of the room. "I've got it."

Whoever had buzzed had gotten past the building's security entrance and was now knocking directly on the door to Colleen's apartment.

Where *were* his shorts?

"Oh, my God," he heard Colleen say. "What are *you* doing here?"

"What, I can't visit my own sister?" Oh, damn! It was Wes. "Sleeping in today, huh? Late night last night?"

"No," she said flatly. "What do you want, Wes? I'm mad at you."

"I'm looking for Taylor. But he better not be here, with you dressed like that."

The hell with his shorts. Bobby grabbed his pants, pulling them on, tripping over his own feet in his haste and just barely keeping himself from doing a nosedive onto the floor. His recovery made an incriminating *thump*.

Wes swore—a steady stream of epithets that grew louder as he moved down the hall toward Colleen's bedroom.

Bobby was searching for his shirt among the sheets and blankets that spilled from the bed and onto the floor as Wes pushed the door open. He slowly straightened up,

"Then take him with you," Colleen said. "I have work to do." She pointed the way. "Go. Both of you."

Bobby moved, and Wes followed. But at the door Colleen stopped Bobby, kissed him. "Sorry about my brother the grouch. I had a lovely afternoon, thank you. I'll see you tonight."

If her intention was to infuriate her brother, she'd succeeded.

She closed the door behind them, with Bobby still holding his socks and shoes.

Wes gave him a scathing look. "What is *wrong* with you?"

How could he explain? He wasn't sure himself how it happened. Every time he turned around, he found himself in bed with Colleen. When it came to her, he—a man who'd set time-and-distance records for swimming underwater, a man who'd outlasted more physically fit SEAL candidates during BUD/S through sheer determination, a man who'd turned himself around from a huge man carrying quite a bit of extra weight into a solid, muscular monster—had no willpower.

Because being with her felt so right. It was *right.*

That thought came out of nowhere, blindsiding him, and he stood there for a moment just blinking at Wes.

"You were supposed to get her to marry you," Wes continued. "Instead you—"

"I tried. I was trying to—"

"That was *trying?*"

"If she's pregnant, she'll marry me. She agreed to that."

"Perfect," Wes said, "so naturally you feel inclined to keep trying to get her pregnant."

"Of course not. Wes, when I'm with her—"

"I don't want to hear it." Wes glared at him. "Just stay the hell away from her," he said, and clattered down the stairs. "And stay away from me, too."

mentioned in his letters and emails down through the years. Joe Cat, Blue, Lucky, Cowboy, Crash. Some of the nicknames were pretty funny.

Spaceman. His real name was Jim Slade, and he was tall and good-looking in an earthy way, with craggy features and the kind of blue eyes that were perpetually amused. He'd followed her around for a while and had even invited her back to the hotel, to have dinner with him later.

Bobby had overheard that, and Colleen had expected him to step forward, to make some kind of proprietary move. But he hadn't. He'd just met Colleen's eyes briefly, then gone back to the conversation he'd been having with Relief Aid leader, Susan Fitzgerald.

And Colleen was bemused—more with her own reaction. It was stupid really. If Bobby had gotten all macho and possessive on her, she would have been annoyed. But since he hadn't, she found herself wondering why not. Didn't he *feel* possessive toward her? And wasn't *that* a stupid thing to wonder? She didn't want to be any man's possession.

She'd spoken to Bobby only briefly before he'd left for another meeting with his team, held back at the hotel. She'd stayed behind and helped discuss plans for TV news coverage of tonight's bon voyage party.

That meeting was brief, and Colleen was on the T, heading toward Cambridge before four o'clock. She was inside the lobby of Bobby's hotel by 4:15.

She used the lobby phone to dial his room.

Bobby answered on the first ring, and she knew right away that she'd woken him up.

"Sorry," she said.

"No, I was just catching a nap. Are you, um… Where are you?"

"Downstairs. Can I come up?"

God, she looked beautiful, in a blue-flowered sleeveless dress that flowed almost all the way to the floor. He'd been hyperaware of her all throughout the afternoon's meeting—aware of how easy it would be to get her out of that dress, with its single zipper down the back.

Bobby crossed the room and opened the curtains, letting in the bright late-afternoon sunshine. "Name it," he said.

"I know we don't officially need your protection until we enter Tulgeria," she told him, "but remember I told you about that bon voyage party? It's tonight at the VFW right down the street from St. Margaret's—the church where I had that car wash?"

Bobby nodded. "I know St. Margaret's." It was in that same crummy 'hood where the AIDS Center was creating a controversy among the locals.

Colleen put her backpack down and came to help as he attempted to make the bed. "We just found out that the local Fox affiliate is sending TV cameras tonight. That's great news—we could use all the public support we can get." Together they pulled up the bedspread. "But..."

"But the cameras are going to attract attention in the neighborhood." Bobby knew just where she was heading. "You're afraid John Morrison's going to show up. Crash your party."

She nodded. "It wouldn't surprise me one bit if he caused trouble, just to get the news camera pointed in his direction."

He took a deep breath. "There's something I should probably tell you. Don't be angry with me, but I checked up on John Morrison. I was worried about you, and I wanted to know how much of a wild card he was."

"There's not much to find out," Colleen countered. "I did the same thing right after he and I...met. He served in the army, did a tour in Vietnam. There's an ex-wife and

doing—if he's gotten that big break as an actor, if he's on Broadway yet."

Oh, God. "The poor man."

"Regardless of that, this *poor man* is responsible for putting cinder blocks through the center's windows. If he gets near you tonight, his health will be at risk."

"You'll be there?" she asked.

"Absolutely. I'll bring some of the guys, too. Rio, Thomas and Mike. And Jim Slade. He'll definitely come. What time does it start?"

"Eight. The camera crew's due to arrive at 7:30."

"We'll be there at seven."

"Thank you." Colleen sat down on his bed. "I liked meeting Rio, Thomas and Mike...Lee, right?" She smiled. "They really think the world of you. Make sure you tell them what you told me about John Morrison. If he shows up, let's try to treat him with compassion."

"We'll get him out of there as quickly—and compassionately—as possible," he promised. "I'm glad you had a chance to meet them—they're good men. All the guys in the squad are. Although some are definitely special. The senior chief—Harvard Becker. Did you meet him? I'd follow him into hell if he asked."

"Big black man, shaved head, great smile?" she asked.

"That's Harvard. Hey, whatdya think of Slade? Spaceman?" Bobby tried to ask the question casually, as if he was just talking, as if her answer didn't matter to him. The stupid thing was, he wasn't sure if he wanted her to tell him that she liked the man or hated him.

Colleen was gazing at him. "I thought he was nice. Why?"

"He's a lieutenant," Bobby told her. "An officer who's probably going to get out of the Teams pretty soon. He's having a tough time with his knees and... He's not sure

divorce and had no intention of repeating that mistake in the near future.

But with Colleen there were expectations.

Although, God help him, it sure seemed as if all the expectations were *his*.

"Wes thinks what we've got going is wrong? Well, what's *wrong*," Colleen countered hotly as she got to her feet, "is strong-arming your best friend into proposing marriage to your sister. What if I'd said yes? Would you have married me just because Wes told you to?"

"No," he said. He would have married her because he wanted to. Because unlike Colleen, this relationship was more to him than great sex. He turned away from her. "Look, maybe you should go."

She moved in front of him, forced him to look at her. "And do what?" she said sharply. "Have an early dinner with Jim Slade?"

He didn't nod, didn't say yes, but somehow the answer was written on his face. Slade was the kind of man she should be with. How could she meet men like him if she was wasting her time with Bobby?

"Oh, my God," she said. "You were, weren't you? You were trying to set me up with your friend." Her voice caught as she struggled not to cry, and as she gazed at him, she suddenly looked and sounded impossibly young and so very uncertain. "Bobby, what's going on? Don't you want me anymore?"

Oh, damn, he was going to cry, too. He wanted her more than he could ever say. He wanted her with every breath, with every beat of his heart. "I want to do what's right for you, Colleen. I need to—"

She kissed him.

God help him, she kissed him, and he was lost.

Again.

In truth, it was no ordinary kiss. It was fire and hunger

THE ELEVATOR DOOR OPENED, and Colleen found herself face-to-face with Wes.

He was getting off on this floor, Bobby's floor, followed by the trio of young SEALs she was starting to think of as The Mod Squad. Pete, Link and Mike Lee.

Wes's expression was grim, and Colleen knew that she looked like a woman who'd just been with a man. She should have taken more time, should have gone into the bathroom and splashed water on her still-flushed face.

Except then she would have been in Bobby's room when Wes knocked on the door.

She went into the elevator, her head held high as her brother glared at her. "Don't worry," she told him. "You win. I'm not going to see him again after tonight."

They were leaving for Tulgeria in the morning. While they were there, she would be sharing a room with Susan and Rene, and Bobby would be in with one or two of the SEALs for the week. There would be no place to be alone, no time, either. Bobby would have no trouble avoiding her.

And after they got back to the States, he'd head for California with the rest of Alpha Squad.

He wasn't interested in a long-distance relationship.

She wasn't interested in one that created limitless amounts of anguish and guilt.

There was no way their relationship could work out. This was what he'd tried to tell her in his room. That was why he'd tried to spark her interest in his stupid friend.

What they'd shared—a few days of truly great sex— was almost over. It *was* over, and they both knew it in their hearts. It was just taking their bodies a little bit longer to catch up.

The elevator door closed, and Colleen put on her sunglasses, afraid of who else she'd run into on the way to the lobby, and unwilling to let them see her cry.

powerful. He'd never felt anything like it in his entire life, and it scared the hell out of him.

"I can't say no to her," Bobby said to Wes, through the door. "She wants me to meet her tonight, and I'm going to be there, because, damn it, I can't stay away from her. It's tearing me up, because I know this isn't what you want for her. I know you wanted better. But if she came to me and told me she loved me, too, and that she wanted to marry me, I'd do it. Tonight. I'd take her to Vegas before she changed her mind. Yeah, I'd do it, even though I know what a mistake it would be for her.

"But she doesn't want to marry me." Bobby wiped his face, his eyes. "She only wants to sleep with me. I don't have to worry about her waking up seven years from now and hating her life. I only have to worry about spending the rest of *my* life wanting someone I can't have."

Bobby sat on the edge of the hotel room bed, right where Colleen had sat just a short time ago.

"God, I want her in my life," he said aloud. "What am I going to do, Wes?"

No one answered.

Wes had stopped knocking on the door. He was gone.

And Bobby was alone.

As the TV news cameras arrived, Colleen glanced at her watch. It was about 7:20.

Bobby and his friends were already there, already in place—Thomas and Jim Slade seemingly casually hanging out on the sidewalk in front of the church parking lot, Rio and Mike up near the truck that held the camera.

Bobby was sticking close to her in the crowd.

"There's a good chance if Morrison's going to try any-thing, he's going to target you," he explained. He was

As Bobby stepped in front of her, he seemed to expand, and Colleen realized that a baseball bat was dangling from Morrison's other hand.

"How about we let those cameras cover some real news?" Morrison asked loudly—loudly enough for heads to turn in his direction.

Loudly enough for the other SEALs to move toward them. But the crowd was thick, and they were having trouble getting through the crush. As were the police officers who'd been assigned to keep traffic moving.

"I'm going down the street," Morrison continued, "just a block or so over, to that AIDS Center they're building down there. I'm going to break the windows in protest. We don't want it in our neighborhood. We don't want *you* in our neighborhood."

He pointed at Colleen with the baseball bat, swinging it up toward her, and just like that, it was over.

She barely saw Bobby move. Yet somehow he'd taken the bat away from Morrison and had the man down on the ground before she even blinked.

The other SEALs made the scene a few seconds before the police.

Bobby lifted Morrison to his feet, handed the man to Spaceman. "Take him inside. There are some empty rooms upstairs." He turned to Rio. "Find Father Timothy. Tell him it has to do with that matter I discussed with him earlier this week." He looked at Colleen. "You okay?"

She watched as Spaceman hustled Morrison inside. "Yeah. I don't think he was going to hurt me."

"What's going on here?" the police officer—a big, ruddy-cheeked beat cop named Danny O'Sullivan—planted himself in front of them.

Bobby touched her arm and lowered his voice. "You want to press charges? Lifting the bat like that could be

been there, but he must've been something of a historian, because he knew the names of the rivers and the towns and the battles in which Morrison had fought.

John Morrison was drunk, but not as drunk as Colleen had first thought. His speech was slightly slurred, but he was following the conversation easily.

As she listened, lingering with Thomas King just outside the door, the two men talked about Admiral Jake Robinson, who'd also served in 'Nam. Morrison knew of the man and was impressed that Bobby thought of him as a friend. They talked about Bobby's career in the SEAL units. They talked about Morrison's bar, and his father who'd served in a tank division in World War II—who had died just two years ago after a long struggle with cancer. They talked about elderly parents, about loss, about death.

And suddenly they were talking about Wes.

"My best friend is still jammed up from his little brother's death," Bobby told Morrison. "It happened ten years ago, and he still won't talk about it. It's like he pretends the kid never existed." He paused. "Kind of like what you're doing with John Jr."

Silence.

"I'm sorry for your loss," she heard Bobby say quietly. "But you've got to find a way to vent your anger besides taking out the windows at the AIDS Center. Someone's going to end up hurt, and that will make my friend Colleen Skelly—and you know who she is—unhappy. And if you make Colleen unhappy, if you hurt someone, if you hurt *her,* then I'm going to have to come back here and hurt *you.* This is not a threat, John, it's a promise."

His friend. She was his *friend* Colleen—not his lover, not his girlfriend.

And Colleen knew the truth. He'd told her right from

repertoire—one of disbelief—flashed across Thomas King's face and he suddenly looked his actual, rather tender age. "Maybe that's something you should tell Chief Taylor yourself."

"Please," she said. "Just give him the message."

Father Timothy had cleared the top of the stairs, and she went down, as swiftly as she could, before she changed her mind.

was empty. He sat down beside her, wishing for the privacy that came with seats that had high backs. He lowered his voice instead. "You okay?"

She wiped her eyes, forced a smile. "I'm great."

Yeah, sure she was. He wanted to hold her hand, but he didn't dare touch her. "The past few days have been crazy, huh?"

She gave him another smile. "Yeah, I've been glad many times over that you and Alpha Squad are here."

God, he'd missed her. When Thomas King had given him her message—don't come over—he'd known that it was over between them. Right up until then he'd harbored hope. Maybe if he went to her and told her that he loved her... Maybe if he begged, she'd agree to keep seeing him. And maybe someday she'd fall in love with him, too.

"You and Wes are on friendlier terms again," she noted. "I mean, at least you seem to be talking."

Bobby nodded, even though that was far from the truth. The final insult in this whole messed-up situation was the damage he'd done to his decade of friendship with Wes. It seemed irreparable.

Wes was talking to him, sure—but it was only an exchange of information. They weren't sharing their thoughts, not the way they used to. When he looked at Wes, he could no longer read the man's mind.

How much of that was his own fault, his own sense of guilt? He didn't know.

"Life goes on, huh?" Colleen said. "Despite all the disappointments and tragedies. There's always good news happening somewhere." She gestured to the bus, to the four other Relief Aid volunteers who sat quietly talking in the back of the bus. "This is good news—the fact that we're going to bring those children back to a safer location. And, oh, here's some good news for you—I'm not pregnant. I got my period this morning. So you can stop

chest was tight and his brain felt numb. "Colleen, are you telling me—"

"Heads up, Taylor. We're getting close," Senior Chief Harvard Becker's voice cut through. "I need your eyes and ears with me right now."

Damn.

Colleen had turned her attention back to the drab scenery flashing past, outside the window.

Bobby stood up, shouldering his weapon, using every ounce of training he'd ever had to get his head back in place, to focus on the mission.

Rio Rosetti was nearby, and he caught Bobby's eye. "You okay, Chief? Your shoulder all right?"

His shoulder? "I'm fine," he said shortly. Dammit, he needed to talk to Wes. Just because Colleen loved him—and she only *maybe* loved him, he didn't know it for sure—didn't mean that gave him the right to go and ruin her life by marrying her. Did it?

"Okay, listen up," Captain Joe Catalanotto said for the benefit of the Relief Aid volunteers, the bus driver and the Tulgerian guard who was leading them down the unmarked roads to the hospital.

All of the SEALs knew precisely how this was going to go down. Swiftly and efficiently.

"We sent a small team in early, to do surveillance," Joe Cat continued. "One of those men will meet us on the road about a mile from the hospital, tell us if there's anything unusual to watch out for. If it's all clear, we'll pull up right outside the hospital doors, but everyone will stay in their seats. Another team will go in to check the place out, join forces with the rest of the surveillance team. Only when they secure entrances and give the all-clear do any of you get off this bus. Is that understood?"

A murmur of voices. Yes, sir.

"At that point," Joe Cat said even though they'd already

Colleen. Killed.

Wham.

Just like that, Bobby's head was together. He was back and ready—200 percent ready—for this op, for keeping Colleen and the others safe.

"Yeah, that's more like it," Wes said, glancing up at him as he checked his weapon. "You're all here now."

Bobby leaned over to look out the windows, to scan the desolate countryside. "I love you, man. Do you really forgive me?"

"If you hug me," Wes said, "I'll kill you."

There was nothing out the window. Just rocks and dust. "I missed you, Wesley."

"Yeah," Wes said, heading toward the front of the bus. "I'm going to miss you, too."

SOMETHING WAS WRONG.

Colleen shifted in her seat, trying to see the men having a discussion at the front of the bus.

They'd stopped, supposedly to pick up one of the SEALs who'd been sent ahead on surveillance.

But instead of picking him up and driving the last mile to the hospital at the outskirts of the small town, they'd all but parked here at the side of the road.

The SEAL had come onto the bus—it looked like the man who was nicknamed Lucky, allegedly from his past exploits with women. Yeah, that perfect nose was unmistakable despite the layers of dust and cam ouflage greasepaint. He was talking to the captain and the SEAL who, according to Wes, had actually gone to Harvard University—the senior chief who was almost as tall as Bobby. The other men were listening intently.

Susan came forward a few seats to sit behind Colleen. "Do you know what's going on?" she whispered.

Colleen shook her head. Whatever they were saying,

to check the children and get them out of there and onto the bus.

"Are there any questions?"

Susan Fitzgerald, head of Relief Aid, stood up. "Yes, sir. You've just basically told us that you and your men are going to sneak into a building where there are twelve terrorists with twelve machine guns waiting for you. I'm just curious, sir. Does your wife know about the danger you're going to be in this afternoon?"

For a moment there was complete silence on the bus. No one moved, no one breathed.

But then Captain Catalanotto exchanged a look with his executive officer, Lieutenant Commander McCoy. They both wore wedding rings. In fact, many of the men in Alpha Squad were married.

Colleen looked up and found Bobby watching her. As she met his eyes, he smiled very slightly. Ruefully. His mouth moved as he spoke to her silently from across the bus. "This is what we do. This is what it's like."

"Yeah, Dr. Fitzgerald," Captain Catalanotto finally said. "My wife knows. And God bless her for staying with me, anyway."

"I don't care," Colleen mouthed back, but Bobby had already looked away.

COLLEEN SAT ON THE bus in silence.

Wes and Jim Slade both paced. Bobby stood, across the aisle from her. He was still, but he was on the balls of his feet—as if he were ready to leap into action at the slightest provocation.

Colleen tried not to look at him. God forbid she distract him. Still, he was standing close, as if he wanted to be near her, too.

"How much longer?" Susan Fitzgerald finally asked.

"We don't know, ma'am," Wes answered from the back

A second one, and then a third. But Colleen couldn't see. She could only hear. Screaming. Was that her voice? Wes, cursing a blue storm. Spaceman. Shouting. For a helo. Man down.

Man down? Oh, God.

"Bobby?"

"Are we clear?" That was Bobby's voice. Colleen could feel it rumbling in his chest.

But then she felt something else. Something wet and warm and...

"We're clear." Wes. "Jeezus!"

"Are you all right?" Bobby pulled back, off her and, thank God, she *was*. But she was covered with blood.

His blood.

"Oh, my God," Colleen said, starting to shake. "Don't die. Don't you dare die on me!"

Bobby had been shot. Right now, right this minute, he was bleeding his life away onto the floor of the bus.

"Of all the *stupid* things you've done," she said, "stepping in front of a loaded gun again—again—has to take the cake."

"I'm okay," he said. He touched her face, forced her to look into his eyes. They were still brown, still calm, still Bobby's eyes. "Breathe," he ordered her. "Stay with me, Colleen. Because I'm okay."

She breathed because he wanted her to breathe, but she couldn't keep her tears from spilling over. "You're bleeding." Maybe he didn't know.

He didn't. He looked down, looked amazed. "Oh, man."

Wes was there, helping him into the seat next to Colleen, already working to try to stop the flow. "God *damn*, you've got a lot of blood. Bobby, I can't get this to stop."

Bobby squeezed Colleen's hand. "You should get out of here." His voice was tight. "Because you know, it didn't

CHAPTER EIGHTEEN

BOBBY WOKE UP IN a U.S. Military hospital.

Someone was sitting beside his bed, holding his hand, and it took him a few fuzzy seconds to focus on...

Wes.

He squeezed his best friend's fingers because his throat was too dry to speak.

"Hey." Wes was on his feet almost immediately. "Welcome back."

He grabbed a cup, aimed the straw for Bobby's mouth. Hadn't they just done this a few months ago?

"The news is good," Wes told him. "You're going to be okay. No permanent damage."

"Colleen?" Bobby managed to say.

"She's here." Wes gave him another sip of water. "She went to get some coffee. Do you remember getting moved out of ICU?"

Bobby shook his head. He remembered...

Colleen. Tears in her beautiful eyes. *I love you....*

Had she really said that? Please, God, let it be true.

"You had us scared for a while there, but when they moved you into this room, you surfaced for a while. I was pretty sure you were zoned out on painkillers, but Colleen got a lot of mileage out of hearing your voice. She slept after that—first time in more than seventy-two hours. She really loves you, man."

Bobby looked into his best friend's eyes. He didn't say anything. He didn't have to. Wes always did enough talking for both of them.

some sweet young tourist that he should've stayed far away from, and I'm thinking about how that's me ten years ago, and how I'm looking for something different now. Something *you* managed to find.

"Scared and jealous—it's not a good combination. I hope someday you'll forgive me for the things I said."

"You know I already do," Bobby whispered.

"So marry her," Wes said. "If you don't, I'll beat you senseless."

"Oh, this is just perfect." Colleen. "Threatening to beat up the man who just saved your sister's life." She swept into the room, and everything was heightened. It was suddenly brighter, suddenly sharper, clearer. She smelled great. She looked gorgeous.

"I'm just telling him to marry you," Wes said.

Bobby used every ounce of available energy to lift his hand and point to Wes and then to the door. "Privacy," he whispered.

"Attaboy," Wes said, as he went out the door.

Colleen sat beside him. Took his hand. Her fingers were cool and strong.

"Colleen—"

"Shhh. We have plenty of time. You don't need to—"

It was such an effort to speak. "I want…now…"

"Bobby Taylor, will you marry me?" she asked. "Will you help me find a law school near San Diego, so I can transfer and be with you for the rest of my life?"

Bobby smiled. It was much easier to let a Skelly do the talking. "Yes."

"I love you," she said. "And I know you love me."

"Yes."

She kissed him, her mouth so sweet and cool against his.

"When you're feeling better, do you want to…" She leaned forward and whispered into his ear.

EPILOGUE

"WHAT TIME DOES THE MOVIE START?" Bobby asked as he cleared the Chinese food containers off the kitchen table.

"Seven thirty-five. We have to leave in ten minutes." Colleen was going through the mail, opening today's responses to the wedding invitations. She looked tired—she'd been getting up early to meet with the administrators of a local San Diego women's shelter who were in the process of buying a big old house. She was handling tomorrow morning's closing—pro bono, of course.

"Are you sure you want to go?" he asked.

She looked up. Smiled. "Yes. Absolutely. You've wanted to see this movie for weeks. If we don't go tonight..."

"We'll go another night," he told her. They were getting married. They had a lifetime to see movies together. The thought still made him a little dizzy. She loved him....

"No," she said. "I definitely want to go tonight."

Aside from her legal work, there were a million things to do, what with finding a new apartment big enough for the two of them and all the wedding plans.

They were getting married in four weeks, in Colleen's mother's hometown in Oklahoma. It was where the Skellys had settled after her dad had retired from the Navy. Colleen had only lived there her last few years of high school, but her grandparents and a whole pack of cousins were there. Besides, softhearted Colleen knew how important it

to do with it. What you really mean is that she's too skinny. She's not stacked enough for Spaceman, is that what you're trying to say?"

"Yes. Don't you hate him now? Thank God he's not coming to the wedding."

She laughed and his chest got even tighter. He wanted to kiss her, but that would mean that he'd have to stop looking at her, and he loved looking at her.

"Didn't he have that friend who started that camp—you know, mock SEAL training for corporate executives?" she asked. "Kind of an Outward Bound program for business geeks? Someone—Rio, I think—was telling me about it."

"Yeah," Bobby said, settling on sliding his hand up beneath the edge of her T-shirt and running his fingers across the smooth skin of her back. "Randy Something— former SEAL from Team Two. Down in Florida. He's doing really well—he's constantly understaffed."

"Ashley wants to do something like that," Colleen told him. "Can you find out Randy's phone number so I can give it to her?"

Ashley DeWitt, in her designer suits, would last about ten minutes in the kind of program Randy ran. But Bobby kept his mouth shut because, who knows? Maybe he was wrong. Maybe she'd kick butt.

"Sure," he said. "I'll call Spaceman first thing tomorrow."

Colleen touched his face. "Thank you," she said. And he knew she wasn't talking about his promise to call Spaceman. She'd read his mind, and was thanking him for not discounting Ashley. "I love you so much."

And that feeling in his chest got tighter than ever.

"I love you, too," he told her. He'd started telling her that whenever he got this feeling. Not that it necessarily

REQUEST YOUR FREE BOOKS!

2 FREE NOVELS
FROM THE ROMANCE COLLECTION
PLUS 2 FREE GIFTS!